The Deadly Fields of Autumn

The woman who alighted from the stagecoach stood for a moment surveying the town, a look of wonder on her face. Her long dress was gorgeous, green-striped on a snowy white background with an extravagance of ecru-ruffled trim. Was it typical nineteenth century style or what passed for it in a Western movie?

I didn't know without consulting a costume book, but I wished I had a dress like that, wished I were coming to a Western town where everything would be new and I'd have a grand adventure.

The woman glanced at the hotel, the Pink Palace, and began walking toward it. The camera came to rest on a man sitting with a white-bearded companion in a Confederate uniform.

He was magnificent. Not White Beard but the other man. In a silvery blue shirt topped with a camel colored jacket and worn with a jaunty Stetson, he was the perennial cowboy. His hair was light brown and wavy, his skin tanned from long hours under a western sun, and his eyes…? I couldn't tell from a distance.

I leaned closer to the screen. Was it my imagination or did the cowboy look like Crane?

Imagination, I decided, but if a dozen men, old and young, had been sitting in front of the hotel, my gaze would have sought him out first.

What an incredibly handsome man!

He was looking at the woman in the green striped dress. I was looking at him. The picture shivered and blurred and disappeared. The music died in mid-note.

Two people were laughing, an intrusive display of hilarity generated by the co-anchors of an early news program.

I'd lost my Western. Lost the connection to the *Twilight Zone*.

At least I knew I wasn't losing my mind. Well, I'd never really thought that was the case, although the television's behavior was odd. What perverse glitch had cut off the movie in mid-scene?

What They Are Saying About

The Deadly Fields of Autumn

Dorothy Bodoin's twenty-fifth installment of her Foxglove Corners Mystery Series, *The Deadly Fields of Autumn*, has arrived.

Time to brew some tea, grab some cookies, and lose yourself in Jennet Ferguson's world, where by profession she is a capable teacher in a high school, but also a skillful and dedicated amateur sleuth in her private life. It is always a good day when a reader can unite with her favorite characters, for along with Jennet we join her husband Crane, friends Camille, Brent, Annica and Lucy, to name a few. They are all equally exciting and compelling in their own ways and bring much depth and interest to these books.

Mystery, intrigue, and collies follow Jennet wherever she goes.

First is the mysterious TV Jennet buys. Every time she turns it on, she sees a Western movie where the lead cowboy looks exactly like her husband. But only she sees it. No one else can.

Involved in collie rescue, Jennet decides to initiate a new program to place older dogs with seniors. This seems like a terrific idea until an owner, Charlotte Gray, disappears along with her dog Bronwyn.

As if this weren't enough mystery, a hit and run crash results in the death of a young girl and a mysterious man sporting a beard harasses Jennet on the freeway.

Not to mention, what is going on with Deputy Veronica the Viper, who baked a birthday cake for Crane and seems to be out to destroy Jennet's and Crane's marriage?

Along with the intrigue are the delightful stories of Jennet's battle to teach English to young people who are not so interested and work under a principal who is far from nice. Her classroom stories add even more dimension to Jennet's complex character.

The book culminates in a breathtaking, heart pounding Halloween party where Jennet comes face to face with pure evil.

The Deadly Fields of Autumn is a book I highly recommend. It is one you will not want to miss.

I also highly recommend the whole Foxglove Corners' series, for I have read every single installment. It is a cozy mystery series to celebrate and a page-turner to investigate the latest goings on with your favorite characters. I am already looking forward to the next one.

—*Suzanne Hurley*
Author of *The Dream Smasher*

The Deadly Fields of Autumn

Dorothy Bodoin

A Wings ePress, Inc.
Cozy Mystery

Wings ePress, Inc.

Edited by: Jeanne Smith
Copy Edited by: Joan C. Powell
Executive Editor: Jeanne Smith
Cover Artist: Trisha FitzGerald-Jung

Wings ePress Books
www. wingsepress.com

ISBN 978-1-61309-649-9

Published In the United States Of America

Wings ePress Inc.
3000 N. Rock Road
Newton, KS 67114

Dedication

Dedicated to the memory of Wolf Manor Kinder Brightstar, my beloved collie, Kinder. You were by my side every day as this book came slowly to life. You are with me now, in my heart. Rest in peace, my dear one, until we are together again.

One

The antique console held a crowded collection of Tiffany lamps, ornate vases, silver picture frames, and a portable television set in a glossy maple case with a dollop of ornamentation. It appeared to be hiding. It appeared to be… Something I had to have.

I lifted the set up and away from its fragile companions. With a weight of about twenty pounds, it would be easy to handle. Moreover, it was an attractive piece. The portable television sets I'd seen in the past had been flat models, plain and strictly utilitarian. This one reminded me of an old-time radio in a Norman Rockwell illustration with a family gathered around it, listening to their favorite program. It was, in a sense, an antique, and would be the perfect birthday present for my husband, Crane.

I ran my finger across the screen, leaving a clear trail in a square of dust. Whoever was in charge of the estate sale had neglected to clean it properly. I wiped my finger with a tissue and called to Miss Eidt who was nearby, rifling through a box of paperbacks.

"Come look at this, Miss Eidt."

Elizabeth Eidt had closed the Foxglove Corners Public Library for the day, but in a light blue shirtwaist dress with a pearl necklace, she still looked the part of an old-fashioned small town librarian. I suspected she had a pair of white gloves in her straw handbag. Holding a paperback with a creased blue and green cover, she joined me.

"That little television? It's charming, but not very practical. I'm used to looking at a larger screen."

"So am I, but this one is unique. I'm going to buy it," I added.

"You'd better find out if it works first."

"It has a cord," I said.

"And there's an outlet on the wall."

"I don't suppose anyone would mind."

I plugged the cord in, turned the set on, and a picture with pale colors swam into focus: a meadow with a dog running toward a lake and a horse in full gallop on the horizon.

"Is this your frivolous gift to yourself for surviving the first week of your new semester?" Miss Eidt asked with a teasing twinkle in her eye. "Because you already have a TV, don't you?"

"Yes," I said, "and we have cable. But I don't watch television unless something momentous happens in the world. I want this for Crane's birthday."

My deputy sheriff husband had taken up a new hobby… making furniture, in an effort to balance long hours patrolling the roads and byroads of Foxglove Corners. The little television set could sit on his workbench, giving him an illusion of company in our basement while he worked.

"Will you still make your frivolous purchase for yourself?" she asked.

I smiled. "Of course. As soon as I see something I want."

I deserved a reward after the grim week I'd had teaching English at Marston High School. In only five days, I could tell I had two rowdy groups that would demand a creative approach and constant attention lest they wrest control of the class from me.

The leisurely day at the estate sale was part of the reward. It had been storming, but we didn't let that stop us.

Miss Eidt was searching for books by such notables as Victoria Holt and Virginia Coffman to fill her new Gothic Nook at the library. I was just looking, always intrigued by antiques.

The purple Victorian house on Grovelane had had one owner, Eustacia Stirling, for seventy years. We both assumed that in that time she had acquired many priceless articles.

"I'm going to look at jewelry next," I said. "But first…" I noted the discreet price tag. Thirty dollars. "I want to pay for the TV and put it in my car."

"I might as well take that whole box of paperbacks," Miss Eidt said. "Some of the covers are in poor condition, and the pages are yellowish; but that adds to the ambiance. Don't you agree?"

I did. At present, Miss Eidt's Gothic Nook was still in the vision stage. Once it began to take shape, there would be no stopping it. She already had two vintage rockers and a Victorian table to lure lovers of the genre.

"Only the box is too heavy," she said. "I can't lift it."

"I'll carry it for you as soon as I pay for the television. The cashier is out on the porch."

"I'll come with you."

We wove through makeshift aisles of chairs and tables out to the porch that wrapped lazily around the stately Victorian. It had stopped raining, and a warm sweet-scented breeze washed over us and set the leaves in the maple trees rustling. A crimson leaf sailed through the air and landed at my feet.

A silver-haired lady in black, whose nametag identified her as Anna Bell, sat at a small desk writing in a ledger.

"That's a little beauty," she said as I set the television on the desk. "It's one of a kind."

I pulled three ten dollar bills out of my wallet. She made a notation in her ledger.

"We're not through shopping," Miss Eidt said. "I have books…"

A strident voice interrupted her. The speaker huffed up to the desk so close to my purchase that I had to resist the impulse to lay a protective hand over it.

"Oh. Are you buying that TV?"

"I just did," I said.

She had stuffed her ample form into a hot pink sundress with a low scoop neckline and a hem that brushed her ankles.

"Oh…" Her lips, painted pink to match her dress, turned down in a childish pout. "I was going to buy it. I just stepped away for a second…"

Sensing an impending conflict, Anna Bell said, "Perhaps you'll find something else. Miss Sterling had several phonographs and television sets."

"Like this one?" she asked with a covetous glance at my purchase.

"I'm not sure. You can look."

"Maybe you'd better go back inside and stand by your books," I told Miss Eidt. "I'll be back as soon as I stash this in the trunk."

I had the feeling I'd better do that before the pink sundress lady grabbed the television set out of my arms and took off.

~ * ~

We had arrived early but still had to park a block away from the sale. By the time I'd locked the television set in my trunk, I was feeling wilted and a bit frazzled. The brief encounter with the disappointed shopper had unsettled me. I hoped I wouldn't see her again.

She was probably inside the house.

Many sales items had spilled out onto the front lawn, with the folded coverings that had protected them from the rain. Oil paintings on easels, white wicker furniture, outmoded luggage that included a hat box, and a rack of clothing from the twenties and thirties. Surely Miss Stirling hadn't been old enough to wear those dresses.

They made a colorful display. Maybe I'd wear a flapper's costume with a long rope of pearls for the Halloween party that Miss Eidt was planning to have in the library. This beaded ensemble would look elegant. It would fall above the knees, which was a departure from the maxi dresses in my closet, but after all it would be Halloween.

As I took it down from the rack, its beads jingled faintly and something uttered a plaintive sound.

I had disturbed a collie who had been lying in the monstrous shadow cast by the clothing rack. She stretched and nudged my hand with her long nose.

"Why, hello, girl," I said.

She was dark sable and white with a silvered muzzle, soulful brown eyes, and a wagging tail. Around her neck she wore a wide collar studded with colored stones that sparkled in the sunlight. Attached to the collar was a sheet of paper with a handwritten note on it:

My name is Bronwyn and I can be yours for twenty dollars.

This sweet old dog was part of the sale? I couldn't believe it. Aside from the questionable practice of selling a dog at an estate sale, who would buy an older collie? Someone who scoured the countryside scooping up unwanted dogs for nefarious purposes? As a collie lover, a member of the Lakeville Collie Rescue League, and a human being with a heart, I couldn't allow that to happen.

The dog laid her head against my hand. I gave her a pat on her silky head, and slipped my hand under the collar.

"Bronwyn," I said. "How would you like to come with me?"

~ * ~

Miss Eidt stood next to Anna Bell's desk, the box of Gothic paperbacks at her feet.

"A nice gentleman carried the box out for me," she said. "Mrs. Bell said we can leave it here while we look for your reward."

"I already found it."

Miss Eidt stared. Bronwyn had trailed along behind me, needing no encouragement.

"You found a collie, Jennet? How unlike you."

"She's for sale," I said.

"No!" Miss Eidt offered her palm to the dog to sniff. "She's an animal. There must be a mistake."

"I hope you're interested in buying her," Mrs. Bell said. "If she isn't sold by the end of the day, she's going to the dog pound."

Where her life would undoubtedly come to a quick end.

"You're not serious," I said.

"It's true. It isn't my decision," she added quickly.

"Well…" I reached for my wallet. Fortunately I'd brought plenty of cash to the sale. I lay two more tens on the desk. "I'm taking her. Does she have any papers? A pedigree? Her health record?"

"None that we found. She was Miss Sterling's dog. Her daughter wants everything gone. That includes Bronwyn."

"Doesn't she have at least have a leash?"

"Mmm. I don't think so. She's had the run of the house."

Miss Eidt nudged my arm. "Will Crane let you have another dog?"

That was a good question, as we already had seven collies. But I didn't plan to add Bronwyn to my household. Sue Appleton, the president of our rescue league, would welcome her. Bronwyn was, after all, a dog in distress.

"In spite of what he thinks, Crane doesn't tell me what to do," I said.

Two

Bronwyn padded along with us to the car without a single backward glance. No one would miss her at the purple Victorian house, and she obviously wouldn't miss the people who had replaced Miss Stirling in her life.

"They didn't even give us her food dish or a bowl for water," Miss Eidt said.

All Bronwyn had was her sparkling collar, the tag, and her name.

"Don't worry. I have everything she needs in my trunk."

As a member of collie rescue, I might come across a collie in dire straits at any time, often in an isolated wooded area. Part of my emergency supplies included a blanket, biscuits, and bottled water, along with collapsible dishes.

Miss Eidt dabbed discreetly at her throat. "My, it's getting hot. Are we still going to stop for lunch?"

"Yes, and if we go to Clovers, we'll be able to take Bronwyn with us. Mary Jeanne, the owner, loves dogs. She has a special room in the back with water and toys where people can leave their dogs while they eat."

"What a great idea!"

"I was thinking," Miss Eidt said. "Someone liked Bronwyn well enough when she was a puppy to give her that pretty name. What happened?"

"Life happened. Bronwyn got old. Her owner died, and the daughter regarded her as a commodity."

A nuisance to be discarded as soon as possible. Possibly she considered a trip to the dog pound a humane solution.

"Poor dog," Miss Eidt said. "If Sue Appleton can't find a home for her, I'll take her."

I reached over and squeezed her hand. Miss Eidt was a definite cat person, owner of the inscrutable feline, Blackberry. I'd never heard her express a desire for a dog.

"You're a sweetheart, Miss Eidt," I said. "Is Clovers okay for lunch?"

"It's perfect," she said. "All this fresh air has made me ravenous."

~ * ~

In the woods along Crispian Road, the leaves were beginning to turn. With new streaks of gold and crimson, this was one of the most colorful drives in town, and autumn was my favorite time of year, even though the heat of summer was determined to linger.

The little restaurant with its wraparound border of green clovers was another favorite, the place I counted on when I wanted to save time with take-out dinners or talk to Annica, my friend and sometime partner in detection. She was a part-time waitress and an English major at Oakland University. Since school started, I hadn't had time to visit Clovers and hear the latest news.

I found a parking place at the end of the lot in the shade and reached for Bronwyn's leash. "We're going to have lunch," I told her, "and there'll be a little surprise for you."

Again she came with us willingly.

"It would be nice to have a collie," Miss Eidt said. "I guess people would say I'm too old to adopt one, though."

"Not at all."

I had no idea how old Miss Eidt was, but whatever her age, she was young in all the ways that count. In her love of sweets, for example, which were displayed in the dessert carousel that greeted Clovers' patrons as they walked through the door.

A glimmer of an idea sprang to life but vanished in the wake of Miss Eidt's cry of delight.

"They have lemon meringue pie!" she said. "I must have some for here and a slice to take home."

Annica came forward to greet us. She was dressed for the season in a burnt orange sheath. Tiny scarecrow earrings danced between strands of her red-gold hair, and a bracelet of autumn leaves made of enamel encircled her wrist.

"We have lemon cake, too," she announced. "It's Lemon Week." She glanced at Bronwyn. "I see you have a special guest.

"Her name is Bronwyn," I said. "Is it all right if I leave her in your dog room?"

"Sure. We have two tables and chairs for people. Shall I serve your lunch there?"

"That might be best. Otherwise she might feel that she's been abandoned."

"She isn't one of yours then?"

"Bronwyn is a rescue. I'm going to take her to Sue Appleton."

"This way then."

Clovers' back room was an airy space furnished with two café tables and chairs. A shelf contained a variety of dishes for dogs.

"I'll bring her a bowl of water," Annica said.

We ordered roast beef sandwiches and two cheeseburgers—without onion or lettuce.

"Is that Crane's dinner?" Annica asked. "Won't he want a few sides and dessert?"

"The cheeseburgers are for Bronwyn," I said. "She doesn't look underfed, but I doubt they gave her cheeseburgers at her last home."

"Lucky dog," Annica said, extending her hand to Bronwyn for a sniff. "Clovers' burgers are the best."

I hoped Bronwyn would be lucky in other ways.

When Annica brought our order, she said, "I love this time of the year. I love my new classes, my life, the weather, the leaves—everything."

She didn't have to add Brent Fowler. Foxglove Corners' illustrious red-haired fox hunter and perennial bachelor had a major claim on her affection. Annica's crush on Brent had developed into a fledgling relationship. She wouldn't talk about her romance with Brent in front of Miss Eidt, though.

"What else is new?" I asked her.

Her eyes sparkled. The topaz eyes of the little scarecrows also sparkled.

"Brent and I are keeping an eye on the mysterious violets," she said. "There are about a dozen of them now. They look as fresh as they did when they first opened."

Miss Eidt looked puzzled. She didn't know about the wildflowers that Brent and Annica had planted on Brent's property where the palatial pink Victorian house had once stood. Or that the first violet had appeared in a cloud of mystery. Some of us thought the spirit of Violet Randall who had lived in the house had sown that first seed.

Annica told Miss Eidt the story. "I won't be surprised if they bloom in the snow," she said in conclusion.

"That will be a sight to see," Miss Eidt said.

"Hey, Miss. A little service here, please." The voice, jarring over the subdued hum of conversation, carried all the way to the back room.

"That was for Marcy. She must be getting busy out there." Hastily picking up her order pad, Annica said, "Gotta go."

Neither Miss Eidt nor I, and certainly not Bronwyn, lingered over our lunch. Miss Eidt was anxious to plow through her box of Gothic novels, and I wanted to get Bronwyn settled in her new home. She had wolfed down the cheeseburgers and lay watching us, front paws crossed.

I had called Sue to inform her of the imminent arrival of a new rescue but had to leave a voice mail. I hoped that Sue wouldn't be too surprised.

~ * ~

As president of the Lakeville Collie Rescue League, Sue was used to collies appearing on her doorstep. At present she had three collies at her ranch, all rescues she had adopted. Sue raised horses and gave riding lessons to several young students, but finding good forever homes for bereft collies was her passion.

She was raking leaves and twigs into an enormous pile that would soon be blazing, sending the smell of burning leaves into the air. Being able to build bonfires was one of the many joys of living in the country. I was glad we were free to do so without having to adhere to pesky home association rules.

As usual her collies, Icy, Bluebell, and Echo, were outside with her, chasing one another around the farm and occasionally lapping water at the dogs' pail. Echo tried to interest Bronwyn in their game, but Bronwyn moved closer to my side, almost smashing me against the corral post. It was clear that she wasn't used to being around other dogs.

Sue pushed her strawberry blonde bangs back and eyed Bronwyn with surprise. Apparently she hadn't received my message.

"Who have we here?" she asked.

"Her name is Bronwyn."

As I summarized the tale of how I'd acquired her, Bronwyn flattened her ears and lifted her left paw in a clever Lassie imitation. She knew how to win a human heart.

"Selling a dog like a decoration is outrageous," Sue said. "There should be a law against it."

"I guess it's one step above being taken to the pound."

"She's beautiful. I hope I can find a home for her, but you know how difficult it is to place older collies. People want puppies or younger dogs."

I *did* know. An idea that I'd had a few days ago resurfaced.

"Some do," I said, "but not everybody. I've heard that some rescues have begun pairing geriatric collies with senior citizens."

"I don't know," Sue said. "Would seniors have time to take care of a dog?"

"More than young people with careers and families. We have to find the right prospective owner and a dog that would blend into the person's lifestyle. No bouncing puppies."

Sue warmed to the idea. "A person who lives alone and might be lonely, or a couple. A gentle dog like Bronwyn would make the perfect companion for somebody who moves at a slower pace. They'd still have to meet our requirements."

"Of course. They'll fill out an application, agree to a home check…"

"Not every senior will have a house with a fenced yard," Sue pointed out.

"Well, people who live in apartments wouldn't be likely to consider a large dog anyway. With this program, we won't have that heartbreaking problem of what to do with an older collie who can't find a forever home," I added.

"Emma Brock is the only one of our members who will foster a geriatric collie. I could keep one here at the ranch, but a dog like Bronwyn might be happier if she were the only dog in the house."

"We'll have to start compiling a list of possible owners," I said. "I have another idea. I know a reporter, Jill Lodge, who works for the *Banner*. Maybe she'll write a story about our rescue and mention our new program."

"We're due for some publicity."

Sue took Bronwyn's leash. Bronwyn cast me a worried look.

"It's all right, girl." I said, giving her a farewell-for-now pat on the head.

She whined and fixed me with her soulful stare. Oh, no. She couldn't have become attached to me already.

Sue pulled a biscuit out of her jacket pocket. Bronwyn sniffed at it politely but didn't take it. Possibly because she was full. She'd just eaten two cheeseburgers. Or apprehensive.

Sue set the biscuit on the grass. "Hopefully we'll find you a nice home, Bronwyn."

"For that article, Jill can take a picture of you with Bronwyn," I said.

"But it's your idea, Jennet. You deserve all the credit."

"I'd rather stay anonymous," I said.

I didn't share Sue's desire for publicity. I'd be happiest working on the sidelines, compiling our list, and waiting for Bronwyn's perfect owner to appear.

Three

Home was a green Victorian farmhouse on Jonquil Lane with a stained glass window between twin gables, gingerbread ornamentation, and a spacious porch furnished with white wicker furniture. I shared my dream house with my husband, Deputy Sheriff Crane Ferguson, and seven collies. Two of the collies had their faces squashed against the bay window, and all of them were barking.

If you want to be sure of your collies' undying love, leave them alone for even a short time. With the estate sale, lunch, and the visit to Sue's horse farm, today's wait had been long. They were accustomed to us leaving for the day during the week, but somehow they knew that today was Saturday. That meant no school. Play time.

They would also soon know that something was different by the scent of another canine on my person.

Carrying the television set, I entered through the kitchen door and greeted every one of my leaping, joyous brood by name.

Halley, a sweet tricolor collie, was the only one of the seven who wasn't a rescue. Then came Candy. When it looked as if I had lost Halley forever, an enterprising urchin had presented a tricolor Halley-lookalike to me hoping I'd give him the reward money.

I'd rescued the timid blue merle, Sky, from an abusive situation, and Gemmy, a sable, who had been accused of causing her owner's fatal accident. Star, also sable, was one of those older collies whose family no longer wanted her.

Misty, my white collie, had appeared on our doorstep one snowy Christmas Eve, and Raven, a rare bi-black who liked to live outside, was recovering in the house from an accident.

To say the humans were outnumbered in our home was an understatement.

I had planned an easy dinner for tonight: steaks, baked potatoes, and salad. After taking a quick shower and changing into a dress, I finally had a chance to sit quietly and try out the new television set.

I plugged it into the counter outlet and turned the 'on' button. An expanse of rolling green meadow filled the small screen. It looked like the same program that had aired when I'd tested it at the estate sale. At least three hours ago.

How was that possible? Unless it was one of those marathons like *A Christmas Story* that play continuously for twenty-four hours at Christmastime.

That was it.

"There's no mystery here," I said aloud.

I turned to the second of the three channels, saw a close-up view of the same meadow and heard background music, a nostalgic, melodious sound.

For heaven's sake! Try the third channel.

Now the scene was different, the main street of a town in the Old West. I saw a hotel named the Pink Palace, a saloon, a general store, and horses. Several horses, some tied to hitching posts, others carrying riders.

Impulsively I played with the channels. All three were airing the same movie. This was certainly not an everyday occurrence.

Did I just say there was no mystery here? I'd spoken too soon.

~ * ~

With their uncanny ability to hear faraway sounds, the collies alerted me to Crane's imminent homecoming while his Jeep was most likely still on Jonquil Lane. They grew restless and gravitated toward the kitchen door, except for Sky and my recovering invalid,

Raven, who still moved slowly. They were both resting under the oak table.

He came through the door, bringing a blast of warm autumn air with him, along with a few flyaway leaves.

Crane is tall and blond although strands of silver have stolen into his hair, complementing his marvelous frosty gray eyes. He is always handsome, but in his deputy sheriff's uniform with its badge, especially so. His presence lit up the house with color and energy.

As usual he had to wade through a wave of excited collies to reach me.

At his entrance, I had turned off the television set. A stagecoach had just lumbered onto the screen. At least the story was moving forward.

"Hi, honey," he said, turning me around for a kiss. "What's that?"

"A TV I bought for you at the estate sale today," I said, "but I decided to keep it."

"Too bad. I would have liked it."

"For your workbench, yes, but inadvertently I picked up a haunted set. You know, ghosts are my province."

"It looks pretty normal to me," he said, running a hand along the top of the case. "What does it do? Transmit messages from beyond?"

I smiled. "Maybe it will in the future. Now it plays the same movie on every one of the three channels. I haven't been watching it that long, but I'll bet it plays them endlessly."

"Let's see," he said. "Turn it on again."

The screen was still warm, but the western town had given way to weather forecaster, Joan Cranby, talking about the unseasonably warm temperatures expected for the coming week and the slight chance of severe weather tonight.

"What the heck? Where's the Western?"

"That doesn't look like a movie to me," Crane said.

"No, it doesn't."

I switched channels. A woman in an apron covered with pictures of kitchen utensils was frosting a layer cake. The third channel was running a commercial for new moisturizing soap.

"Perfectly normal," Crane said. "I guess I can have my birthday present back."

"I guess. It was a false alarm."

He locked his gun in the special cabinet in the living room, as he always did, while I checked the steaks.

"Dinner will be ready in about twenty minutes," I said.

"I'll go take a quick shower."

I moved the TV into the living room, moved from the realm of the *Twilight Zone* into a familiar routine of salad and biscuit making. It looked as if I wasn't going to have a new mystery after all.

I gathered ingredients for the salad and started tearing lettuce. My good friend and neighbor, Camille Ferguson, who was also my aunt by marriage, had given me tomatoes from her vegetable garden, so this salad would be special. I added spinach leaves and let my thoughts wander back to the TV.

Why should I summarily dismiss the possibility that I'd purchased a mystery at the estate sale? I still couldn't explain why the Western movie had been playing on all three channels, both at the estate sale and in my kitchen.

Miss Eidt had seen it, too.

I had to think about that. Had she? Or had she been looking at something else when I'd turned the TV on? Darn. I didn't remember. I'd have to call her.

I sliced a tomato into the bowl of torn lettuce.

Finish making the salad and forget about the vagaries of the TV.

I found myself remembering the disappointed woman in the pink sundress. She had wanted to buy the TV set herself. I was almost afraid she was going to grab my purchase and make off with it. Was there something special about the set? There had to be, and perhaps she was aware of it.

Stop! I ordered myself.

It was an antique. Unique. A well-crafted piece. Period.

I backed up to get a cucumber from the refrigerator and narrowly missed stepping on Candy's paw. She yelped in protest. It was her way of telling me to watch where I put my foot.

Candy wouldn't eat vegetables, but I'd brought out one of her favorite foods to add to the salad. Cheese. She was hoping for a hand-out.

I heard Crane's footsteps on the stairs. Candy heard them, too, and, cheese forgotten, took off to escort him to the first floor.

I took the steaks out of the oven. It was time for dinner, and by mutual agreement we banned distressful topics from the table—and also electronics.

That included a haunted television set.

Four

On Sunday, as soon as Crane left for his patrol of Foxglove Corners, I took Halley, Sky, and Star for a long walk to Sagramore Lake. Then I came home and went straight to the television set, now moved to the credenza in the dining room. I turned it on and consulted the *TV Guide*. The three channels were showing exactly what they should be showing.

I turned back a page to scan the programs scheduled for yesterday, hoping to see a movie with a Western title. Nothing came remotely close to one.

Where was my Western?

Not liking the noise and mindless chatter of contemporary television, I turned the set off. Immediately an unwelcome thought forced its way to the forefront of my mind.

What if I had never seen those lovely scenes? The meadow, the main street, the stagecoach? The dog and the horse? Was it possible that my imagination had played a cruel trick on me? Perhaps my gruesome first week of classes had dredged up a past trauma I'd endured at Marston High School.

It was possible. Anything was possible. Still, I rejected the idea. I was used to coping with the ups and downs of teaching high school English. I was an experienced professional, for heaven's sake. I might be highly imaginative, but I wasn't delusional.

That Western movie existed somewhere, if only on another plane. I had to find it again.

But it wasn't on today.

Going into the living room, I pulled my cell phone out of my shoulder bag and called Miss Eidt.

"How's your Sunday going?" I asked.

"It couldn't be better! I'm enjoying those books immensely. I've already read *Thunder Heights, The Lute and the Glove, and Scarecrow House*."

"Since yesterday?"

"That's all I've done. I can't put them down. When I finish one, I have to start another." She paused, no doubt wondering about the purpose of my call. Usually we held our conversations in the library.

"Did you take Bronwyn to Sue Appleton?" she asked.

"She's there now, and we have a great idea."

I told her about our new plan to match geriatric collies with senior citizens, then took a deep breath while she exclaimed how innovative it was and wondered why nobody had thought of doing that before.

"I want to ask you something, Miss Eidt," I said. "Do you remember yesterday at the estate sale when I turned on the TV to see if it worked?"

She did, of course.

"Do you remember what you saw on the screen?"

There was another pause. It lengthened.

Finally she said, "I couldn't say. I'm afraid I wasn't paying attention."

"Didn't you even glance at the screen? Just for a second?"

"I noticed a picture, but nothing registered except that the TV was working. Why is it important?"

I could have told her. I *should* have told her.

Not yet, I decided. Not until I knew more about the strange television set I had bought.

I said, "I'm not sure that it is. I'll try to stop at the library next week. I can't wait to see the Gothic Nook."

Whether I'd be able to do that depended on what the coming week brought. An impromptu teachers' meeting? Extra preparation or papers to grade? My schedule was no longer mine to make.

"I'll see you then," Miss Eidt said. "Enjoy the rest of your weekend."

I ended the call and sat back in the rocker. Misty padded up to join me. I stroked her velvety head, waiting for the act of petting a dog to soothe me, to banish the thought that had settled in my mind.

Was I the only one who was privileged—or cursed—to see the Western movie that didn't exist?

It had become a tradition for Brent Fowler to stop by our house just before the dinner hour knowing he would be invited to join us. Brent wasn't a freeloader. He was a millionaire and an extremely generous man. He never appeared without flowers or wine for me and treats for the collies, usually from Pluto's Gourmet Pet Shop.

I wasn't surprised to see him that evening. I had more or less anticipated his visit and had baked two apple pies, then cooked a roast in the oven. Today's gifts were a sumptuous bouquet of autumn-hued flowers and an assortment of homemade dog cookies.

"Liver chip," he announced. "Every dog's favorite."

I took the flowers and cookies, and Crane hung Brent's jacket in the closet. It was Brent's favorite outer garment, a rich forest green which set off his dark red hair.

"How was your first week of school?" he asked, as I filled a vase with water for the flowers.

"Same as last year. Busy. Rowdy classes. An overbearing principal."

"You'll survive," he predicted.

"Possibly."

"Jennet is a good teacher," Crane said. "Her students don't know how lucky they are to have her."

I smiled at him. It was no secret that Crane thought he could manage my classes better than I could, even without his gun strapped on. "The key is discipline," he always told me.

I wished there were some way I could prove him wrong.

Misty leaped into Brent's lap, confident she'd be welcome, and Sky lay at his feet. Of all our company, Brent was their favorite.

"How is Raven doing?" he asked. "I don't see her."

She was lying under the dining room table, Sky's special retreat.

"She's healing slowly," I said. "She sleeps in the house and can't go for walks yet."

"Poor girl.

I knew Brent would slip Raven a bite of his dinner.

"Is anything else new?"

I glanced at Crane. He nodded slightly.

"I may have another mystery," I said. "Miss Eidt and I went to an estate sale yesterday, and I bought an old portable television set."

"And?"

"It appears to be haunted."

"It would be if you selected it," he said with a teasing glint in his eyes.

I chose to ignore that. "My TV has a mind of its own. It only displays its haunted properties when it feels like it."

"I'm intrigued."

"I'll show you."

I moved the TV to the living room and set it on the table nearest an outlet.

"It was supposed to be my birthday present, but Jennet decided to keep it," Crane said.

"I'll buy you something else."

Turning the television on, I waited for the main street of a western town and a stagecoach to form. Instead two distinguished gentlemen were deep in a political conversation.

"Darn."

"That isn't very ghostly," Brent remarked. "It's scary, though."

I shouldn't have bothered to switch to the other two channels, already knowing they'd be airing contemporary programs. Admitting defeat for the present, I turned the TV off. feeling like hitting it with a hammer.

"Well," I said. "This is one of the times my TV is keeping those ghostly properties under wraps."

"What did you see before?" Brent asked.

"Scenes from a Western movie."

I added the uncanny facts. "The movie was playing on all three channels, and it had apparently been on for several hours."

"That *is* mysterious," Brent said, "but I can think of an easy explanation. Almost every movie ever made is out on CD. Maybe there's a CD of this western embedded in your set."

Crane leaned forward. "Interesting theory, Fowler, but how exactly would that work? I can't visualize it."

"And why does the movie come on only some of the time?" I added.

"I'm not a scientist, Jennet," Brent said. "It just seems logical to me. What's the name of this movie?"

"I didn't see the title or the stars' names. When I first turned the TV on, the movie had already started."

I hadn't thought of that. It was something I should know.

But how was I going to find out more about the elusive Western if the temperamental TV kept serving me a diet of contemporary fare?

Five

"I bought a dog at the estate sale," I said. "She's an older sable and white collie named Bronwyn."

In his surprise, Brent almost spilled Misty out of his lap. "They were selling a dog?"

"For thirty dollars," I added. "If Bronwyn wasn't sold by the end of the day, she was going to the pound."

"That's outrageous. Is she here?"

"Sue Appleton has her," I said.

Brent didn't hesitate. "If Sue can't find a home for her, I'll take her. I always have room for one more."

Bronwyn was indeed lucky with two offers of a home, one from a kind and gentle older lady and one from a man in his prime who already owned two collies.

"I'll let you know," I said, "but we're starting a new program at the Rescue League. We always have trouble placing collies past the age of six or seven. From now on, we're going to look for senior citizens to adopt our geriatric collies."

"I'll bet you'll find a lot of people willing to open their hearts to an older collie."

"I hope so."

"If not, give me a call."

"I will and thank you."

That reminded me. I was supposed to call Jill Lodge about writing an article for the *Banner* to help promote our new program. Well, it was Sunday. I'd call her tomorrow after school.

And because it was Sunday and the weekend was winding down, I'd better make the most of every minute.

While Brent and Crane discussed the possibility of embedding a CD into an old portable TV, I set the table with the autumn bouquet in the center and lit the tapers in the candlesticks that had belonged to Crane's Civil War ancestress, Rebecca Ferguson.

As always I counted on them to bring a blessing to our home.

~ * ~

The next morning, I fixed Crane a big breakfast, made a sandwich of leftover roast beef for my lunch, and set out to pick up Leonora, my longtime friend and fellow English teacher. I didn't have to worry about the dogs as Camille always took care of them when I was at school.

Ever since Leonora's move to Foxglove Corners, she and I had carpooled to Marston High School, which made the hour-long commute pass more quickly. We never ran out of conversation. Among today's topics were the haunted TV, Bronwyn, our new program at the Rescue League, and the newlywed Leonora's struggle to combine marriage with her career.

She would learn the ropes. We all did, and with time life would get easier.

This year Leonora was experiencing something different for her—a difficult class. With her blonde good looks, charisma and calm, in-control personality, she rarely had a discipline problem, let alone a surly, disruptive class, the kind I had at least once every semester.

"From the moment they first walked in the door, they were unruly and obnoxious," she said for about the sixth time. "Usually kids are on their best behavior, for a few days at least."

"The honeymoon period. It never lasts."

"With this class, it didn't even start."

We both had sections of American Literature, which was required for all juniors who hoped to graduate. This year our classes were scheduled at the same time.

"Fourth hour is a bad time," I pointed out. "The kids are anxious for lunch, then still wound up after lunch and tired."

"That's no excuse for bad behavior," Leonora said.

"There must be something about that age. Most of my trouble has been with juniors."

"If only we had more appetizing material to teach."

That was part of the problem. Our survey started with the beginning of American literature, which meant staid Colonial writing, Puritan sermons, and devotional poetry as thick as mud.

"Cheer up," I said. "We have witches to look forward to."

"The Salem witch trials. Even those excerpts are boring."

I couldn't resist teasing her. "Never say that. They're scintillating, profound, and reflective of an exciting time in American history."

"May I borrow that sentiment for my lecture?" she asked.

"You may."

The freeway exit loomed ahead, seeming to float in a light September mist. From the car, I could see the colors of autumn swim by. Crimson, russet, and gold, touched by early morning light. How beautiful it was! How much more beautiful in the countryside we'd left behind.

A new day, a new semester, the first literary efforts of a new country to teach, I thought. *Monday, please be a good day.*

~ * ~

I couldn't complain about my first three classes, Journalism, a section of World Literature, and a conference hour. In Journalism, it was always exciting to train a new staff for the school newspaper, and my tenth graders in World Literature, were, so far, enthusiastic about their study of the short story. My conference period was next, scheduled at a time when I didn't need a break.

Then came fourth hour American Literature. They stormed into the classroom like an invading horde of barbarians, thirty-four strong. Some went to their assigned seats, some to the desks they had assigned themselves, and a few remained standing. The window ledge with a view of school-owned woods was a popular place to hang out.

The bell rang. I pulled the seating chart out of my gradebook. It was too early in the semester for me to remember everyone's name.

"Class," I said. "Take your assigned seats."

My reasonable request elicited a round of grumbling from a disgruntled few and a demand to know why they couldn't sit near their friends.

Well, that should be obvious.

"Sit in your assigned seats."

I waited for the inevitable shuffle to be completed, then took attendance. Four students were absent. Would those four not being present today make a difference? It didn't seem so. Correction. Didn't *sound* so.

I glanced at the clock. Ten minutes had gone by. Principal Grimsley would call this a rocky start to class. I couldn't disagree. It was certainly noisy.

But so was Leonora's class next door.

Well, this class was mine, my responsibility.

"Quiet!" I said, hoping to drown out the last hold-outs. "Settle down. Today we're going to review Friday's material on the early American settlers."

"Review?"

The speaker was a pretty blonde girl who wore far too much makeup and looked older than the average junior.

"We don't need a review," she said, adding in a lower but still audible voice, "It was bad enough the first time."

"Fine," I said, quickly consulting the seating chart. "Brianna—perhaps you can tell me the title of the first piece of American writing and its author."

"I know that!" she said. "It's *The Legend of Sleepy Hollow* by Washington Irving.

I suppose I should give her credit for knowing the name of an American author.

"You're about a century off," I said. "We *do* need that review. I have a quiz for you tomorrow," I added. "It would be to your advantage to pay attention today."

Predictably this ushered in another muttered protest.

The quiz was a spur-of-the-moment inspiration. All right. A punishment. I'd have to create it tonight and print copies.

Ten more minutes had passed. That flippant response to my announcement wasn't part of my plan.

"That's a nice dress, Mrs. Ferguson," said a girl in the first row, another blonde. How many blondes did I have in this class, for heaven's sake, and how could I tell them apart? This girl was Jessica.

I'd chosen the outfit, a navy polka dot dress with a high waistline, because I always felt pretty in it and needed to feel confident when standing before a classroom. Still, I recognized the compliment, timed as it was, as a delaying tactic.

"Thank you," I said. "Now, back to the early American writers. Who can give me the gist of the Puritan sermon we read yesterday?"

"Gist?" someone said.

"Why do we have to know that?" Jessica asked. "How's it going to help us when we graduate?"

I had my answer ready, not that they believed it.

It had taken us almost a half hour to reach what I'd thought would be the beginning of the day's lesson. If Grimsley had been sitting in my class—heaven forbid—he would be certain to comment on that.

At this point in fourth hour, I always got hungry, so hungry that I didn't know how I could last until the bell rang without eating.

Don't think about it, I told myself. *Try to summon up a little enthusiasm for the lives and perils of those courageous people who sailed across the ocean to settle a new land.*

In truth, it was a marvelous adventure.

In college, I'd had a Classics professor who had entertained us with tales of Odysseus and company as if they were his personal friends. He'd kept us laughing. I'd been enthralled and for the first time read the Classical writers eagerly. How had he done it?

Apparently he truly regarded these austere personages as his friends. Could I do that with the likes of William Bradford and Jonathan Edwards?

Not in a million years.

The class grew restless with the review. In the back of the room, two or three students initiated their own conversation. The noise level rose. Another conversation started close to the front door. My demand for quiet fell on deaf ears.

It was also noisy in Leonora's room next door.

Even without looking at the clock, one could tell it was almost time for the period to end, almost time for lunch. Three minutes.

"Remember the quiz tomorrow," I said. "You might reread a few of the selections tonight…"

And the lunch bell rang.

Six

Our lunch hour was a twenty-minute reprieve in a hectic day. It wasn't an hour, nor was it strictly speaking twenty minutes. Teachers and students had ten extra minutes to travel to and from the cafeteria. To redeem that time, Leonora and I brought our lunches and ate in her classroom or mine.

"Did you see Grimsley in the hall just before fourth hour?" Leonora asked.

I unwrapped my sandwich. "I didn't notice him."

It was his habit to patrol the halls, ostensibly sending malingerers back to class. We all knew he was really spying on us, which was his right as principal, I supposed.

"My class was diabolical today," Leonora said.

"Mine, too."

"We can look forward to a lecture on discipline in our next meeting," she added. "Because the way our class behaves is our fault, of course."

"There's no meeting today. Thank heavens."

I took a bite of my sandwich. The roast beef tasted even better in a sandwich, but the slices of white bread were too small. The Hometown Bakery was closed for vacation. Our current loaf had come from Blackbourne's Grocers.

"We'll have a Rescue League meeting tomorrow, though," I said. "Sue wants to tell the members about the new program before they read the story in the *Banner*."

"That's a good idea, but I hate meetings. They take away from my home time."

She fell silent, no doubt thinking about Jake. After their marriage he had transferred from Ellentown to the sheriff's department in Foxglove Corners, and they were going to stay in the house Leonora had bought, which made her happy. It was a pink Victorian on wooded acreage, perfect for Leonora, Jake, and the two collies.

I was quiet as well, wishing I'd made two sandwiches but happy I'd brought an oatmeal-raisin cookie for dessert. Whatever I had would have to sustain me until the end of the school day.

~ * ~

As soon as I got home, I called Jill Lodge and told her about the new program. She was happy to write a feature story on placing older collies with senior citizens.

"Why aren't all the rescues doing this?" she asked.

"They should be."

"My aunt had a collie, Pilot, on her farm in Harrisville," she said. "It broke her heart when she had to sell the farm and move to town. She bought a small house with a yard, but after Pilot died, she never had another dog. I'm going to tell her about your program."

"So far we have only one geriatric collie," I said. "But we're always getting dogs. Ask your aunt to check our website."

"I'll do that. I'd like to take pictures to go along with the story, if I may."

"Sue Appleton is our president," I said. "She has a horse farm on Squill Lane. It's close to me. Maybe Bronwyn will still be there."

If by chance she had found a home, Sue still had Bluebell, Icy, and Echo, all beauties, although not elderly. Along with Sue, they would be photogenic enough to draw people to the article.

"I'll try to get down to Foxglove Corners later this week," she promised, "and I'll stop by for a visit."

I said goodbye and ended the call. Now…

I looked around the kitchen. The stew was bubbling merrily away. Nevertheless, I scraped the bottom of the Dutch oven with a spoon. Candy materialized at my side, licking her chops.

"Not yet," I said.

Everything was under control. I had free time, about an hour, until Crane came home, and what better activity could I choose than a few minutes of watching television on the haunted set? Just to see what was on.

I turned the TV on and beheld the stagecoach I'd seen before.

Yes! I was back in fantasyland, this time with music. The theme was familiar. A heart-stirring melody from Copland that invoked open spaces and campfires and an infinity of stars in a black sky.

The woman who alighted from the stagecoach stood for a moment surveying the town, a look of wonder on her face. Her long dress was gorgeous, green-striped on a snowy white background with an extravagance of ecru-ruffled trim. Was it typical nineteenth century style or what passed for it in a Western movie?

I didn't know without consulting a costume book, but I wished I had a dress like that, wished I were coming to a western town where everything would be new and I'd have a grand adventure.

The woman glanced at the hotel, the Pink Palace, and began walking toward it. The camera came to rest on a man sitting with a white-bearded companion in a Confederate uniform.

He was magnificent. Not White Beard but the other man. In a silvery blue shirt topped with a camel colored jacket and worn with a jaunty Stetson, he was the perennial cowboy. His hair was light brown and wavy, his skin tanned from long hours under a western sun, and his eyes…? I couldn't tell from a distance.

I leaned closer to the screen. Was it my imagination or did the cowboy look like Crane?

Imagination, I decided, but if a dozen men, old and young, had been sitting in front of the hotel, my gaze would have sought him out first.

What an incredibly handsome man!

He was looking at the woman in the green striped dress. I was looking at him. The picture shivered and blurred and disappeared. The music died in mid-note.

Two people were laughing, an intrusive display of hilarity generated by the co-anchors of an early news program.

I'd lost my Western. Lost the connection to the *Twilight Zone*.

At least I knew I wasn't losing my mind. Well, I'd never really thought that was the case, although the television's behavior was odd. What perverse glitch had cut off the movie in mid-scene?

None of the actors had spoken yet. Would the handsome cowboy speak to the woman in the green-striped dress as she passed him? Probably not, if they hadn't been introduced. On the other hand, this was the Old West where, presumably, people didn't adhere to stuffy custom.

The co-anchors' constant babbling was getting on my nerves. I snapped the TV off and realized that it was later than I thought. I'd better get the rest of my dinner together.

As I went back to the kitchen, I found myself wondering what was going to happen next in the movie. I hoped it wasn't still airing, somewhere on another plane, because if it were, I was missing a significant chunk of the plot.

~ * ~

The melody played in my mind over and over again. After a period of quiet concentration and a search of my music library, I identified it as the introduction from *Billy the Kid* by Copland.

I made a salad, brought out ingredients for biscuits and resisted the impulse to turn the television on again.

Crane, on the other hand, couldn't wait to see the mysterious Western movie I'd talked about. Even before he locked his gun in the cabinet, he turned the TV on to breaking news. A tornado had touched down in the western part of the state, smashing barns and a lakeside restaurant. No lives were lost.

"That's a surprise," he said.

Quickly I looked out the window. Jonquil Lane lay quietly under a placid blue sky filled with white cotton candy clouds, a summer sky with no storms brewing. Still…

"Should we take the dogs and go to the basement?" I asked. "We can all eat there."

"No, this was a freak. Listen."

The forecaster was talking about a thirty percent chance of severe weather in towns located a comfortable distance from us. Thank God.

The weather alert was followed by a grim story of a carjacking.

"I *did* see some of the movie a while ago," I said. "The actor looked like you."

Crane's gray eyes sparkled. "I'd like to see him. Usually when people say a man looks like me, I can't see the resemblance."

"Who says that?" I asked.

He shrugged. "People."

"Well, I want to know what's going to happen," I said. "I hate seeing only a part of a movie that looks good."

"You don't have to wait for your magic TV. Find out the name of the movie and see if you can find it on a CD."

I had been going to do that. Unfortunately school work left little time for leisurely research.

"Come to think of it, though, I have a history of Western movies somewhere and one of period costumes," I said.

"You're all set then. I'll go take a shower."

"And I'll make the biscuits."

I rolled up my sleeves and began to roll the dough. Was nineteenth century life in a western town so mundane, so predictable?

Probably more so. But I had to remember. I was thinking about a movie.

Seven

The next day after school, I took Halley, Gemmy, and Star for a long walk. We ended up on Squill Lane so close to Sue's horse ranch that it made no sense not to stop and visit her.

The trees were glorious with autumn tints of scarlet and yellow. Falling leaves floated languidly in the air and crackled when we tread on them. A light smoky scent wafted across the lane. Someone was burning leaves. Maybe they were about to roast hot dogs or marshmallows. Crane and I should do that one evening.

Time in the fresh country air with my dogs was a much-appreciated blessing at the end of another chaotic day at Marston.

We turned in at the ranch and walked up the driveway to the house. Sue was resting on the porch with four collies to keep her company. They were all wagging tails and frantic excitement as they welcomed the newcomer who had brought three of their kind to visit. Bronwyn was the first to reach my extended hand.

"I found the perfect owner for Bronwyn," Sue said by way of greeting.

I climbed the steps and sat beside Sue on one of the two matching wicker rockers.

"So soon?" I said.

"And with little effort. I took Echo with me to Carmenelli's yesterday. They have an outdoor seating area where you can bring your dog on a leash and drink your coffee. No one bothers you or makes unkind remarks. Well, everyone there made the greatest fuss over Echo. The lady at the next table asked me so many questions about her that I finally asked if she ever had a collie.

"Dogs are a guaranteed icebreaker," I said.

"Turns out she grew up with a collie. Did I mention she was a senior citizen?"

"Not yet."

"She was."

"I was thinking the other day," I said. "Mentioning age might be a little drawback in an opening conversation. Some people may not want to admit they're that old."

"She brought up her age. Her name is Charlotte Gray, by the way. She said she was too old to keep up with a young dog like Echo and couldn't even consider raising a puppy, no matter how much she longed for one. That was my cue to tell her about Bronwyn."

"In what ways is Charlotte the perfect owner?" I asked.

"She has a small house with a large back yard near Sagramore Lake. Charlotte is a retired music teacher. She was having her coffee and pastry all alone. How sad."

"Well, so were you."

"Not at all," Sue said. "I had Echo. But that's beside the point. I told her about our collie rescue and the new program, then about how we came to have Bronwyn."

Hearing her name, Bronwyn looked up, her eyes on Sue, waiting to hear another word she knew.

"Doctor Foster says Bronwyn is in good shape, and I know from experience she's very sweet, very much a lady. Quiet and dignified."

"Like Charlotte?"

Sue nodded. "They're a perfect match. Charlotte is coming to see Bronwyn tomorrow. If you're home from school around four, I'd like you to meet her."

"Just think. We may have our first success before Jill even writes her article."

"And before I have a chance to tell our members about it."

"Let's hope this adoption will be the first of many," I said.

~ * ~

It was encouraging to be able to celebrate one success. In other matters I wasn't so lucky. My reference book on the history of Western movies contained extensive write-ups and illustrations of both major and minor films, some of which I'd never heard about, but it ended with the sixties. I didn't think the movie that played (sometimes) on the haunted TV was that old. Unfortunately I wouldn't have time to go to the library until the weekend.

As for my temperamental television set, I turned it on for a few minutes whenever I passed it, but I never saw the movie or heard the music.

In school the days were all the same, nerve-wracking—no, nerve-destroying—with the constant threat of Principal Grimsley interrupting my class to tell my students to be quiet. He had done that to two other teachers.

In my fourth period American Literature class, I was involved in a 'hall pass' war. In a short impromptu meeting, Grimsley had claimed that every time he left his office, he saw more students in the halls than in class, some without passes. That had to be an exaggeration, but he'd made his point. Henceforth, he decreed, we were not to sign passes for any student except for the most serious reason. He left it to our discretion to decide what was serious and what was frivolous.

I imagined signs of imminent death would qualify as serious.

By then I had identified three troublemakers in my fourth hour classes: Brianna, Rachelle, and Jessica. Privately I called them the blonde demons. Because I had a hard time remembering who was who, I mentally assigned them distinguishing physical traits.

Brianna was the prettiest of the three and wore the most makeup. Rachelle's hair was the longest and the straightest, and Jessica was taller and slimmer than her friends. The girls always had to go somewhere: to the lavatory, to their locker, to the attendance office, to the counselor. And it was always an emergency.

The following day was no exception. I was giving the class notes on Puritan poetry when Brianna sidled up to the podium and slapped a slip of paper down on its top.

I ignored her.

She stepped closer, her heels making a tapping sound on the tile floor.

Try ignoring that.

"Mrs. Ferguson…"

"What is it?" I demanded.

"I don't feel well. Can I go to the bathroom?"

She looked fine, glowing with youth and good health. Her cheeks were a bit rosy, but that could be expertly-applied blush. And her smile? It was smug. I didn't believe her.

"Class is almost over," I said.

"Yeah, in twenty minutes."

"Surely you can wait."

"Surely I can't." She emphasized the word 'surely' as if to mock me.

The attention of the class began to slip away. Not that I'd had a tight hold on it to begin with.

"I'm sorry," I said. "I can't."

"Why not?" She pushed the pass closer to me. "Can't you sign your name?"

What would Crane do? Give her the kind of answer she deserved? Something like 'I can. Can *you*?' I decided to stay with the facts.

"Principal's orders," I said.

"No way. I got out of Chemistry last hour."

"This is American Literature," I said. "Go back to your seat."

She grabbed the pass, crumbled it, and tossed it into the wastebasket. At a safe distance, she muttered something I couldn't make out.

What a brat!

I took a breath and glanced at my index card. I'd forgotten what I was saying. If only I could skip poetry and turn the pages to the section on the Salem witch trials.

It seemed appropriate.

~ * ~

A storm brewing in the west cut my walk with the dogs short. We just missed getting drenched. Inside, I looked for something to do. The haunted TV beckoned.

I turned it on to discover that it was playing the Western movie, and the story hadn't moved forward. It was as if I had put it on 'Pause.' We were still with the handsome cowboy in front of the Pink Palace as he gazed boldly at the lady who had come to town on the stagecoach. Trying to restrain my excitement, I pulled a chair close to the TV and turned up the volume.

He spoke. "Welcome to Jubilee, Miss…"

He had a slight accent, Texan I'd guess. When he smiled, the fine lines around his eyes crinkled in a bewitching manner. Just like Crane's.

Who was the actor? I didn't recognize him. Certainly I would remember if I'd seen a man this ruggedly handsome. If I knew his name, I could google it and find a list of his screen credits.

He stood. "My name is Luke Emerson, ma'am," he said.

The lady gave him a shy smile and swept past him, her green-striped skirt almost brushing against him.

She hadn't seen fit to introduce herself. In her place, I wouldn't have missed the opportunity. He had issued a clear invitation.

Women weren't as forward in the nineteenth century. But then, they were still women.

My hands gripped the arms of the chair. "Please don't turn yourself off now," I begged the TV.

Thinking I was talking to her, Misty appeared at my side and trained her eyes on the screen. Odd. She'd never even been aware of television programs before.

The lady walked through the doors of the Pink Palace, and the camera moved outside, resting on the face of the bewhiskered Confederate.

"She sure is pretty," he said.

Luke nodded. "That she is."

Inside the hotel, the lady stood waiting to be noticed.

As luck would have it, Crane wouldn't be home for an hour. Would the movie still be playing then? And where was Brent? He must be due for a visit. Only Brent and Crane knew about the haunted television set. I'd started to tell Leonora, then stopped. Why not wait until I had more to tell—and proof, whatever form that would take?

Suddenly it was important to me that I have a witness. Otherwise, after a while, people would think I was hallucinating when I spoke of a movie that came and went on my new TV at will.

If only I could record the movie, but the old VCR was in the basement, and I didn't know how to record on the DVD player. Even if I did, an attempt to capture the film might inadvertently interfere with the broadcast, might kill it. I certainly didn't want to do that.

Eight

Several scenes unfolded without interruption. Finally I knew the name of the girl in the green-striped dress: Susanna Cade. She had come to Jubilee, Colorado, to live with her married cousin, Alicia.

Susanna needed a room at the Pink Palace for one night only. She also hoped they served dinner at the hotel. Why her cousin didn't meet her when she arrived was unclear at present.

We went along with her, seeing the frontier hotel room, the restaurant, and the morning sun rise on the mountain top from Susanna's window. With each changing scene, I hoped the movie would keep playing. I wanted to see the cowboy who looked like Crane and more of the story.

Grabbing a stray envelope, I jotted down what I knew so far. The cowboy's name was Luke Emerson; the town was Jubilee in the state of Colorado. Or Colorado Territory. It would depend on the year. The time had to be after the Civil War, which would be 1864, based on the Confederate uniform worn by Luke's bewhiskered companion. Perhaps as much as ten years, as the diehard Confederate was elderly and the gray uniform had seen better days.

What else?

Susanna was new in town, obviously. Alicia, whom we met the next morning, lived in a cozy house with comforts I didn't realize a frontier woman would have, such as china teacups and lacy scarves on tables. Or was Alicia's home a movie set, not necessarily historically accurate? Her husband was the town's doctor.

The name of the movie might be *Jubilee*. Or *Susanna*. Or something vastly different.

Somewhere, not too far away, thunder rumbled. The storm was reforming. From her safe place under the dining room table, Sky whined. She hated storms and knew what the sound meant.

I took my eyes off the screen for a second.

Misty was sitting on a chair with the best view of Jonquil Lane. I stood beside her, wondering when the sky had darkened. Puffy clouds hovered low over the earth, and the trees across the lane swayed frantically in the wind.

"Who has to go out before it rains?" I asked.

Halley padded to the door and stood watching me to see if I was going to open it. Misty followed her. The other dogs responded by not stirring from their various resting places.

I opened the door and stepped back out of the wind.

"Hurry," I told them.

While Misty and Halley rushed outside, I checked the meatloaf in the oven. Another half hour. Then I glanced at the clock and was surprised to find it was so late. Not that dinner wouldn't be ready when Crane came home, but I had no idea I'd been watching the movie so long.

I hurried back, only to find the early news on again and a lightning icon in the lower right corner of the screen.

Once again, my movie was gone. I couldn't have been away from the set for five minutes.

~ * ~

"It's blowing up a monster storm out there," Crane said as he locked his gun in the cabinet.

I shooed Candy away from the stove. "This is like summer weather."

A few more windstorms like this would tear the leaves from the trees before the color season peaked.

While Crane showered, I comforted an agitated Sky who had crept out from under the table and stood trembling at my side. Poor Sky. I hated to see her distressed but couldn't tune out the storm. With seven collies, I was lucky to have only one who feared thunderstorms. To be honest, I didn't care for them myself.

By the time Crane came downstairs and I was bringing the dishes to the table, rain fell in slanting sheets, pounding the windows. The lane would be a muddy mess. I lit the tapers in the heirloom candlesticks, and we sat while Sky scurried back under the table.

Alicia had candles in her living room. Candles and ornamental oil lamps and wildflower bouquets in crystal vases.

"I was watching my Western movie a little while ago," I told Crane.

"I thought the haunting had played itself out," he said.

"It only started. Then I left the room for a second and lost it. The news was on."

"I guess I'm never going to get my birthday present."

"Not until I figure out what's going on."

"Do you think you will?" he asked.

I thought about it. "Yes, eventually. I have enough information now to track down the movie."

"How will that help you understand what's going on with the TV?"

"It won't, but it'll be something." I passed him the platter. Meatloaf, a prosaic entrée with parsley garnish that would taste as good as it looked.

I looked forward to my new challenge. Research, after all, could be restful and never dangerous. In the haunted television set, I had the perfect mystery.

~ * ~

Charlotte Gray was crying.

Bronwyn had come to her readily, with wild enthusiasm. Her pretty face radiated with a collie smile. It should be a happy moment, not a time for tears.

I sat on Sue's porch keeping my collies back while Sue, looking uncomfortable, searched in her basket for a box of tissue.

"Is anything the matter?" she asked.

Charlotte wiped her eyes. "No, nothing. She's just so beautiful."

"She is."

So was Charlotte, graceful and ladylike with her ash brown hair arranged in a shoulder-length pageboy and sweet smile.

She reached out to pet Bronwyn who wriggled joyfully under her caresses.

Charlotte wasn't dressed for a visit to a horse farm to pick up a collie. Her black wool jumper had already attracted several dog hairs, and her white silk blouse wouldn't stay pristine for long. But who was I to judge another's choice of clothing?

"You'll take her then?" Sue asked.

"I've been waiting for her all my life."

Bronwyn's new owner had a touch of drama in her makeup.

"All right, then," Sue said. "I have some of her food for you and a box of treats. Let's go over the paperwork."

"I'd better go home," I said. "Coming, girls?"

As Charlotte was going to join our rescue league, I knew I'd see her again. I couldn't have hoped for a better launch for our new program.

~ * ~

Jill Lodge, the vivacious brunette who was a cousin of the *Banner's* owner, took a whirlwind tour through Foxglove Corners, taking pictures of Sue with Icy, Bluebell, and Echo. By then, Bronwyn had left with Charlotte for her new home. Because Jill wanted to illustrate her article with a picture of an older collie, she asked if she could photograph Star.

"Will you match her with a senior citizen?" she asked.

I'll swear Star understood the question. From that moment she moved closer to me. Her face acquired a worried look. Perhaps she was missing her collie sisters who were inside, pacing and barking at being excluded from the company.

"Good heavens, no," I said. "Star isn't a foster. She's part of our family, part of the pack."

"If you hadn't adopted her, what would have happened to her?" she asked.

"Sue would have held onto Star until we found a family that wanted her, unlike the people who raised her."

"She might have been with Sue a long time," Jill said.

"That happens more often than not. It's what inspired our new program. I hope your article will make older owners realize that they still can have a collie companion. Sue and I plan to keep a list of prospective owners."

"I'll try my best," Jill said. "Could I have a picture of the two of you together? You and Star?"

"Well…"

I wanted to refuse. Previously I'd invited trouble when one of my collies—no longer mine—had received an award for saving a child from drowning. The wrong person had read the article written to commemorate the event and recognized the dog.

Finally I said, "All right, as long as you don't include my address or write anything about me and just identify Star as an older collie."

"But I can use your name?"

"Yes, Jennet Ferguson."

"You should be proud of your work with the Rescue League," she pointed out.

"I am, but I don't want any publicity."

"Oh, that's right. You teach high school students. But not in Foxglove Corners."

"No," I said, "but it doesn't matter. Once your name is in the paper, you're vulnerable. You'd be surprised how enterprising teenagers can be if they want to find you."

"I guess I understand," she said. "Where would you like to pose?"

I looked around. We'd been sitting on the porch, but there was one bright patch of color in the yard. "In front of the purple coneflowers. They're exceptional this year. Come, Star."

She came down the stairs with me and sat beside me. I smiled for Jill's camera, but I thought Star still looked worried. I was surprised. We'd had her long enough for her to feel secure with us. Perhaps that was the fallout of having been surrendered to a rescue league. A loyal, sensitive collie never forgot.

Nine

For Crane's birthday I planned to cook all of his favorite foods for dinner and bake an orange chiffon cake for dessert. As for his present, I'd decided to hold on to the haunted television set. Its replacement was a Civil War-era print depicting a minor Confederate battle.

I was reasonably certain it didn't come with supernatural properties.

His birthday fell on a weekday, a day which had been relatively free of discord at school. On hearing about Crane's birthday, Brent had invited us to dine with him at the Hunt Club Inn on Saturday. Tonight's dinner was just for us.

I turned the roast over, checked the potatoes and carrots, and set about decorating the cake with orange blossoms and a sentiment: 'Happy Birthday, Crane.' The dogs crowded into the kitchen, lured by the enticement of roasting beef. I had to be careful not to step on paws as I wielded my decorator's tools.

When I had finished my masterpiece, I turned on the haunted TV. It wasn't haunted today. The early news was on, practically a repetition of yesterday's events with the same weather pattern. Quickly I turned it off again.

Would I ever see the rest of the movie? More to the point, would I ever know why it came on, then vanished for days?

I fussed with the table, brought the cake from the kitchen counter to the credenza, and added birthday candles, the final touch. With everything ready, I sat in the living room and relaxed.

A commotion rose at the side door as the dogs rushed to greet Crane. He stepped inside, carrying something in both hands. A cake carrier? He set it on the oak table.

I melted into his 'hello' kiss. "What's that?" I asked.

"Some devil's food cake," he said. "About a quarter."

"Did you buy your own?"

Foolish question. Who buys half a quarter of a cake and a glass carrier for it?

"They had it at the station for me," he said. "During lunch."

"The sheriff?"

"No, Veronica."

Veronica the Viper. The female deputy sheriff who had set her sights on my husband, knowing full well he was married to me.

"Veronica baked a cake for you? How did she know it was your birthday?"

"That I don't know."

"Does she bake cakes for everyone's birthday?" I asked.

"I don't think so."

"It isn't a new tradition in the sheriff's department, then?"

"This is the first time it's happened."

I detached myself from his embrace. "I baked you a cake, too. The kind we had for Leonora's wedding shower last month. You said you loved it."

"I did. I do."

"Well, if you had too much cake today…"

"That was at lunchtime," he said quickly.

He locked his gun in the cabinet while I pushed Veronica's cake to the back of the kitchen counter. How dare that Viper bake a cake for my husband? Wasn't it bad enough that she asked Annica for news of him every time she came to Clovers for lunch?

What else had she planned? And should I let Crane know how angry I was? He *did* appear to be a trifle guilty about the cake. Probably because of my reaction. I was never skilled at dissembling.

I couldn't seem to help myself, though. I felt as if Veronica had intruded on our evening. Perhaps that had been her intention. In which case, I wouldn't let it happen.

But what to do? I could keep quiet and let my anger boil over or express what I was feeling. Well, a censored version of it. I decided to speak.

After Crane had taken a shower and changed out of his uniform and before I served dinner, I said, "It seems that Veronica is carrying your work relationship a trifle too far."

"She's just friendly," he said. "After all, she's new in town."

I'd heard that before. "She's been in Foxglove Corners for a while now, hasn't she? She must have made new friends."

He couldn't deny it.

"Veronica is grateful because I lent her a helping hand when she was new in the department," he said.

I didn't believe gratitude was her sole motivation. Perhaps Crane didn't believe it either, although once he may have. He couldn't possibly be that naïve.

"We can throw it out the window for the birds," he said.

"If I did that, the dogs would find it in a heartbeat, and it's chocolate. Poison."

"Then I'll take it back to the department for the other deputies," he said.

And have them wonder why he was returning the cake? And what would the Viper think? That she'd won?

"You can leave it," I said.

Not that I'd eat it. I could take it to school tomorrow for Leonora.

I'd give Crane his present after we ate, while we sat in the living room over coffee and my orange chiffon cake.

I could only hope that Veronica hadn't given my husband a birthday present, too.

~ * ~

I didn't have to stop at Clovers after school the next day, but I wanted to see Annica and knew she'd be working a late shift. Turning on Crispian Road, I found myself driving through an enchanted forest of color—crimson and yellow and crispy brown.

"It'll be nice to have a cup of tea anyplace but at school," Leonora said. "I still hear the noise of kids shouting. When I close my eyes, I can see those idiotic grins. I heard one of them saying 'Pass it on' today. I don't know what 'it' was, but fortunately I nipped it in the bud."

"You must have had a bad day," I said.

"The worst. Jake won't be home till later."

Hence her willingness to dally on the way home.

"I might buy some cloverleaf rolls," I said.

There wasn't much left of the orange chiffon birthday cake. Crane and I had each had two pieces. Veronica's devil's food offering remained on the kitchen counter, unmentioned and unlamented.

Leonora, who excelled in cake making, had commented on it: "Too sweet and there's an unpleasant aftertaste. The frosting is like paste."

I pulled into Clovers' parking area, admiring the bright green clovers on the border with brilliant maple leaves gleaming in the background. Red and green, Christmas colors.

"I wonder if Veronica will bake Christmas cookies for Crane," I said.

"Let it go, Jennet. You'll drive yourself crazy."

"Would *you* let it go? Suppose the next cake is for Jake."

"She wouldn't dare."

"I guess not. Unless she can concentrate on two men at the same time. I want to ask Annica if she's been in Clovers lately," I said as I pushed open the door.

Someone had tracked leaves onto the welcome mat and even a small twig. Well, it was autumn and one couldn't escape the great unleaving.

Annica, who liked to harmonize with the season, wore a black midi dress patterned with falling leaves in unleaflike colors of rose, turquoise, and lavender, with gold leaf earrings.

"Did you come for take-out?" she asked. "We have something new. Shepherd's pie. It's delicious."

"Just tea this afternoon," I said, "and a dozen cloverleaf rolls if you have them."

My favorite booth by the window was free. Here we could enjoy our tea while watching the leaves blow across Crispian Road.

Annica reappeared with a tray. Tea for three and chocolate biscuits on the house, and she sat with us. I poured boiling water over my tea bag and came directly to the point.

"Has that female deputy sheriff been in asking about Crane lately?"

Annica stirred a teaspoon of sugar into her cup, then another, then a third.

"Are you sure you want to know?" she asked.

Oh, no!

"I don't want to be a harbinger of bad news," she added.

"You promised to keep me informed," I reminded her.

"Yes, but you haven't been in. I guess I could have called." She took a sip of her tea. "Good but too hot."

"You'd better tell her," Leonora said.

"She's been here three times since we last saw each other and yes, each time she quizzed me about Crane. I didn't tell her anything," she added. "It's the truth. I haven't seen Crane in ages. But don't worry. I'm willing to lie for you."

"Is that all she did? Ask about him?"

"She said he had a birthday coming up, and they were planning a surprise for him."

"They?"

"They meaning her. What was the surprise?"

"She baked him a cake."

"That doesn't sound too terrible."

"She's trespassing on Jennet's property," Leonora said. "It wasn't very good cake."

"I don't own Crane," I said. "But that horrible woman is intruding on my life. I baked Crane a birthday cake, too."

"I'm sure that's the one he ate," Annica said. "Anyhow, Jennet, I think you need a love potion. You'd better pay Lucy a visit."

That made me smile. "Lucy doesn't mix love potions. And I don't think I need supernatural help. Yet."

But Lucy *did* read tea leaves. I had a sudden, pressing desire to know what the future held for me and the Viper. Forewarned is forearmed, after all.

Ten

Saturday was shaping up to be a busy day. I planned to visit Lucy Hazen in the morning and afterward research Western movies in the library. In the evening Brent was taking us out to dinner. During the school year I had to cram too many activities into my weekends. I missed the long, carefree days of summer.

Lucy lived in a many-gabled house that fairly dripped with Gothic atmosphere and ambiance. In a whimsical moment she had christened her home Dark Gables. The interior was indeed dark, except for her sunroom at the back where summer bloomed forever with white wicker furniture and a profusion of green plants. French doors offered a view of Lucy's fountain against a background of woods. Like trees all over the county, the leaves were brilliant shades of crimson and gold.

Lucy wrote her horror novels for young adults in the sunroom. Here she'd authored *Devilwish*, which was currently being made into a movie in and around Foxglove Corners.

My visit was long overdue. Lucy didn't know about the haunted television set. It was the kind of story that would appeal to her and perhaps inspire one of her future stories.

"This visit is a treat, Jennet," she said.

Her black midi skirt swished and her gold bracelets jangled as she and her pretty blue merle, Sky, escorted me to the sunroom in the back. "I'll put the kettle on for tea."

"Good. I want to see if Veronica the Viper is still hanging around in my cup. She's certainly messing around in my life."

"I'll see if she's there," Lucy said.

"Annica suggested a love potion."

"For whom?"

"For Crane, I guess."

"You don't need a love potion," she said. "Crane is devoted to you."

"It's the Viper I don't trust."

Lucy nodded. "You don't want to take your eyes off a snake. Annica is so silly. Speaking of love potions, she asked me if I had a recipe for one."

I was curious. "Do you?"

"Of course not, Jennet. I'm not a witch, not even a good witch. Annica will have to settle for a tea leaf reading. Annica is such a beauty she doesn't need magic," she added.

While Lucy boiled water, I made myself comfortable on the wicker sofa with Sky lying close by, her head resting on my lap. Like all collies, Sky was clever. She knew the inevitable progression: company, tea, cookies.

Lucy brought a tray of tea and shortbread to the sofa and said, "What has Veronica done now?"

I told her about the devil's food cake she'd baked for Crane's birthday.

"She's certainly forward."

We drank our tea, nibbled on shortbread, all three of us, and I prepared my teacup for a reading. After knowing Lucy for so long, I knew the procedure. Drink the tea, drain the excess liquid, turn the cup toward you three times, making your wish while the leaves formed patterns gleaned from your life—and your future.

"You don't have to believe this," Lucy always cautioned, often adding, "It's just for fun."

I was ambivalent about having my tea leaves read. 'Just for fun' it might be, but on occasion the events Lucy foretold actually happened.

Veronica was still in my teacup, skulking around too near my home for comfort. Lucy pointed to a leaf that resembled a coiled snake.

"That's her. It looks like she's making herself at home."

Unfortunately she couldn't see what Veronica would do next. Nobody could.

I sat back and offered a cookie to a patiently waiting collie.

"Has she moved?" I asked.

"I'd say she was in the same place as she's been before."

"There must be single men in the sheriff's department," I said. "You'd think she'd set her cap for one of them."

"Don't let her rattle you. She was probably hoping Crane would take the cake home."

"The cake holder is still on the kitchen counter," I said.

"You should return it filled with doughnuts. Let her know her little gift to Crane doesn't bother you."

That was worth considering. I might do it. But suddenly I didn't want to waste another minute of my time with Lucy talking about Veronica, so I launched into the tale of the haunted television set.

Lucy's eyes lit up. "I would *love* to see it, Jennet. Do you think I could?

"Sure, but so far, I'm the only one who's seen the movie. Come over anytime. We'll turn on the TV, and maybe it'll play for you."

"So you have another mystery to solve. It's a fascinating one. I've read about rogue appliances and electronics, but this is something new."

"It takes my mind off Veronica and school problems."

"That's good."

"The trouble is, they'll still be there, waiting for me at the end of the day," I said.

~ * ~

The Foxglove Corners Public Library was an old white Victorian on Park Street, named for the park that gave its residents a colorful view in all seasons.

It had been Miss Eidt's family home before she donated it to the town, along with several books from her own collection. The library was a unique place where new-fangled innovations such as computers mixed in harmony with vintage series books and an old-fashioned card catalog.

The cat, Blackberry, kept a vigil on the wicker chair she'd chosen for her own use. The creature stared at me with shining jewel-like eyes as I approached the porch, without a flicker of welcome.

Well, as I always thought, she wasn't a dog.

Miss Eidt was at her desk sorting Halloween cut-outs. She wore her blue shirtwaist dress again with a three-strand pearl necklace, looking cool and serene as always.

I handed her the box of doughnuts I'd bought at the Hometown Bakery. "It's a little late for doughnuts, but they look good."

"Never too late, Jennet. What brings you to the library?"

"Research," I said. "I'm interested in Western movies today?"

"For school?"

"For myself."

It was time to tell Miss Eidt about the mystifying properties of my purchase.

She was astonished. "I had no idea. How could you go to an estate sale and buy the only haunted item in the house?"

"Just luck," I said. "I'd love to know the title of the movie or, better still, to see it."

But Miss Eidt wasn't finished talking about the new mystery. "A normal TV doesn't act that way. It's like it has a soul."

I'd never thought of it that way. Miss Eidt's simple observation led to a chilling thought.

Not that it was possible, but… What if it did have a soul? If an article acted like a sentient being, how could it be considered insentient? And suppose that very strange television set was alive. What was its purpose?

Preposterous notions, all.

"Brent suggested there was a CD inside it," I said. "Outside of taking it apart, I don't know how to prove it."

"But if you *did* find a CD inside, what would activate it? It's almost as if that TV is toying with you."

For a moment I wished I'd never taken Miss Eidt into my confidence. Inadvertently she'd given rise to a host of unsettling possibilities.

"If you find the title, I have some CDs out on the shelves," she said. "There are some Westerns, mostly classics like *Red River* and *The Searchers*."

"This movie isn't a classic," I said. "I don't recognize the stars. I'm assuming it's an obscure film."

"There's bound to be a record of it somewhere." She held up a cardboard cut-out of a black cat wearing a witch's peaked hat. "It looks like Blackberry, doesn't it?" she asked.

"A dead ringer," I said, just as something furry brushed against my leg.

The cat had followed me inside.

Eleven

After poring through the library's resources for an hour, I came to a conclusion. My own books on Westerns were as good as anything Miss Eidt had to offer. Tired of skimming repetitious material, I moved on to the shelves containing the CDs she had mentioned.

Several well-known favorites were there. I decided to check out *The Searchers* and three other classics to watch with Crane. At the last moment I added *The Old West on the Small Screen,* attracted by the rainbow-colored horses on the cover.

Blackberry followed me up to the desk. I didn't realize she'd stayed with me. Strange. Didn't she know I was a dog person?

Miss Eidt said, "Did you see the new Gothic Nook?"

How could I have missed it? Although, being a nook, it might be out of sight.

"Follow me," she said, leading the way to a cozy space by the back windows. The nook was furnished with Queen Anne chairs and antique side tables. The lamps were Tiffany style chosen primarily for their colors and nineteenth century atmosphere. All the shelves in the nook were well-stocked with Gothic romances, most of them paperbacks that had sold for a pittance decades ago.

At present no one was there.

"It's been popular from day one," Miss Eidt said. "Some people read books right here in the library and ask me to hold them until the next day."

"Can't they check them out?" I asked.

"Oh, definitely, if they choose, but some readers prefer our peace and quiet to their own homes."

I took *The Lute and the Glove* down from the shelf. Its cover, depicting a bonneted woman strolling among gravestones, had a long tear, neatly taped by Miss Eidt or her assistant, Debby.

"I loved this one," I said, recalling the young woman who had seen the ghosts of a pair of ill-fated Elizabethan lovers. "Few writers can create a ghostly atmosphere like Katherine Wygmore Eyre."

Still, I'd like to try. I thought I could write an equally thrilling Gothic. Some day. Once I figured out the secret of the haunted television set. Our green Victorian farmhouse had its own kind of atmosphere, every bit as enthralling as that of an English manor.

"I think I'll check it out," I said. "I'd like to read it again."

Miss Eidt said, "The words are small, and the pages are yellow and fragile."

"I can see that," I said. "I'll be careful."

I hadn't found the title of my movie, but, in all, my morning at the library had been satisfactory. Perhaps I wasn't meant to know any more about Susanna's story than the TV was willing to give me.

~ * ~

Brent had invited Lucy to join us for Crane's second birthday celebration at the Hunt Club Inn. Both Lucy and I wore black. Lucy had added her signature gold chains and bracelets while I chose my crystal heart and teardrop earrings for accessories. We were all in a festive mood as was the Inn, dressed in autumn colors, both somber and bright.

The fox head wreath, the one decoration I always tried to avoid, glared down at the diners. In honor of the season, it wore a circle of crimson and yellow leaves interspersed with red berries. It made me feel like crying.

I supposed I was the only person in the Inn, with the exception of Lucy, who decried the sport of fox hunting, which was why I tried not to think about the poor fox who had lost his body or about Brent, an enthusiastic fox hunter who owned his own pack of foxhounds.

When we'd given our orders to the waiter, Brent said, "The cook baked a birthday cake for dessert."

Cake? This would be Crane's third cake, but neither he nor I—nor Lucy-—mentioned that other cake, the one Veronica the Viper had gifted him with.

Crane was speechless.

"That was thoughtful of you, Brent," I said.

"We have to show the sheriff how much we appreciate him, and we do. He keeps the peace and keeps us honest."

I glanced at Brent. What an unusual sentiment for Brent to utter, and why would we be anything but honest?

Finally Crane said, "I appreciate the gesture, Fowler, but I'm not having any more birthdays. This is the last one. Just don't sing "Happy Birthday," he added.

"I'm staying the same age, too." Brent turned to me. "What's the latest on the haunted TV?"

"One time, it played a little more of the Western, but usually when I turn it on, I see today's news or weather."

"I still think there's a mini CD player inside," Brent said. "If Jennet would let me take it apart, I could prove it. What do you make of it, Lucy?"

"I don't know. I'm hoping to see what Jennet saw. I don't agree with you, though, Brent. An embedded CD player simply couldn't work."

"I think the movie is a Western romance," I said, hoping to divert a lively debate.

"What kind of Western is that?" Crane wanted to know.

"It's for women. Sort of like a Hallmark movie. Women were a part of the frontier, too, you know."

"A minor part," Brent said. "Dance hall gals and schoolmarms. Oh, and rancher's wives, of course."

"Don't forget Belle Starr and Rose of the Cimarron."

"Rose who?" Brent demanded.

"Google her," Lucy said.

"In my movie, a young woman, Susanna, comes to a town in Colorado, Jubilee, and right away attracts a cowboy who looks like Crane."

"According to Jennet," Crane said. "I never met a man who looks like me—except for my Uncle Gilbert, and he's a much older version."

"This actor is a dead ringer for Crane, and he's young," I insisted. "I'm pretty sure they'll fall in love."

"Maybe I don't want to see it then," Brent said.

"Remember the mystery," I reminded him.

"Oh, yes."

"Jennet brought *Red River* from the library," Crane said. "You can watch it with us, Fowler. You, too, Lucy."

At that moment a waiter appeared with our food. Prime rib for the men, pecan-encrusted whitefish for Lucy and me. We dropped the subject of Westerns and rogue televisions to enjoy our dinner.

The cake was a marvel, three layers of chocolate decorated with a jaunty fox, of course, who wore the badge of a deputy sheriff.

"The fox has your eyes, Sheriff," Brent said.

As host, he offered to cut the cake but mangled the first piece.

Lucy took the cake server from his hand. "Let me. Since Crane isn't going to keep track of the years from now on, we'll dispense with candles."

Which was good, as Brent hadn't thought to bring them.

The cake was delicious. By the time we were drinking our after-dinner coffee, there was scarcely a crumb left on the plate.

I sighed happily. We were a solid circle, my well-loved husband and our friends. Try as she might, Veronica the Viper couldn't trick her way into it.

~ * ~

The dogs marked our homecoming with enthusiastic barking, although Misty included a prodigious yawn.

I hadn't taken my phone with me. It lay on the oak table faithfully informing me that I had a missed call from Sue Appleton.

Should I wait till tomorrow to listen to the voice mail? I didn't want to deal with a rescue emergency at midnight. On the other hand…

Curiosity won. Sue had a question or, rather, a request.

Jennet, will you do the follow-up home visit for Charlotte and Bronwyn after school one day soon? I'm sure everything is fine with them, but we have to follow procedure.

"All right," I said as if I were talking to the voice mail. "Nothing easier."

And trailed by Halley and Misty, I hurried up the stairs to join Crane in our bedroom.

Twelve

Sagramore Lake was still and blue, a smooth mirror reflecting the autumn-turning landscape. I drove to the end of Sagramore Lake Road and found the address Sue had given me.

Charlotte Gray's house was a pretty bungalow painted light yellow with black shutters. It had an enviable view of the lake, being the last house on the block. A white picket fence enclosed the entire property, and the grass was hidden under a thick blanket of dark red maple leaves.

Charlotte had a driveway with a narrow strip of grass in the middle but no garage and no car in sight.

I opened the gate and crunched down the leaves that covered the walkway. Charlotte hadn't raked them or even swept them off the pavement. In fact, it didn't look as if she were home, as the drapes were closed. I knocked on the door, waited, then rang the doorbell.

Nothing. Not even a dog barking inside the house.

I glanced again at the Post-It note in my hand. I was at the right address, but obviously I wasn't going to see Charlotte today.

Well, I could come back another day. The bungalow was within walking distance of Jonquil Lane. I often took my dogs walking down to the lake, sometimes meeting my young friends, Jennifer and Molly, playing with their collie, Ginger, on the way.

I turned to leave as the door of the neighboring house opened. A woman with glossy auburn hair brushed back stood on the porch. She wore an orange sundress, its princess lines spoiled by a bulky apron.

"Wait… Miss?"

I smiled, wondering if she recognized me from one of my previous walks.

"I'm Charlotte's neighbor, Sylvia Eastbrook," she said. "Charlotte isn't there."

"I guess I'll have to try again. I'm Jennet Ferguson."

"Are you a friend of Charlotte's?" she asked.

I paused. I could be, but, "I only met her recently," I said. "I'm with the Collie Rescue League, here to check on Bronwyn."

"Oh, yes, her new dog. Well, you're the first person to come by since she left. Charlotte has been gone for four days. I saw her drive away early one morning. She had the new dog with her."

"Maybe she went on vacation," I said.

"Unlikely. Charlotte never goes anywhere."

Until now, I thought.

"Where do you think she is then?" I asked.

"I can't imagine, and I don't know what to do about it. I'm leaning toward calling the police. Only…"

I waited. Cutting across the driveway, plowing through the maple leaves, she came to a stop next to me, close enough so that I could see the smoky eye makeup she wore.

"Only what if I'm wrong and it's all innocent? Charlotte would be upset if I reported her missing and she wasn't. She's a very private person."

"You seem to know her pretty well," I said.

"I'd say so. We share a garden in my backyard. Sometimes we go out for dinner. If Charlotte is doing something unusual, she'd tell me. She told me all about Bronwyn," she added.

I frowned, looking down at the unraked leaves. Then I glanced at the mailbox which appeared to be empty.

"I've been taking in her mail," Sylvia said. "What would you do if you were in my place?"

I didn't have to think about it. Suppose Lucy or Annica were unaccounted for? Lucy not at Dark Gables and Annica missing her shift at Clovers?

"I'd talk to the police and let them take it from there," I said. "It's better to be safe than sorry."

"That's what I'll do."

"And please let me know what you find out. I live nearby, on Jonquil Lane." I wrote my cell phone number on the Post-It note.

Sylvia promised to call me as soon as she had news. I said goodbye and walked back to my car, taking one last look at the tranquil Sagramore Lake.

Sylvia had transmitted her concern to me.

Disappearances weren't unusual in Foxglove Corners. On the contrary. Huron Court, one of the roads near the lake, had been known to sweep people into another season and time. There was also Brandemere Road where—if you believed one of Foxglove Corners' more outrageous legends—the unsuspecting traveler reached the end of the earth and dropped off the planet.

Then people vanished for purely natural reasons. Sometimes they met with foul play. And here was Charlotte, retired piano teacher, living a quiet life centered around her home. She had just adopted a dog—our latest rescue collie.

What could have happened to her?

I drove back down Sagramore Lake Road, and turned on Jonquil Lane, anxious to be home where I didn't anticipate any turmoil greater than collies clamoring for their dinner.

That adoption had gone too smoothly. The circumstances were too neat. The perfect owner turning up just as we planned to launch our geriatric match program. It was almost suspicious.

It looked as if another mystery had landed in my life.

~ * ~

I didn't have time to think about Charlotte Gray's vanishing act, nor of Bronwyn, that afternoon. Planning dinner at the last minute, feeding seven collies, and writing a test for World Literature swallowed up my time and energy.

The next day, all too soon, I found myself facing another day at Marston High School. The unseasonably warm weather continued. Once again, kids were attempting to come to class in beach wear, prompting a special announcement—make that warning—from Principal Grimsley during a rare interruption in second period.

My American Literature class, the Class from Hell, Number Two, was reasonably civilized, which should have been a flying red flag. During lunch an office aide brought me a message from the principal:

Mrs. Ferguson, please see me during your conference hour.

Fortunately I'd almost finished my sandwich. The last bites were certain to be tasteless.

"I wonder what I did," I said.

Leonora handed me one of her chocolate chip cookies, a guaranteed remedy for whatever ailed me.

"He might be giving you a compliment or a reward."

"I'm not that optimistic where Grimsley is concerned."

"Did you have a run-in with a student?"

"Not lately."

"Maybe a parent complained."

"About what?" I shrugged. "I can't imagine."

I'd know soon. The bell rang. One more period to wait. It could be worse. Grimsley's favorite tactic was to issue a summons on a Friday afternoon, asking for a Monday meeting, which gave a teacher the whole weekend to worry.

I bit into the cookie. Chocolate can cure any ills. Except for a visit to the principal's office.

~ * ~

He greeted me with his pasted-on smile and came to the point, wasting no words on pleasantries.

"I assume you recall my policy on hall passes."

He handed me a yellow Post-It note similar to the one Sue had used for Charlotte's address.

I read: *Rachelle to Duncan's Donuts, 4th hour,* with the day's date. It was signed *Jennet Ferguson.*

"How do you explain this?" he demanded. "The hall monitor found it on the floor by the drinking fountain."

"It's obviously forged. This isn't my signature."

"Are you sure? It looks like your handwriting."

I bristled. Grimsley had just crossed a line, not that he would care.

"No, it doesn't," I said. "And I didn't sign this pass."

"Was the girl in your class today?"

I tried to remember.

Think! It was only a few hours ago.

All I could see were two blondes, not the third.

"I'll check my gradebook," I said.

His eyebrows rose.

"To be absolutely sure. Offhand, I don't think so."

I imagined her having a snack at Duncan's Donuts, soaking up sunshine and possibly flirting with one of the boys who had also skipped school.

"You check and let me know," he said. "If she forged the pass, it's a grave infraction."

"Have you talked to Rachelle?" I asked.

"She wasn't in her fifth period class."

Well, then…

Her subterfuge could have had serious consequences for me. Suppose she had been hit by a car as she crossed the street, her attention on licking the frosting from her lips? I would be liable.

Unless I'd marked her absence. If Grimsley had kept the forged pass as proof.

He picked up a folder, indicating that our meeting was over. Dismissed, I hurried back to my room and checked my gradebook, relieved to see that I had indeed marked her absent.

Another hurdle in the pass wars overcome.

Thirteen

After school I took Halley, Gemmy, and Misty with me to visit Sue at her horse farm. I hoped I'd be able to walk off the anger I still felt at Rachelle for forging my signature and at Grimsley for believing I'd sign a pass to Duncan's Donuts.

I can't say I felt any happier about the situation, but the woods of Jonquil Lane and the blessed silence wrapped me in a crimson and gold embrace. The grayness that pursued me slipped quietly away.

Take comfort from us, the trees seemed to say. *Rejoice in the fall.*

It was warm, but the air had a subtle autumnal scent, fresh and piney with a hint of burning leaves. You would never mistake it for spring air.

The incident at Marston would pass with the waning days of summer. In the meantime, I had a Rescue League problem to deal with. Sue needed to know about Charlotte's apparent disappearance with Bronwyn.

She listened to my report quietly, her expression grim, while Icy, Bluebell, and Echo lay panting near their water pail, and my trio looked on. The dogs appeared to be listening to the tale of Bronwyn, too.

"It certainly is strange," Sue said. "Charlotte gone, Bronwyn unaccounted for. How can we know that our rescue collie is all right? Charlotte didn't say anything about taking a trip when she picked her up."

"I'd be more concerned if she left Bronwyn alone in the house or even in the care of her neighbor," I said. "At least they're together."

"Here I thought Charlotte was the perfect owner for Bronwyn. You never can know about a person until something like this happens."

Sue blamed Charlotte for the situation, which was premature, given the little we knew about the circumstances.

"She may still be the perfect owner," I said. "Something unforeseen must have happened. I'm going to try to find out what it was."

"How do you propose to do that?" Sue asked.

"Her neighbor is going to call me if she hears anything, and the next walk I take with the dogs will be to Sagramore Lake Road."

"You'll just see the same thing. A closed-up house and unraked leaves."

"I'm going to be optimistic," I told her.

It occurred to me that I might have another source of information. Molly and Jennifer would know immediately about a new collie on the block. They would have introduced themselves and Ginger to Charlotte. For all I knew, they might already know her, might have taken piano lessons from her.

Which didn't mean Charlotte would discuss her plans with two young girls in the neighborhood and not her friend next door. But it was a lead, however slim. All I could do was ask.

Sue said, "This isn't an auspicious start to our new program. Did you read Jill Lodge's story in the *Banner*?"

"Not yet. Is it in today's paper?"

"Yesterday's," she said. "It was a wonderful story and the pictures turned out really well. Even *I* took a good picture for a change, and the dogs are adorable. I already had two calls from people interested in adopting an older collie."

"That's good news. Do we have any collies to offer them?"

"Unfortunately, not at this time. I had to explain that we don't have any dogs that qualify at present, but that's bound to change.

Now we have to tell people our first adoption didn't go according to plan."

"You don't have to tell people anything," I said, feeling exasperated. "Let's concentrate on finding out where Charlotte and Bronwyn went. It may all be simple."

In an ideal world, every geriatric collie who entered Rescue would have a group of potential owners eager to bring a collie into their lives. We had to be patient.

So I told myself. Nevertheless, it would be to everyone's benefit to solve the mystery of Charlotte's disappearance as soon as possible.

~ * ~

As we kept newspapers for a week, finding Jill's story was easy. She was a talented writer whose enthusiasm for her subject was infectious. It made me want to adopt an older collie myself, although I was still comparatively young and already had seven dogs. 'Our limit,' as Crane often said.

I was glad Jill had left my name out of the story. Maybe I was being paranoid, but an enemy had once tracked me down after reading about an award given to one of my collies, and for a while, it hadn't gone well.

Before I returned the *Banner* to the stack, I noticed a familiar name in an article below Jill's story: Huron Court.

That little-travelled road was seldom if ever in the news, but earlier this week it had been the scene of a hit-and-run accident that had left a young girl hospitalized in critical condition. I remembered the curves that seemed to go on forever and the long stretch of woods that lulled a driver into inattention or tempted him to speed.

Nothing good ever happened on Huron Court. Was it possible that Charlotte had taken Bronwyn for a leisurely ride on that accursed road? If so, we might never hear from her again. But I was determined to remain optimistic.

I found one of my collie note cards and wrote a note to Jill to express our thanks—on behalf of the Rescue League—for writing the article. Now to find Charlotte and Bronwyn.

~ * ~

Except for more leaves beyond the picket fence, Charlotte's house was unchanged. Someone had raked leaves off the sidewalk and driveway but ignored the walkway. A neighbor, perhaps, who had run out of energy.

I led Halley, Sky, and Star to the beach and stood looking out over Sagramore Lake, admiring the blue of the sky and the shimmer of the water. The scene seemed unreal, like an oil painting, every color true and intense.

A dog barked in the distance. Misty gave an answering yelp while Sky moved closer to me and Star lay down, anticipating an interruption in our walk.

"It's Ginger," I told them, "and Molly and Jennifer."

The girls had turned into lovely young ladies with long shining hair and lightly made up faces. It seemed that only last summer they were selling lemonade and cookies at their homemade stand.

Of course it wasn't.

"Hi, Jennet." Molly gave Sky a gentle pat while Jennifer fluffed Star's fur and shook Misty's paw.

"It's a collie reunion," Jennifer said. "Sit, Ginger. Let's visit."

"How's school this year?" I asked.

"We *love* it, Molly said. "We have most classes together and we joined the Drama Club."

"And our teachers are the greatest," Jennifer added.

Would one of my students ever say something like that? I wondered for a moment and thought it doubtful. I'd better change the subject to the one that preyed on my mind.

"Have you seen Ms. Gray's new collie, Bronwyn?"

"We met her. She's so pretty and friendly. Sometimes she's in the yard when we walk by."

I gave them a brief version of Bronwyn's history, telling them how I'd found her at an estate sale and taken her to Sue's horse farm where Charlotte had adopted her.

"I want to visit Charlotte," I said. "But she's never home when I come by. Do you girls have any idea where she is?"

Molly and Jennifer exchanged a look.

"I saw Ms. Gray drive away one morning when I was waiting for Molly's mom to drive us to school," Jennifer said. "I waved to her, but she just drove by."

"Maybe she didn't see you."

"She looked right at me."

That was all the information I was going to get. But it told me something. Charlotte was distracted or upset or worried. Something was the matter. It had kept her away from her home for days. I needed to know what it was.

"Jennifer thought she was mad at us," Molly said, "but I don't know why she would be. We've been helping her with yard work this summer."

"We went ahead and raked her leaves," Jennifer added. "She asked us if we'd do that and shovel snow this winter."

"I'm sure it's nothing you did," I said. "Look, if you or Molly see her, would you let me know? It's important.

"Is she in trouble?" Jennifer asked.

"I don't know. Maybe. Or maybe she's just enjoying a fall vacation."

I didn't think they believed me. I didn't believe it myself.

Fourteen

The clouds over the lake had darkened imperceptibly, and a scent of rain stole into the fresh air. Moments ago I had been standing in the sun with Molly and Jennifer. I hadn't given a thought to raincoats and umbrellas when I changed into my orange sundress.

It was time to go home before the storm developed.

I led the dogs back to Sagramore Lake Road, pausing for a moment at Charlotte's house, hoping for a sign that she had returned…like a car in the driveway or a dog barking, but nothing had changed in the short time I'd been walking on the beach. Only the weather.

Thunder rumbled overhead, and lightning streaked across the sky, clear signals that we'd better be on our way. And incidentally we'd better move away from the trees that lined Sagramore Lake Road. Sky pulled on the leash, ears flattened, anxious to retreat to her safe place under the dining room table.

Luckily we reached the house before the real downpour started.

At home I assembled stew makings—the beef and vegetables cut up this morning—and tossed them into the Dutch oven. With dinner more or less taken care of and a little bit of leisure time before Crane came home, I turned on the haunted television set. Maybe there'd be news of the storm.

Instead a gracious nineteenth century living room filled the screen. A gathering or a party was in progress. Susanna was talking to Luke while they drank something pink and frothy. She wore a soft silvery green dress with a bodice full of white ruffles. He'd donned a dark suit, circa 1870s. Gone were the blue cowboy shirt and camel vest, but he still looked rugged and handsome.

Excited to see my Western movie again, I turned up the volume.

"If you want to see a real ranch, Miss Susanna, let me take you out to the L Bar E," Luke was saying.

Susanna smiled demurely at him. "I'd like that, Mr. Emerson."

Ah, the budding romance! But I'd missed something. Susanna and Luke had moved from a first encounter in front of the Pink Palace to a gathering in a private house. The movie must have gone on without me while I'd been away from the TV.

Conversation swirled around them, the actors out of sight. The music faded.

"Then that's what we'll do," Luke said. "Tomorrow morning? Bright and early?"

"Tomorrow morning." Susanna sipped her drink. "I'm looking forward to it."

They sat at opposite ends of a divan that looked as if it were covered with rich blue velvet. Behind them, against the wall, stood a piano. To their right, an ornate wooden table held a three-tier server stacked with cookies and tiny sandwiches, alongside a silver tea or coffee service. This was hardly the kind of refreshment you'd offer a man of the West.

The scene looked so homey, so inviting, that I could imagine myself a part of it. Like Alice stepping through the looking glass to enter a strange and wonderful world. I saw myself wearing a quaint, charming dress, nibbling on the cookies that resembled miniature stars, and flirting with the man who looked like Crane: lean, strong, more at home on horseback than in a living room or parlor, as it was possibly called then.

Except I'd have to get rid of Susanna.

Luke didn't seem to mind the dainty fare, although I imagined he would have preferred a thick steak or a bowl of stew. His attention was focused on Susanna, his expression betraying his fascination with her.

A woman in gray, a slightly plumper version of Susanna, who was possibly her cousin, Alicia, descended on them, plate in hand. She asked Luke if he'd like another sandwich.

He accepted and, while he ate, regaled Susana with the virtues of Jubilee, which in his view offered a visitor the latest modern innovations, among them a genuine theatre and a weekly newspaper, the *Jubilee Tribune*.

He was a master at description. With an artist's hand, he painted snow-topped mountains, clear blue streams that matched the color of the sky, and green meadows. Jubilee was, in short, a veritable paradise of which he owned several hundred acres. He raised cattle and horses.

"We have the most beautiful country west of the Missouri out here," he said.

"I know I'm going to like living in Jubilee," Susanna said.

Living in Jubilee? This wasn't a short vacation, then, as I'd assumed. *What would she do to support herself?* I wondered. What choices did a woman have in the eighteen seventies?

A good question.

Suppose *I* lived in 1876. Would I be a schoolmarm in a one-room schoolhouse? Or a seamstress? Wait, not that. I couldn't sew. What else? I recalled Brent's sexist classification of women in the West. They were dancehall girls or rancher's wives.

Perhaps Susanna had come to Colorado to stay with her married cousin and look for a husband. Marriageable men were scarce in her time as many young men, from both the North and the South, had lost their lives in the Civil War. Still, I remembered, those who survived often moved out West, hoping to build new lives.

Somehow, though, I didn't think marriage was Susanna's only goal.

But this idle speculation was making me miss more of the movie.

Susanna glided gracefully to the piano and began to play a familiar piece, Stephen Foster's *Old Dog Tray.*

How I loved that song, both the melody and the melancholy lyrics!

A commotion at the side door yanked me from my reverie. The dogs were gone from the living room, even my faithful Halley. They were quite literally raising the rafters with their raucous barking. The mellow strains of Susanna's song lingered as I made the transition to my reality.

Crane was home.

So soon? I glanced at the clock.

No. A little late. I'd lost track of time, mesmerized by the movie. Odd. I had experienced this kind of loss once before, and yet the story of Susanna and Luke hadn't moved out of the parlor. Outside, in my world, the light was slowly building in the sky. The rain was over, leaving the earth soggy.

A savory smell reminded me of a real world concern. The stew!

I rushed to the kitchen, stopping to swirl a spoon through the bubbling meat and vegetables before greeting Crane. Fortunately my dinner wasn't burning—yet.

I turned down the heat as Crane emerged from the yelping pack to claim a kiss.

"It sure looks good," he said, eying the stew.

"It will be." I took his hand and led him to the TV. "My movie is back on. Hurry!"

Alas, we were too late. A new weathercaster was explaining that the storm had blown over but was expected to return around midnight.

"It looks like I missed it again," Crane said. "I want to see this cowboy who looks like me."

I wondered if he ever would.

"He really does resemble you," I said. "But he's a wealthy rancher, not a cowboy."

~ * ~

After dinner, while Crane read the sports page, I turned on the haunted TV again.

News—darn it. Shootings, wildfires in the West, turmoil in the South as opposing groups clashed. What was happening to our world?

I gave the 'off' knob a turn as an unwelcome thought slipped into my mind. Why couldn't Crane see the movie? Was it happening again?

I didn't want to think about the time not so long ago when I was haunted by a sound of gunfire that nobody else heard, but the thought, once surfaced, appeared to be here to stay.

Admittedly, I often saw spirits or heard sounds I couldn't explain, but conjuring an obscure Western movie was surely beyond even my fragile power.

Still, it was happening. How many times? I couldn't remember, only knew it was too many.

Lucy had a strong connection to the supernatural. She was waiting for an invitation to put my TV to the test. To my dismay, I realized I was pinning all my hopes on her. If she couldn't see what I saw on the screen, what did that mean for me?

Nothing good.

"I see where Gail Redmond died," Crane said.

"Is she a sports figure?" I asked.

He looked up from the paper. "She's the girl who was injured in the hit and run on Huron Court. The driver will be facing a murder rap when they find him."

"What do they have to go on?"

"A white Ford, possibly a Taurus, with substantial damage."

"Was the victim able to describe the car that hit her?" I asked.

"No, a witness did. Now the witness is missing, too."

"Three cars were travelling on Huron Court at the same time? That's unusual."

"Now that you mention it, yes, it is."

"Maybe the driver is afraid to come forward," I said. "He may know he killed her."

For all we knew, he was reading the article at this moment.

"He should own up to it," Crane said. "We'll find him. It's just a matter of time."

How enviable to be that confident.

"Now," he said, "Are there any dogs who want to go for a walk?"

He was immediately besieged by the pack, with Candy in the lead.

Raven regarded the excited collies gravely. My poor girl. Her leg was mending nicely, but a vigorous walk was still beyond her. She who had lived happily outside had been the best of invalids, and my heart broke every time I had to exclude her from an outing.

"Soon." I stooped to pat her head, heartened when her tail thumped on the floor. "Pretty soon you'll be able to go out, too."

I'd have to check with Doctor Foster. I shouldn't forget that I had plenty of concerns in the real world.

Fifteen

Among my concerns was the whereabouts of Charlotte Gray, who still hadn't returned home. I held out hope that she had left on an autumn vacation, perhaps on a color tour up north. But a strong premonition told me this wasn't the case.

Another premonition suggested a grim possibility. Charlotte disappears for days on end. A hit and run driver is responsible for a fatal injury on Huron Court. Could there be a connection? Could Charlotte possibly be the hit and run driver?

No, not the gentle woman who had adopted Bronwyn. There must be another explanation for her leaving town.

"What do you think I should do?" I asked Crane that evening when he came back from walking the dogs.

He hung their leashes on the hooks in the kitchen and took off his jacket while the collies made a dash for the water pails.

"Her neighbor reported her missing?" he asked.

"That same day."

"And this neighbor saw her drive away from her house?"

"Yes, and so did Jennifer, but Charlotte didn't acknowledge Jennifer's wave, which is suspicious."

"We'll have to wait for somebody to recognize her or her car. Or for her to use a credit card."

Waiting was all I'd been doing. I'd already called Sylvia twice. Nothing had changed at Charlotte's house. Molly and Jennifer had been by to rake leaves, and she had taken in Charlotte's mail. She'd been listening for a phone call that never came, growing more concerned with each passing day.

"Waiting isn't good enough," I said. "I have a feeling that Charlotte may be in trouble."

And also Bronwyn, who was presumably still with her.

"Someone has to help her," I said.

"I'll see if Mac knows anything," Crane promised.

That we didn't know where Bronwyn was continued to bother Sue.

The next day, I took the dogs for a walk to the horse farm. It was a downtime for Sue and her collies. Bluebell, Icy, Echo, and a fourth dog were playing Frisbee. Fortunately the day's sunshine had dried the mud left from yesterday's downpour.

My dogs longed to join the game, but I didn't let them off their leashes.

Sue hurled the bright red disk across a sloping stretch of meadowland. The dogs scampered after it, the new collie trailing the others. She was a pretty sable and white girl with a charming white blaze, a little smaller than Bluebell.

"I named her Taffy," Sue said. "She was found scrounging for food outside a restaurant in Lakeville—without a collar. She isn't microchipped. The vet says she's around seven. I'm almost afraid to contact one of our prospective owners after what happened with Charlotte."

Icy brought the Frisbee to Sue, who set it on a table. "Game's over."

"Come, Taffy," I said, and she loped up to me as if she hadn't heard a kind word from a stranger in a long time. Her coat was soft and warmed from the sun, and her dark eyes had a haunted look.

I fussed over her and immediately Sue's other collies crowded me, all seeking attention.

"Have you heard anything about Charlotte yet?" Sue asked.

"Not yet, but her neighbor and two girls I know are watching for her. As soon as she pulls in her drive, I'll know."

"It's so irresponsible, not to be in touch with us. She knew we were going to do a follow-up visit."

It disturbed me that Sue blamed Charlotte for whatever had gone wrong in the adoption. If indeed, anything had.

"We don't know what happened with Charlotte," I said. "She may be home tomorrow with a simple explanation for her absence. Probably she didn't think she had to answer to anyone. You didn't tell her she couldn't leave town."

"That's true. I hope you're right, but I had an awful thought the other day. Suppose Charlotte is one of those people who collect dogs to sell to laboratories or dog fighting gangs."

The nightmare images she invoked caused icicles to form in my veins. The very suggestion of our Bronwyn in evil hands was unbearable.

"What gave you that idea?" I asked.

"Charlotte was too perfect, right from the beginning, and the adoption went through so quickly."

"She could also be a lonely woman who longed for the companionship of an older, more settled collie."

"Maybe. It was just a thought."

"A person shouldn't be penalized for perfection," I said. "In the meantime, we can't let our new program die. It has the potential for bringing so much joy to senior collies and humans."

"I won't," she assured me. "There's still the matter of what to do with Taffy. Here we have an older dog who would have been hard to place before you thought of matching geriatric collies with seniors."

"Which is why we initiated the program in the first place," I said. "You'll have to investigate people thoroughly and hope for the best. Anything can happen to jinx an adoption—or a sale for that matter. Once a collie leaves our protection, her future is out of our hands."

~ * ~

With so much going on, I'd almost forgotten that tonight was movie night, but Brent didn't. He called to tell me he was bringing popcorn, soft drinks—and Lucy. Forewarned, I baked two batches of chocolate fudge brownies and sprinkled them with powdered sugar.

What movie should we watch? The CDs I'd borrowed from the library were on the coffee table. I decided to let Brent and Crane choose. I had liked all of them once upon a time and hadn't seen them for years.

I didn't consider the television Westerns with the multi-colored horses on the cover. I'd watch them another time when I was alone.

"Good," Brent said a little later as he viewed my selection. "No chick flicks."

Lucy helped me set out the plates of brownies and bowls of popcorn. "*Are* there any so-called chick flicks?"

"*Westward the Women*?" I said. "*She Wore a Yellow Ribbon*?"

Crane helped himself to a brownie.

"*She Wore a Yellow Ribbon* is about the seventh cavalry, Jennet. The girl is there strictly for decoration. Pick one, Fowler, so we can get started," he added.

"That's easy," Brent said. "*Red River*. I always wanted to go on a cattle drive."

We settled back to watch Brent's choice while most of the collies dispersed to various private corners for before-bedtime naps. The exception was Raven, who kept her eyes trained on the screen as enthralled by the action as if she were watching Lassie gallop to the rescue.

We took a break at the movie's mid-point. I went to the kitchen to add the rest of the brownies to the empty plates.

"Do you have *How the West Was Won*?" Lucy asked when I returned. "That's my all-time favorite western."

"In my CD case. It'll just take me a second to find it."

"I always had a crush on James Stewart," she confessed.

"For me it was Gregory Peck."

"Him, too."

We brought plates and bowls into the living room. "Before we go home, could we see if your other TV is working?" she asked.

"Oh, it's working. You mean if the mysterious movie is on. Well, sure, but don't count on it."

It only plays for me.

I didn't say this, but I thought it.

~ * ~

After finishing *Red River*, we watched *How the West Was Won.* The brownies were gone, a handful of popcorn remained in the green bowl, and Raven had lost interest in television, drifting off to sleep.

Crane and Brent took the dogs out, then went down to Crane's workshop in the basement to see the bookcase he had made for my Gothic paperback collection.

"Now is the time," Lucy said, with a hopeful glance at the television set. "May I?"

"Be my guest."

She touched it. "That's strange. It's warm. Like it's been on for a long time."

"It hasn't been, though. Let me see."

I lay my hand where Lucy's had been and felt both sides. "It feels cool to me."

"Something's going on," Lucy said. "This is no ordinary television set. Of course we already knew that."

She turned the 'on' knob. I held my breath and waited for a glimpse of blue sky and green grass or a Victorian parlor. Instead we found ourselves watching Kevin James falling backwards down the stairs in a rerun of *The King of Queens*.

"Darn," I said.

Was Susanna's story rolling on its merry way while I baked and prepared the house for our movie watching night? And had it then stopped for some inexplicable reason?

"I really wanted you to see my movie, Lucy."

"I hope I will eventually," she said. "Only not tonight."

~ * ~

That night I dreamed that Lucy turned the television on and I stepped through the screen right into a set designed to resemble a rustic living room lit by oil lamps

A man rose from a roughhewn chair. His gray eyes gleamed with admiration and delight. He had blond hair with silver streaks and sideburns a bit too long to be fashionable. Tiny lines crinkled around his eyes.

He was a dead ringer for Crane.

"Welcome to the L Bar E, Jennet," he said. I've been waiting for you."

Sixteen

The dream stayed with me the next morning as dreams sometimes do. It had ended abruptly like a TV program cut off at a particularly exciting point. Like the Western movie that had no doubt inspired it. I longed to return to the dream, to see what would happen next.

That being impossible, I wondered if Crane and I could visit Colorado someday. I wasn't deluded enough to think I'd find the Wild West as depicted in the movies we'd watched last night, but it couldn't be all concrete and freeways. Surely there were also ranches and horses and cowboys. Maybe we could find Jubilee.

As we drove home from Marston the next day, I mentioned the idea of a western vacation to Leonora.

"What would you do with the dogs?" she asked.

That was a drawback. Taking care of seven collies for two weeks was too much to ask of my obliging neighbor, Camille.

"Well, I can dream," I said.

We were on our way to Clovers for take-out dinners, thanks to Grimsley's overly long staff meeting. Leonora, a veritable newlywed, was unenthusiastic.

"I promised myself I'd prepare a hot meal from scratch for Jake every night," she said.

"Scratch is overrated. Clovers' food is so good he'll never know the difference."

"But I will." She paused, twisting the handle of her handbag. "Okay, I'll do it. Just this once."

"Good decision, and there's Clovers," I said.

The painted clover clusters on the restaurant's border shone through a rising haze, and the woods along Crispian Road blazed with crimson and gold color, overwhelming the green. We were driving through a Technicolor world.

Inside Clovers, chrysanthemums in autumnal hues brightened the tables, and the gingham checked tablecloths matched the centerpieces. Annica, looking radiant even in brown, rushed forward to greet us in a jingle of silver bell earrings.

"Beware the snake," she whispered.

"There's a snake in the restaurant?" Leonora asked, dropping her gaze to the floor.

I was quicker to interpret Annica's cryptic remark. The snake was Veronica the Viper, the last person in the world I wanted to see. Still, perversely, I glanced at the tables, searching for her.

Only one woman was dining alone, Veronica, but I wouldn't have recognized her. She wore a white sheath—in September—and her black hair was styled in a short pageboy. It had a blue sheen in the overhead light.

Brilliant heart-of-summer white in September? Not exactly seasonal, but her choice of color and her beauty made her stand out. In uniform or civilian clothes, Veronica was the kind of woman who attracted male attention.

"She means Veronica," I said to Leonora. "Let's order and get out of here."

I scanned the menu, settling quickly on two stuffed pepper dinners. "Do you have a whole apple pie, Annica?"

"Sure do. It's cooling in the kitchen."

"I'll have that," I said, and Leonora added, "Same for me. I'll take a pie, too. Cherry, if you have it."

"Coming right up."

I opened my purse, searching for a twenty dollar bill.

"Jennet?"

That voice. That sultry voice. As she left me no choice, I turned, and there stood Veronica. Nemesis. Arch-enemy. She was too close to me, invading my space. I stepped back.

"It *is* Jennet Ferguson, right?"

Pretend you don't remember her.

"Yes," I said. "Do I know you?"

"I'm Veronica Quent. Don't you remember? I work with Crane."

"In the sheriff's department?"

"I'm a deputy sheriff, yes, the only woman in the department. I baked a cake for Crane's birthday," she added. "He's been so nice to me."

"That was—thoughtful."

Annica set our orders before us, took the money, and handed us our change, as quickly as I could have hoped. Now we could leave. I dropped coins and bills into my purse, not caring where they fell.

I felt Veronica's eyes on me.

"Since I work with your husband, we should get together sometime," she said. "You and me and Crane. We could go out to dinner…"

"I don't know," I said. "We're both busy. Crane makes our social engagements."

Leonora stifled a cough.

"Ask him then," Veronica said. "My favorite restaurant is the Adriatica."

Leonora rattled her bag. "Jen, our food will cool off."

"We're going. Good afternoon, Ms. Quent."

How stiff that sounded. How unlike me. I didn't care.

Without a backward glance, we left Veronica standing alone at the counter. I felt shaky and hoped my nervousness hadn't been obvious. I was never able to conceal my true feelings, and I would as soon encounter a Massasauga rattlesnake as that woman.

Outside, Leonora said, "You handled that well, Jennet."

"Did I?"

As we walked back to the car, a dozen better responses occurred to me. Where were they a few minutes ago when it had mattered?

"Yes, very well," she said. "Crane makes all your social engagements. That's rich. You wouldn't go anywhere if it were left to him."

I had to smile. "I hope Veronica wasn't serious about our getting together. Why would she want to do that?"

"Mmm, you're right," Leonora said. "You'd think she'd want Crane to herself. I'm so glad she isn't going after Jake."

"I hope she drops the idea."

"I don't think she will."

"I don't either," I said. "How will I get out of it?"

~ * ~

I decided not to mention the encounter to Crane. I had a suspicion that Veronica would, the next time she saw him. Well, let her. But what if she asked him about our getting together?

He wouldn't be likely to agree, not after the birthday cake fiasco.

I set the stuffed peppers on the platter and spooned mashed potatoes into a large bowl, as usual dodging Candy's prancing paws.

Dinner was ready, the tapers in the heirloom candlesticks burned brightly, and I heard Crane's footsteps on the stairs. It was time for dinner, time to ban stressful conversations and even thoughts. After dinner, the ban would still be in effect. I'd had enough stress for one day.

As soon as I did the dishes, I'd see if by lucky chance the Western was playing on the haunted television set. Later Crane and I would take the dogs walking on the lane. This was my life, for which I was everlastingly grateful, and I wasn't going to allow a poisonous viper to slither any closer to my home.

~ * ~

The television gave me contemporary fare which was, as always, disappointing, but then Crane was home, within calling distance. It would keep its supernatural properties under wraps. Our walk with the dogs was perfection with a warm September wind, rustling leaves, and collies who miraculously behaved when Crane led the pack.

After that, our evening took an unexpected turn. Crane picked up the *Banner*, and I chose a novel from my reading basket intending to end the day in a shadowy gloom-begotten Gothic world.

I hadn't finished a single paragraph when my cell phone rang.

Jennifer said, "I just saw Ms. Gray drive by, Jennet. She parked in her driveway. You said to let you know when she came home."

Finally.

"Thank you, Jennifer," I said. "You have no idea how important this is. Could you tell if she had Bronwyn with her?"

"I didn't see her, but I heard barking."

"That's good. I'm going right over and see her."

I powered off my phone.

"Did you say you're going out?" Crane asked.

"Charlotte and Bronwyn are home," I said.

"Look at the time, honey. It's past ten."

I came abruptly back to reality. "I guess it's too late for a visit or even a call."

"Especially if she's just come home from a trip. She's probably exhausted, maybe in bed."

"Tomorrow she may be gone again," I said.

It wasn't likely, but something told me I needed to seize my opportunity.

"You'll have to chance it."

I tried to dismiss Sue's idea of Charlotte as an opportunist who had acquired Bronwyn to sell her into a hellish life. It was outlandish. Still… The possibility remained. On the other hand, as Bronwyn was still with Charlotte and barking, I could dismiss that ghastly notion.

Out of the mood for reading, I dropped my book back in the basket, cheered by the thought that tomorrow was Saturday. I could be on Charlotte's doorstep early. Nine would be a reasonable hour for an important visit.

Maybe delay was for the best. I was exhausted myself and wanted to be rested and alert when I talked to Charlotte.

Crane said, "Let me know what kind of car Charlotte has."

He must still be wondering if she'd driven the car that had killed the young girl on Huron Court.

Seventeen

The car was bright blue, a shade rarely seen on the roads. Its lines were sleek, reminiscent of the old Plymouth Volare, and it was liberally caked with mud, a sign that it had been driven significant miles.

More important, it wasn't white, therefore, not the vehicle that had been involved in the fatal hit and run on Huron Court. Also, the body was in pristine shape, obviously well cared for, without a scratch in sight. I was relieved to put my suspicion to rest.

Still, Charlotte's recent trip remained a mystery. I'd have to find a way to ask her discreetly about it.

In a swirl of leaves, I stood on the porch and rang the doorbell. Bronwyn's head appeared in the picture window. Her bark was loud, even from outside. Charlotte joined her collie, meeting my gaze through the glass, no doubt curious to see who was visiting her so early in the morning.

The door opened. Her smile seemed surprised and somewhat forced, but she was dressed for the day in dark checkered pants and a lacy sleeveless top. Good. I hadn't called too early. She had her hand hooked in Bronwyn's collar as if afraid the collie would bound through the door.

"Why, Jennet," she said. "You're up early on a Saturday. Come in."

I gave Bronwyn a pat on the head. "I came to see how you and Bronwyn are doing."

"We couldn't be better. She's the best companion I ever had. I was just having a cup of coffee," she added. "Could I interest you in some?"

"I'd love that," I said. "Coffee is exactly what I need."

And time, I thought. I had to set the stage before interrogating her.

"Let's go in the kitchen," she said. "I have a good coffeecake."

I had a fleeting impression of cool colors and furniture with clean, classic lines that brought to mind the sea or, in this instance, the lake. The kitchen was different, small but cozy and painted a sunny shade of yellow.

Bronwyn pulled a toy out of a basket filled to the top with stuffies. Her creature of choice was a pink bunny who wore a green and yellow ribbon. She shook it with mock ferocity and dropped it at my feet, which told me that Bronwyn wasn't too old to play with toys and that Charlotte was pampering her new dog.

Experienced in this game, I picked the bunny up. I sat at the table, and Bronwyn stood in the doorway, eyes alert, waiting for me to throw it.

"Bronwyn appears to be adjusting well to her new home," I said.

"I haven't had her long, but already I can't imagine my life without her."

I threw the bunny across the kitchen. She scampered after it.

"Obviously she eats well."

"She licks every dinner bowl clean."

"Does she sleep through the night?" I asked.

"I go to bed earlier than most people, so sometimes Bronwyn whines to go out around four or five."

"That's understandable."

"And she's a good traveler."

Ah, the opening I needed.

"You must have been away the last few days," I said. "I stopped by before."

She turned to rummage through an old fashioned bread box on the counter. "I took the coffeecake out of the freezer last night. It'll be thawed."

"But you weren't home," I added.

Charlotte brought out a coffeecake sprinkled with powdered sugar and unwrapped it. She poured coffee for me and refilled her own cup.

"Do you take sugar or cream?" she asked.

"Just black will be fine."

Bronwyn had brought the bunny back to me and stood waiting for me to notice her.

I tried to think of another way to introduce the subject of Charlotte's trip. She saved me the trouble.

"I have a cabin up north," she said. "I took a short vacation now that I have someone to go with."

"That someone being Bronwyn."

"It makes a difference. She's protection, and I can talk to her. I'll swear she knows what I'm saying."

"A collie is all of that," I said, "But why do you need protection?"

"You know how it is. A woman traveling alone…" She trailed off.

"Did Bronwyn like the north?" I asked.

"I didn't let her run free. I kept thinking she'd make a beeline for the woods and get lost or tangle with a wild creature. Actually I spent most of the time inside cleaning. You know, a place gets dusty even though you don't live in it every day."

I *did* know. Crane and I had a log cabin which, with our schedules, we rarely had a chance to use. When we did, my first jobs were to mop and dust.

I took a bite of coffeecake. It was plain but delicious, not too sweet, with prune filling. When I complimented Charlotte on it, she said, "It's my grandmother's recipe. To be truthful, she didn't use a recipe, but I used to watch her make them."

I was learning little details of Charlotte's life, but I had the feeling she was being deliberately evasive. Having received a glowing report about Bronwyn, I'd have to leave when I finished my coffee and cake. I might as well be direct.

"While you were gone, there was a terrible accident in Foxglove Corners," I said. "It was a hit and run. A young girl died."

She hesitated a telling moment before speaking. "How very sad. Was she a child?"

"No, a college student."

"Where did this happen?" she asked.

"Very close to Sagramore Lake Road," I said. "On Huron Court."

"I know where that is. It isn't built up."

"Not now. There used to be a lovely pink Victorian house on Huron Court, but it burned to the ground."

"I remember," she said. "Now all sorts of flowers are blooming there. At this time of year, most of them are dying out, but the goldenrods are spectacular, so tall and bright."

I tried again. "Huron Court has a fair number of curves. I can see how an accident could happen there. You're driving along and think yours is the only car in miles. Then you find yourself about to collide with another one, head on."

Charlotte shuddered. "Do you think that's what happened?"

"I really don't know," I said. "The killer just drove away, leaving the girl seriously injured. The police are looking for him—or her."

"And you say she died?"

"In the hospital, some days later. Her name was Gail Redmond.

Charlotte drained her coffee cup and picked up the pot. "There's never an excuse not to own up to what you did," she said. "More coffeecake, Jennet?"

~ * ~

With a glance at the lake that lay still beneath an increasing wind, I drove the short distance home. I had my report for the Rescue League and Charlotte's excuse for leaving town, but I was certain she had withheld a portion of the story, a major part.

Did it make sense to adopt a new dog and promptly drive up north to a cabin which presumably she'd had for a while?

Maybe.

She hadn't impressed me as the impulsive kind. If she'd said she'd gone to the cabin to close it for the winter, I'd be more inclined to believe her. That was what cabin owners did at this time of year.

Lacking evidence to the contrary, however, I had to believe her. At least her car wasn't white. I could lose the suspicion that she was the hit and run driver.

At home I typed a brief report on Bronwyn's new life and sent a copy to Sue who would add it to our website. Bronwyn's success story was a rousing endorsement for our new program.

But why was I still uneasy?

Eighteen

A call from my sister, Julia, drove questions about Charlotte's mysterious trip to the back of my mind. Julia was finally returning to the states after studying in England and taking an extended vacation in Italy. Her flight would arrive on Monday afternoon, and she insisted on renting a car and driving to Foxglove Corners.

"I don't want you or Crane to alter your schedules," she said. "Besides I'll need my own transportation when I'm home in the states."

It was no use arguing with her. Julia was independent and self-sufficient. I suspected that her time overseas had sharpened these qualities.

"If you get there before we do, Camille has a spare key," I said. "Have a safe flight."

Now I'd wait and hope nothing happened to prevent our reunion.

On Sunday afternoon, when sunlight turned the autumn-colored leaves to fiery brilliance, I took Halley, Sky, and Misty walking to Sagramore Lake, hoping we'd run into Charlotte or perhaps see Bronwyn in the yard.

We met a collie on the way, but it was Ginger padding along between Jennifer and Molly. The girls were wearing beige shorts and the tops that Miss Eidt had designed for her summer reading club.

The dogs all knew one another and were overjoyed at the chance to share their walk, even Sky who usually tried to melt into the background when confronted with unexpected company.

"Did you ever get to visit Ms. Gray?" Jennifer asked.

"Yes," I said, "and I saw Bronwyn too."

"That's good because they're gone again," Molly said.

"What? I just saw them yesterday."

Charlotte hadn't said anything about leaving town again, but I recalled my nagging feeling that she was withholding some of her story. In that case she would hardly advertise her plans. But to take another trip so soon?

Jennifer said, "She left a note asking us to keep raking her leaves. She's going to pay us later."

"That's strange," I said. "When did you find the note?"

"This morning."

That meant she must have left late Saturday night or early Sunday morning, which suggested haste. Or fear?

We soon reached the lake and Charlotte's house. The blue car was indeed gone. A new layer of crimson maple leaves blanketed the lawn and the driveway, seeming to hide secrets. A thick newspaper wrapped in yellow plastic, probably the Sunday *Banner*, lay on the porch in a bed of leaves, undisturbed.

"Very strange," I added.

Molly's eyes lit up. I recognized the look. "Do you think it's a mystery?" she asked.

"Don't be silly, Molly," Jennifer said. "Ms. Gray isn't a mysterious lady. Before this, she hardly ever went anywhere."

"Then something must have happened," Molly countered. "She's always been so nice to us. If she's in trouble, we want to help."

The girls fancied themselves modern day Nancy Drews. They were always eager to leap into my mysteries and at times had provided valuable clues. But did I want to involve them in this one? I didn't think so, not until I knew what was going on in Charlotte's life. It might be innocent; it might not. What to tell them?

"There could be trouble, but it's too soon to tell."

"If there *is* a mystery, we'll help you solve it," Molly said.

Jennifer, easily convinced, said, "We can keep an eye on the house and let you know as soon as she comes back. She will. She has to pay us for raking leaves."

"You can do that," I said. "It'd be helpful."

We stayed together along the lake and around the block while Molly and Jennifer regaled me with tales of their new classes, the boys they liked, and Ginger's adventures in agility.

With the girls brimming with the enthusiasm of the young, and the dogs finding their pleasure in sniffing new scents, everything seemed so normal that it was difficult to believe Charlotte might be involved in a dangerous situation. Even with this second disappearing act.

Still there might well be mischief afoot, and because of Bronwyn, my concerns went beyond curiosity.

As soon as I took the collies home, I'd better call on Sue Appleton.

~ * ~

Sue set the brush on the porch step. "Now I *know* something's wrong."

Seeing her opportunity, Bluebell, half brushed, escaped to a safe distance where she lay between Icy and Echo watching us.

"You're probably right," I said.

"Our Bronwyn is in the middle of it."

I settled myself in a wicker rocker and told the dogs to Sit and Stay. Misty gave a whimper to express her displeasure. She wanted to run with Sue's collies.

"You have to remember, Bronwyn belongs to Charlotte," I pointed out.

"If our rescue is in danger, all bets are off."

I sighed. Charlotte had adopted Bronwyn. She had her papers. The Rescue League had a clear policy on rescinding an adoption. Unless, of course, the collie was being abused.

"Maybe she'll return in a few days," I said.

"And maybe she won't."

"She has to," I said. "Her home is here."

Sue was determined to look on the dark side. I hoped everything would work out, but I was baffled and couldn't think of any way to find out where Charlotte had gone and why.

Then I remembered the neighbor who had been collecting Charlotte's mail. Possibly Charlotte had revealed her plans or at least left a note with more details than the one Jennifer had received.

At my feet Sky trembled, and in the next instance, thunder rumbled across the sky. Until then I hadn't noticed the dark clouds amassing above the woods.

"It wasn't supposed to rain," Sue said.

The weather continued to amaze me. "When we left the house, it was sunny and beautiful."

It was beautiful still, if a little darker. Rain has a way of creeping up on you, especially when you don't read the paper or listen to the weather news on television.

I rose and took the leashes. "Let's outrace the storm, girls."

Sue called to her dogs. "This problem with Charlotte isn't over," she said.

"I'll let you know as soon as I hear something," I said and hurried the dogs down the driveway out to the lane.

~ * ~

Raindrops began to fall before we reached the house. We increased our speed and arrived home, wet and breathless, with a roll of thunder.

Water landed on me from three sides as the dogs shook. I toweled myself dry and changed clothes, put a roast in the oven, and thought about the haunted television. I hadn't even looked at it for two days.

I turned it on and saw Luke's face. He was talking again, extolling the virtues of the Territory in general and his ranch, the L Bar E in particular.

Good! Great!

I settled down to listen and watch. Luke's face was aglow with passion for his home, for life, for his success. The fine lines around his eyes crinkled bewitchingly. What an absolutely handsome man this Crane lookalike was!

He made me forget I was watching a movie, perhaps filmed in a state far from Jubilee. I could almost believe I was standing beside him, listening to the story of his first days in the Territory when the ranch was only a dream.

Except Susanna was the girl at his side, wearing one of her long beribboned, beruffled dresses, a sunny yellow in color. She was the one who listened to him.

He appeared to be giving her a horse or the loan of one.

This should be interesting. She could hardly mount the large creature wearing one of those long, full skirts.

He'd keep it for her, he was saying. She could ride it whenever she came visiting.

The scene changed. We were back on the main street of Jubilee in front of the Pink Palace Hotel. The white-whiskered man in the tattered Confederate uniform sat on a bench observing a lady alight gracefully from the stagecoach. She was a showy woman, elaborately coiffed and clothed.

The plot thickens. Was she competition for Susanna?

Outside in the real world, the rain continued. It sounded like pebbles of ice landing on the windows.

Windows!

They were open in the bedroom. Lightning crackled across the sky as I rushed up the stairs to close them.

Now to see who the gorgeous newcomer was. I hoped she hadn't come to Jubilee to make trouble for me.

For you?

For Susanna. I meant Susanna.

I slipped back into my chair. On the screen cereal flakes danced around their open box to a catchy little tune.

It had happened again. Why was I not surprised?

Crane must be on his way home. On the lane. In front of the house. All of the dogs had fled to the side door, barking all the way.

I turned off the television in mid-tune. The movie played only for me. It stopped when anyone else entered the house. I should have remembered that.

For the rest of the viewing audience, it was dancing cereal.

Nineteen

I came home from school the next day to find a strange car in the driveway and Julia sitting in the kitchen with the table set for tea.

The collies circled around me excitedly, eager to tell me about the visitor who had appeared in my absence, all except Raven and Sky, who shared space under the table in the dining room. They all remembered Julia from her last visit.

Misty had apparently coaxed Julia into a game of Fetch as the white goat lay on the floor.

I sidestepped it and Julia rose to hug me.

"Welcome home, Julia," I said.

Julia's eyes were misty. "It's so good to see you looking well and happy."

After a day in the Marston trenches, I thought I looked bedraggled. An ink blot stained my white sleeve, my hair was windblown, and… Oh, what did it matter? Julia was home, this time to stay.

She was the one who looked good, dressed in a soft aqua sheath and as cool as a lake breeze. Her bright blonde hair was longer, and she wore a new ring, a turquoise stone set in a golden claw.

"I bought cameos in Naples for you," she said. "A nice assortment of bracelets and brooches."

"That's lovely, but all I wanted was my sister home."

As she poured the tea, I noticed a loaf of pumpkin bread on a china dessert plate.

"Camille just brought it," Julia said. "You have no idea how much I've missed American baking."

I cut thick slices for us. "You can have as much as you like now."

"Not if I want to stay thin," she said. "And I do. Tell me what's new. Then I'll tell you about my travels in Italy."

"I don't know where to begin."

But I did. "I have a new ghost," I said. "It's a different kind of ghost, truly unique."

She listened to my tale of the movie that had haunted me ever since I'd found the old television set at the estate sale.

"I was watching it yesterday," I said. "It comes and goes like a… Like a ghost, and every time this happens, the story is at the same point where it left off."

"I don't know how that can be."

"When anyone else is with me, there's regular programming on," I said.

I had clearly impressed her. "That's unusual even for you. What do you think causes this—anomaly?"

"I don't know. Brent's idea is that there might be a tiny CD embedded in the set."

"Seriously? I can't imagine how that would work. Shall we take it apart and see?"

"No," I said quickly. "I don't want to risk losing my movie."

"Good heavens, Jennet. All this angst over a Western?"

"It's more than that," I said.

I didn't know how to explain the hold it had on me. The movie had intrigued me from day one, both the story and the mysterious way it came and went. What if I never saw it again? If Luke, Susanna, the old Confederate veteran, and the as yet unnamed newcomer from the stagecoach never returned?

I'd be devastated and frustrated that I'd never solved the mystery.

"I'd miss it," I admitted. "I want to know what's going to happen next. The actor who plays Luke is a dead ringer for Crane."

"Finish your tea and we'll see if it's on now," Julia said.

I did, in a few gulps. "I don't think it will be."

The dogs followed us into the living room where I'd moved the set, all except Sky and Raven. I turned the TV on. Western movie or dancing cereal? I held my breath.

Neither. It was a trailer for a new science-fiction movie.

"The ghost isn't cooperating today," Julia said.

~ * ~

We had a quiet evening with no surprise company and a silent cell phone. No Rescue League emergency and no call from Jennifer or Molly about Charlotte Gray.

"What do you plan to do now?" Crane directed his question to Julia as we settled in the living room with our after-dinner coffee.

"I'd like to stay in education, on the college level, if possible," she said. "But for the immediate future I'm going to relax and unwind. I feel like I've been on a merry-go-round."

"Just on a jet plane." I touched the bracelet that Julia had given me, seven large pink cameos, all with different faces, joined by delicate scrolls of gold. It had a rosy shine in the lamplight.

"Maybe you can help me solve my television mystery," I said.

"Not if I never see this entrancing movie and you won't let me dissect the TV."

"I haven't seen it either," Crane said.

"What's it about?" Julia asked.

"A girl comes to Jubilee in the Colorado Territory around the 1870s and meets a handsome rancher. He seems to be enamored of her. A new lady just came to town."

"It doesn't have much action for a Western," Crane said.

"I'd classify it as a women's Western." I refilled our coffee cups.

"A new genre." Julia glanced at the television. "Shall we see if it's on now?"

I set my cup down and walked over to the set. As they had before, the top and sides of the cabinet felt warm as if it had been on for hours.

"It's definitely vintage," Julia said. "Before the invention of the remote."

"I'd like to see the dancing cereal flakes," Crane said.

I smiled. "Crane is one of the few people in the world who likes commercials. I have to admit that was a cute one."

As I had anticipated, a contemporary program was playing. It looked like one of those ghastly reality shows. I couldn't turn the set off fast enough.

We sat quietly for a few minutes, drinking coffee.

"I'm sorry," I said. "It's disappointing."

True to her nature, Julia was philosophical. "Tomorrow is another day, as Scarlett O'Hara said."

"What are you going to do tomorrow, Julia?" Crane asked.

"Go shopping. I need a new fall wardrobe, clothes appropriate to wear while I stand in front of a class expounding on Victorian literature. Then I'm going to look for a car. I'm not sure what kind I want."

"I wish I could go with you," I said.

"We have all the time in the world now," Julia reminded me. "I'm not going anywhere in the immediate future."

Nor was I.

In spite of the mysterious threads that continued to wrap around me, having Julia home was wonderfully energizing. I felt that I could find out what Charlotte was up to and perhaps solve the mystery of the elusive movie. Maybe I'd even have an ally in my conflict with Veronica the Viper.

~ * ~

The peace and quiet of our evening was too good to last.

Crane had built a fire more for atmosphere than warmth, although the fall evenings and mornings were chilly. Firelight makes everything softer and in general better.

Julia said, "You two are living the American dream. A house in the country, dogs, important jobs. This is what I'd like for myself someday."

The rippling notes of my cell phone woke Misty, who had fallen asleep at my feet and propelled me out of my chair. I'd left the phone on the credenza in the dining room.

Molly's name came up on the screen.

"Hi, Jennet, it's Molly. Is it too late to call?"

"No, it's okay." I glanced at the clock. It was nine-thirty. "What's happening?"

"Ms. Gray came back. But here's something funny. She didn't park in her driveway. She left her car parked at the other end of the street. She didn't have to. We raked all the leaves."

"Are you sure it's her car?" I asked.

"It's the only blue car around here," she said. "Besides, we checked the license plate. It has her birthday, March, on it, and she has a sticker on the back window that says *I (heart) Collies*."

That was indeed odd, and I was thankful that the girls had been so observant. They really wanted to help Charlotte.

"I hope she stays put for a while," I said. "I have to go to school tomorrow."

"Yeah, so do we."

But I could call her. Yes, I'd do that.

Thanking Molly for the information, I ended the call and punched in Charlotte's number. Her phone rang six times, then a voice directed me to leave a message.

Should I? It was so easy to ignore or delete a voice mail. Well, nothing ventured, nothing gained. In any event, it was too late for a visit tonight. I'd have to take a chance that she'd be curious to know why I wanted to contact her again. I left a short simple, message:

It's Jennet, Charlotte. I have to talk to you soon, tomorrow if possible. It's very important."

I hoped I'd finally have some answers. Incidentally, I wondered why Charlotte had avoided parking in her own driveway. I could think of only one reason. She wanted it to appear that she wasn't home.

The next question was why.

Twenty

I was so busy in school the next day that I didn't have time to dwell on the mystery of Charlotte Gray. My first American Literature class was extremely annoying. I tried to interest them in *Rip van Winkle*, only to be bombarded with requests and, in some cases, demands for hall passes.

I refused them all and continued giving them background notes on Washington Irving's contributions to American literature.

"That's a nice pin, Mrs. Ferguson," Amie said.

This comment was typical of the female fringe of Fourth Hour. A compliment at an inopportune time designed to disrupt the business of the class.

"Thank you," I murmured.

I had pinned a cameo brooch, Julia's gift, to the collar of my white blouse. It was glossy brown in a gold oval, with an unusual forward-facing head.

For a moment I allowed myself a delicious fantasy, standing at a podium, wearing the same long navy blue skirt and white blouse, giving a lecture on Emily Bronte to a college class. Oh, rarest of miracles, they were listening to me. Taking notes. Asking relevant questions.

That *could* happen at some time in the future. If I wanted it to.

"Sign this, Mrs. Ferguson." Rachelle sidled up to me and thrust a piece of paper in my direction. "I need a drink of water."

"No, you don't," I said. "Go back to your seat."

"But I have a sore throat. The fountain's just outside the door," she added as if I weren't familiar with the building.

"No passes," I said.

"I'm going to choke."

When I didn't answer, she stamped her way back to her seat by the window, muttering something that sounded like, 'I hope *you* choke.' Her two blonde cronies giggled. I glared at them.

Should I interrupt class to write a discipline referral? I wondered.

No, not this time. Not for this *sotto voice* defiance. By rights, that wish for a choking spell should have been aimed at Principal Grimsley, whose rule I was enforcing.

I gave the class the last note about thunder being caused by men playing nine pins, or bowling, in the sky, and we were ready to begin the story. If only it had a catchier opening.

~ * ~

Thunder rolled in as the echo of the last bell faded. Wonderful. Stormy weather on the way home. It was my week to drive.

Leonora stood at the door. "Ready, Jen?"

I slipped my raincoat on and grabbed my gradebook. I wasn't taking any schoolwork home tonight.

Leonora had the foresight to keep an umbrella in her closet. Mine was in the car.

"Let's hurry," she said.

The storm caught up with us on the freeway. Thunder and lightning and slick pavement. Was it raining in Foxglove Corners? I hoped to take the dogs walking to Sagramore Lake. *If* the rain turned the lanes to mud, I'd have to drive to Charlotte's house. Feeling suddenly tense, I turned on the lights.

She'd had all day to return my call but hadn't left a voice mail for me. I suspected she didn't want to talk to anyone. Why was Charlotte so secretive? I didn't think it had anything to with Bronwyn; therefore it could be argued that her comings and goings weren't my concern. I could be wrong, though.

Halfway to Foxglove Corners, I left the freeway to travel on a country road strewn with downed branches. I had to drive more slowly and steer around occasional obstacles which included a deer leaping out of the woods into my path.

Leonora screamed. I slammed on the brakes, sliding to the verge where, thank God, the car stopped. When I looked for the deer, it had vanished. By the time I dropped Leonora off at her house, my nerves were frazzled. At least the storm had passed.

I didn't see Julia's rental car, and it was too early for Crane to be home. Even after all these weeks, it felt strange not to see Raven rushing out to the car, the first of the dogs to greet me.

I'd had to get used to this low key homecoming because Crane and I were in agreement. From now on, Raven would live in the house with the rest of the collies.

Inside, I made time to drink a cup of tea with a slice of pumpkin bread. Nicely energized, I left fresh water and bones for the dogs and set out for the lake.

The rain had washed the countryside clean and left a myriad scents in the air—and more leaves on the ground. I left the windows open, breathing in the freshness.

Freshness for new beginnings.

On reaching Sagramore Lake Road, I was happy to see Charlotte's blue car parked a block away from her house. I'd been half afraid she'd be gone, and indeed, the house had a sad abandoned look. The drapes were drawn, and the interior dark. And empty?

Nonetheless, I parked and walked up to the porch.

Was that a bark quickly hushed?

I was about to ring the bell when the door opened. There stood Charlotte with a suitcase in one hand and Bronwyn's leash in the other.

A flush spread over her face. "Oh," she said. "Jennet. I'm on my way out."

Bronwyn wagged her tail but didn't utter a sound. This was far from the welcome I'd expected, but at least I'd arrived in time to intercept Charlotte.

"Do you have a minute to talk?" I asked.

"Not really."

"You didn't return my call."

"No, I was going to. I had so much to do." With a sigh, she set the suitcase on the floor.

"Come in then," she said. "I suppose I have a minute. No more."

Such an enthusiastic welcome. It wasn't in my nature to be pushy except when I was trying to solve a mystery.

I stepped inside, past the suitcase, past Bronwyn, and took a seat on the sofa. The living room reminded me of the ones we'd recently seen in the ghost town, Ashton. Clean and sparse, all personal possessions stored away. Charlotte remained standing.

How was I going to begin? Express concern for Bronwyn? Or come right to the point?

"Is something wrong, Charlotte?" I asked.

She didn't meet my eyes. "Why would you say that?"

"I have one of my feelings. I've learned to trust them."

She hesitated. "Well, something *did* come up. I decided to leave Foxglove Corners for a while."

I waited. Surely she was going to say more. Or not.

"When a person adopts one of our dogs, she becomes family," I said. "Whatever the problem is, we're here to help."

She was silent. I couldn't think of anything else to say, to encourage her confidence, except: "Please let me help you."

She sat at the other end of the sofa. "There *is* something, but I don't know what you could do."

"Tell me," I said. "You may just need a new perspective."

"I need more than that." She sighed again. "That hit-and-run on Huron Court. Do you remember it?"

"Of course," I said. "The victim died."

"Yes, well, I was a witness."

A witness, then. I was afraid she was going to say something else.

"I thought there was only one witness," I said, "and the witness disappeared."

"I don't know what you heard. There were two of us. Do you know the field of flowers on Huron Court?"

"I do. My friends are the ones who planted it."

"It's still beautiful in the autumn. That day I took Bronwyn for a ride. I'd just passed the field when I heard a crash. Beyond the next bend in the road, I saw the wreckage. I pulled off to the side and dialed nine-one-one. Someone else had stopped, a young man who kept saying he was a medical student. His name was Jeff."

One aspect of Charlotte's story didn't sound right. Unless I was mistaken the one witness was a man in a gray car. The police were looking for him. I told Charlotte what I'd heard.

"There were two of us and the man who was in the accident," she insisted. "The girl had been thrown out of her car. It didn't look good. She was still. Her raincoat was covered in blood. I knelt on the ground to see if there was anything I could do. Thankfully she was unconscious.

"It was all blurry, but I remember Jeff suddenly shouting, 'Hey, get back here. You can't leave.'

"I looked up to see the man who hit the girl speeding past us. The front end of his car was damaged but not too badly.

"The young man told me to stay with her. He was going after him.

"But he came back a few minutes later saying he'd lost him. Then we heard the ambulance."

"What do you remember about the hit-and-run driver?" I asked.

"Not much. I just glanced at him. He looked at me. His hair was thinning, and he had a black beard. He wore sunglasses."

"The police still haven't found him," I said.

"I know. And that young medical student talked to the police. Then he drove off and wasn't seen again."

"How terrible," I said. "Especially now that the girl has died. But I don't understand why you've left town twice. Not because of this accident, surely?"

She leaned back and stroked Bronwyn's fur absently. "That's only half of my story," she said.

Twenty-one

Charlotte said, "The next day I found a printed note in with my mail, unsigned, of course. It said, 'Forget what you saw or you'll be sorry.'"

She kept her hand on Bronwyn who rested her head on Charlotte's lap.

"What I saw could only refer to the accident. The driver's face."

"I take it you gave your name and evidence to the police," I said.

She nodded. "At the time I did. But how could they protect me? We have a small force. They can't be everywhere."

I started to contradict her, but she was right. Even with a Personal Protection Order, a person couldn't be one hundred percent safe if she were the target of a determined assassin.

"Do you still have the note?" I asked.

"No, I threw it away. The same day I saw the driver at Blackbourne's Grocers. I don't think he saw me. When I came home, I grabbed food and water and drove up north to the cabin. It's located on eighty acres. After a while, I thought it was safe to go home. But then I saw his car on the expressway and had a glimpse of his face with that ugly beard."

"Did he see you that time?"

"I'm sure he did. I took the next exit, and he didn't follow me."

"And now you're going away again?"

"Yes, back to the cabin. I packed more clothes and picked up some medication I need. There's a shotgun at the cabin. Bronwyn and I should be safe. You can see why I said you couldn't help me."

"Not at all. First, you should definitely report this man's threat to the police. It sounds like he's still in the area. If they find him, he'll be arrested for murder, and you'll be safe."

He saw Bronwyn too. I'm afraid for both of us."

"My husband is a deputy sheriff and our friend, Lieutenant Mac Dalby, is on the force," I said. "Let's see what they say."

As she seemed unconvinced, I added, "If this man tracked you down on your eighty acres, they'd never find your body. You do *not* want to isolate yourself."

"I'm afraid," she said.

"I would be, too. How do you think he found you?"

"Possibly because of my car's color," she said. "I had it painted. There aren't many blue cars that shade on the road today. When I stopped for the accident, he had time to see my license. It doesn't matter how he found me. He did. And I think he got to Jeff and made him disappear."

The other driver was dead and apparently one witness was taken care of. That left Charlotte—and Bronwyn. In her place I'd be terrified, too.

"Don't leave today," I said. "Let me talk to Lieutenant Dalby."

"That man knows where to find us."

"Is there any other place you can stay for a few days?" I asked.

"My neighbor, but that's right next door, and I don't want to involve her."

"There's a new inn in Maple Creek," I said. "The Shell House. He'll never think to look for you there."

"That wouldn't work. I have Bronwyn. We're staying together."

"Call and find out if they allow dogs. Give me a little time to think of something, Charlotte. It'll all work out."

"You can't know that."

"We can hope," I said. "Anyway, I believe it's better to stay and fight than run away. I'll think of something."

When I left, I thought she looked a little more hopeful.

On the short drive home, my thoughts were a jumble. I'd encouraged Charlotte to stay in Foxglove Corners. Now I was responsible for what happened next. The safest place for Charlotte and Bronwyn was with Crane and me, but we already had seven collies and Julia was occupying our only guest room.

Leonora and Jake were newly married and unlikely to want a houseguest.

Sue? She'd probably be willing to help, especially since Bronwyn was part of the package, but I recalled her tendency to blame Charlotte for not providing a safe home for our rescue, which was unfair. What had happened and might still happen was beyond Charlotte's control.

Lucy was a better choice. She lived alone at Dark Gables with one collie. I was sure she'd welcome Charlotte, and with all the pines on Lucy's property, it would be impossible to see a blue car from the road.

How to find Black Beard was the main problem. Fortunately the police were already looking for him.

~ * ~

I was relieved when Lucy agreed to let Charlotte and Bronwyn stay at Dark Gables as long as necessary. Charlotte planned to report the threatening note to the police, while Mac promised to do everything in his power to apprehend the elusive hit-and-run driver, no easy task with the little he had to go on.

Having done all I could to help Charlotte, that night I fell asleep with a clear mind and tumbled into a rare, pleasant dream.

I strolled through a tranquil blue and green world with Luke Emerson at my side. We were at the L Bar E. In the distance, snow-capped mountains reached up to the sky.

"I've been waiting for you, Jennet," he said. "What took you so long?"

"I couldn't find my way back."

As I walked, I felt the unaccustomed weight of material against my legs. I was wearing boots rather than heels, and I clutched the edges of my shawl with one hand. Who needed a shawl? The weather was warm with a gentle breeze that smelled of lightly scented spring flowers. It was weather fit for a dream.

I was wearing one of Susanna's dresses, and Susanna was gone. I had taken her place.

Luke reached for my hand. "You're here now. That's all that matters." He added, "And here you'll stay in the great state of Colorado."

"I thought Jubilee was in Colorado Territory," I said.

"It was. As of now, we're a real honest-to-goodness state."

Thunder rumbled over the mountains, magical little men playing a perpetual game of nine pins in the sky.

"Looks like we're in for some rain," Luke said.

Hand and hand we walked toward a sturdy ranch house that looked as if it had been made by hand, all of the neighbors pitching in to erect a structure in the wilderness, using materials native to the region.

It swam in the lightest of mists that thickened until I couldn't see the house. It was lost in a dense white fog. But I could still hear the thunder.

I woke, clutching the sheet. The dress was gone. In its place I wore a long nightgown of lightweight cotton that twisted around my knees.

Luke no longer held my hand.

He had gone, too.

~ * ~

I felt a little guilty for being happy in a dream with a man who wasn't my husband, Crane—until I realized how ludicrous that was. A dream had no more substance than a wish. I hadn't created it. Except it had been incredibly real at the time. I'd felt the press of the heavy fabric and the warmth and strength of Luke's hand in mine. I'd seen the color of the grass and the sky.

I wondered why I had dreamed of my Western on a night when thoughts of a menacing hit-and-run driver should have filled my mind. And that scene in which Luke and I walked away from the threat of rain toward the ranch house? That hadn't been part of the movie I'd seen on the haunted TV. It was purely a product of my mind.

A worrying thought surfaced. Suppose the next time the TV decided to cooperate with me, I saw my dream scene played out. That would be way too bizarre.

Highly unlikely. Something else was going to happen. For example, that fancy newcomer from the stagecoach was going to make her presence known.

I turned on my miniature bedside flashlight and glanced at the alarm clock. I had one more hour to sleep. I'd close my eyes and maybe the dream would return.

It didn't, of course. A dream isn't a dessert featured on a menu board. You can't order it and sit back while you wait for it to appear. If you could, though, how wonderful that would be.

Inevitably the alarm clock rang. Just in case I hadn't heard it, Misty added her high-pitched yelps to the disturbance. I didn't worry about her waking Julia up as she usually slept until seven-thirty. Beside me, Crane stirred and got out of bed. Immediately the day filled up with activity.

Take care of the dogs, get dressed for school, pack a lunch, make a hearty breakfast for Crane.

In the hustle and bustle of the real world, the last fragments of my Western dream disintegrated.

Twenty-two

With Charlotte and Bronwyn safe at Dark Gables, I had to decide what to tell Sue about their situation. How would she react if she knew that our rescue and her new mistress were the targets of a killer who was determined to keep his identity a secret?

In two words—not well.

Eventually I decided not to tell her. Not yet, anyway. Immediately a sense of well-being settled over me. For two whole days my classes were somewhat civilized. If Veronica had approached Crane about our getting together for dinner, he didn't tell me. Julia was considering applying for a position at her first-choice college.

And the sun shone on the sweet fields of autumn as the many-colored leaves stirred in the wind.

As I walked with Gemmy, Misty, and Star down to Sagramore Lake Road, I had an almost irresistible desire to see Brent's wildflowers on Huron Court in the fall of the year. I especially wanted to view for myself the mysterious violet that we associated with the spirit of Violet Randall who haunted the road. Was it still in bloom?

Of course I wouldn't go. I'd vowed never to set foot on Huron Court again, and that was one vow I planned to keep.

Misty slowed as we approached Charlotte's house. How desolate it looked. You could tell when a house's people had left it, even with the walkway and driveway neatly raked. The cloud of sadness that enveloped its walls was almost palpable.

Jennifer and Molly were running with Ginger on the deserted beach. All three came to a stop, the girls aglow with the energy of the young and Ginger panting. The exhausted collie touched noses with Misty and flopped down in the sand.

"I want to thank you girls for letting me know Charlotte was back," I said. "It really helped."

"Why did Ms. Gray go away again?" Molly asked.

"She took Bronwyn and went to stay with a friend," I said. "And, oh, I forgot. She gave me an envelope of money and a note for you girls. Stop at my house after school and pick them up."

"Don't forget to tell Jennet about the man, Molly," Jennifer said.

"Oh, yeah. It may not be important but, we were walking home from school the other day, and…"

Molly reached down to take a stone away from Ginger. "You can't eat that, girl."

Jennifer continued. "We saw a man at Ms. Gray's house. He went up to the porch and knocked on the door. Then he rang the bell. When no one answered, he tried to look inside, but the drapes are closed, so he went around to the back."

"Can you describe him? I asked.

"He was going bald and had a long beard," Jennifer said. "He was mean-looking."

The hit-and-run driver. Charlotte was right to leave her home when she did. I shuddered to think what might have happened if she'd opened the door.

"Did you notice what kind of car he had?"

The girls exchanged glances. "It was beige," Molly said. "He came back the next day about the same time and knocked on the door again."

"Do you think you can keep up the surveillance?" I asked. "And let me know if you see him again or if you see anything unusual?"

"Sure," Jennifer said. "This turned into a mystery, didn't it?"

"That man is a mystery," I said. "I don't know exactly what his intentions are, but I *do* know they aren't good."

"We *are* helping, then."

"Very much. But whatever you do, don't approach him. Don't let him know you're watching him."

I didn't want to alarm the girls, but I had to add, "He could be dangerous. Just give me a call if you see him."

"We will," Molly said.

"Tell Ms. Gray ' hi' for us," Jennifer added.

I agreed to do that, and we parted company. On the way home, I gave Huron Court a wide berth. There was enough danger in the air without courting more.

~ * ~

Brent's before-dinner visit that evening was a surprise. We hadn't seen him for several days. As usual he didn't come empty-handed. He had a two-pound box of candy for us and make-believe fudge from Pluto's Gourmet Pet Shop for the collies.

The dogs were so accustomed to Brent's largesse that they began to lick their chops as soon as he stepped through the door.

"Liver fudge," I said. "Yuk."

Crane took Brent's jacket. "Our girls will love it."

"Did Julia ever come home?" Brent asked.

"She's visiting a college," I said. "She'll probably stay there overnight."

"I'll see her next time around then." Brent settled into the rocker with Misty on his lap. Raven limped up to lie at Brent's feet, beating Sky to her favorite spot. Refusing to be discouraged, she lay down next to Raven.

"What's new around here?" Brent asked.

"Not much," I said.

Crane sat beside me on the sofa. "Is Charlotte's story a secret?"

I glanced at him. "Well, not anymore."

I'd thought that if only a few people knew Charlotte had witnessed the fatal hit-and-run, she'd be reasonably safe. Brent could keep a confidence, though. Besides, as Lucy's friend, he might see Charlotte at Dark Gables. With this in mind, I told him about her dilemma.

"No one should have to leave their home unless there's a disaster like a tornado or flood," he said.

"Charlotte is an older woman alone with a geriatric dog. She can't have round-the-clock police protection. What else can she do? Jennifer and Molly saw the driver at her house," I added. "I'm glad she decided to stay with Lucy."

"Let me know if I can help," he said.

Crane frowned. "Catching a killer is a police matter."

"I can still do something," he countered. "Have the cops found him yet?"

"They're still looking."

After a moment, Brent said, "I'm surprised there was any traffic on Huron Court. People must not know how dangerous it is."

The peculiarities of Huron Court weren't commonly known at this time. People simply didn't talk about it. Or perhaps, like Brent, they didn't give in to their fears.

"Maybe your wildflower field is the draw," I said.

A sudden frown darkened his face. "Hey, Jennet, you don't suppose the accident happened because he was distracted by my wildflower field, do you? Because, if it did, I'm partially to blame."

"That didn't happen," I said, remembering what Charlotte had told me. "She'd already passed the wildflowers when she heard the crash around the next curve in the road."

"That's a relief. Speaking of my flowers…" He pulled out his phone, a larger, newer version of mine. "I took these yesterday."

I could hardly believe my eyes. Amidst the tall goldenrods and stalks of spent coneflowers, the dark blue violets looked as healthy and new as if they had just arrived from a flower shop.

"The babies," he said.

"It's uncanny," I murmured. "It's fortunate you can't see the violets from the road. That *would* be a draw."

"It's a curiosity," he said. "Well, I can't do anything about it now. Pretty soon everything will die."

"Even the violets?"

"We'll have to wait and see. How about your other mystery, the temperamental TV?"

"I haven't thought about it lately," I said.

"Let's see if your movie is on."

I crossed the room and lay my hand on the top of the television. It felt warm while all the other surfaces in the house would be room temperature. I didn't have to touch them to be certain of it.

I turned it on, and a kitchen came into focus. The cook, who wore a gaudy sequined top, wielded a butcher's knife over a slab of undetermined meat.

"We don't want to watch that," Crane said.

"Jennet already knows how to cook," Brent added.

"Thank you."

"Maybe," he continued, "you imagined that movie."

"I certainly did not. I'm surprised you'd say that."

"If Jennet said she saw it, she did," Crane said.

"And I'm going to see it again, straight through to the end," I said, even though I knew whether or not I did wasn't up to me.

Twenty-three

Somewhere in the house, an old phonograph was playing the waltz from *Billy the Kid.* That evocative music never failed to transport me to the Old West.

The well-loved strains invaded every corner of the room. At first the music was soft, as if heard from a distance. Gradually the volume increased until it was so loud that I feared Crane would wake. Then abruptly it stopped.

I was awake, the sheet pulled high over my face. Still I heard the melody, now from far off. From downstairs or maybe outside.

How could I hear music from a dream?

You can't possibly.

I listened intently. All I heard at the moment were normal accounted-for sounds in a house steeped in nighttime silence. In any event, it had been decades since I had owned a phonograph.

What a weird dream! No scenic background, no people, no action, only the music and the feeling that I was waltzing on a dance floor—without a partner. What on earth had inspired it?

I remembered then. The haunting melody was the theme of the Western movie.

Did that mean the antique TV had turned itself on?

I almost got out of bed to go downstairs but stopped myself in time. The television was bizarre but not so bizarre that it could turn itself on and off at will.

Besides, the house was quiet now. My appearance on the first floor would disturb the dogs. They'd think they should go out. Misty, who slept with Halley in the doorway, padded up to the bed and nudged me with her nose. I hadn't made a sound, but she knew I was awake and wanted to know why.

"It's all right, girl," I whispered. "Go back to sleep."

To myself I repeated a sentiment that had become a mantra: *A dream is only a dream.*

~ * ~

Lucy and Charlotte had made an instant connection, as had Bronwyn and Sky. Still Charlotte wanted to go home, or at least take refuge in her cottage up north which was her second home.

On Saturday morning I did my grocery shopping for the week and stopped at Dark Gables. I didn't want to give Charlotte anything else to worry about, but thought she should know that the man who had almost certainly driven the death car had been seen at her house.

"Unless you're prepared to deal with him, you can't go home yet," I said. "He could come again anytime."

Charlotte had grown progressively paler as I told her what Jennifer and Molly had witnessed.

"I guess I'd better stay here a little longer, if it's all right," she said.

Lucy smiled. "Stay as long as you like, Charlotte."

"If only the police would catch him."

"Gail Redmond's family offered a reward for information leading to his capture," I said. "Three thousand dollars."

"I hope that tempts someone to betray him. But how could anybody know what he did?"

"By his damaged car?" I said. "Or maybe he's one of those dumb criminals who can't resist bragging on Facebook about it."

Lucy filled the teakettle with water and set it on the stove to boil. "Let's see what the leaves have to say."

"The leaves?" Charlotte asked.

"Lucy reads tea leaves," I said. "She's very good at it."

"Oh… But do I want to know the future?"

I sighed. "Forewarned is forearmed. Why doesn't everybody believe that?"

"We have coffeecake, thanks to Jennet," Lucy answered.

Collie ears pricked up in attention.

Charlotte said, "Well, I'm game."

~ * ~

Lucy peered into the teacup and frowned at the arrangement of leaves. That wasn't a good sign.

"Am I going to live?" Charlotte asked.

She had been reluctant to have Lucy read her tea leaves, claiming she didn't believe in fortune telling.

"It's your choice," Lucy had said, "but think of it as a parlor game. You don't have to believe what I tell you. It's really all in fun."

I didn't believe her. That is, I *told* myself I didn't believe her. How to explain those events Lucy saw in my cup that later happened in real life? I couldn't.

"I guess it's all right, then," Charlotte had said, and we'd all had tea and the coffeecake I'd brought from the Hometown Bakery.

"I'm sure you're going to live," Lucy said. "If you weren't, I'd see… Well, nothing."

Lucy had told me about a frightening incident that had happened years ago. She'd been reading tea leaves at a party. When a certain woman tried to drain the excessive liquid from the cup, part of the ritual involved in preparing the teacup, all of the leaves fell out onto the saucer.

Several months later she died. She didn't have a future.

"That frightened me," Lucy had said. "I didn't tell her what it meant, of course. I pretended she wasn't doing it right, and, after a few more tries, she lost interest. After that, I didn't read tea leaves for a long time."

That grim little story frightened *me*.

Charlotte had a good cup, though, filled with fascinating patterns which Lucy was able to interpret.

"There is danger, but we know that," Lucy said. "I see a large rolling barren field. And here's something odd. It looks like a cross." She showed it to us. "This dark leaf is a man."

"How can you see all that in a little teacup?" Charlotte asked.

"Well, the patterns are very, very small."

"Remember, Charlotte," I said, "think of this as a parlor game."

"It *is* sort of fun."

"Your wish will come true," Lucy added. "That's all I see this time. Jennet, is your cup ready?"

"Ready as ever." I handed it to her.

Her frown was back. "You still have a serpent in your teacup," Lucy said. "It's right close to your home. Next to it is an initial 'V'."

She didn't have to say anything more.

That wretched female deputy sheriff, Veronica Quent, had taken up residence in my teacup months ago and reappeared every time Lucy read my tea leaves. I had no idea how to send her on her way—away from my cup, away from my life. Most of all, away from my husband.

"A snake is a symbol of evil, right?" Charlotte asked.

"I don't know what else it could be," I said, and added, "I loathe snakes."

"Who doesn't?"

I wasn't about to enlighten her further. My undeclared war with Veronica was a secret known only by a few friends.

"Your wish will come true," Lucy added.

That was good, but Lucy always saw my wish, which was to live happily ever after with Crane. If my wish were meant to come true, why then should I worry about Veronica the Viper?

There was no reason.

Momentarily cheered, I cut myself another slice of coffeecake.

Twenty-four

Leaves continued to fall in Foxglove Corners, turning the landscape into a crimson and gold wonderland. They rustled overhead and crunched underfoot as I walked up Jonquil Lane with my collies. Leaves flew in our faces and blew into high mounds in the woods. On the lanes no one raked them except perhaps into the flowerbeds.

I wished this glorious season could last forever. I had a feeling that something wondrous was waiting to happen and it would happen in the fall.

Julia had applied for a position in the English Department of Maplewood University. She liked the school and the town, which had a whole block of picturesque old Victorian houses. She had no doubt she'd soon be teaching there.

I wished I had a modicum of her optimism and confidence. All I had were my feelings.

"As soon as I sign the contract, I'm going to look for a house," she said. She'd already purchased a light green Ford Focus and was wasting no time in establishing her new life. She had reconnected with old friends and made new ones. This evening she had a dinner date with an English professor.

So strong was my feeling that some wondrous happening was imminent that the short news story in the *Banner* jolted me back to reality.

Police have found the body of Jeffrey Handlon in a heavily forested area west of Spruce Road. Handlon was reported missing five days ago from his Lakeville apartment by a friend. The police are asking anyone with information about his murder to notify them.

A picture of an attractive light-haired young man accompanied the story.

I recalled that Jeff was the name of the other witness in the fatal hit-and-run, the medical student who had subsequently disappeared. Could that Jeff and the murder victim, Jeffrey Handlon, be the same person?

Charlotte would know. She might not know Jeff's last name, but she had seen him at the crash scene, albeit briefly.

Another question occurred to me. Could the driver have killed Jeff to keep his identity a secret? And if so, did he intend to eliminate Charlotte as well? With both of the witnesses gone, he would be home free. I didn't even consider the possibility that somebody else might have killed Jeff.

Although I hated to give Charlotte another reason to be afraid, she had to know if the long-bearded driver intended to kill her, too.

Her voice on the phone was subdued. "Thank you for letting me know, Jennet, but I read the story and saw the picture. It was Jeff. I don't know what to do," she added. "Now that Jeff is gone, I guess I'm next."

"Stay at Dark Gables with Lucy," I said. "Now that the driver—I wish I knew his name—has left a body behind, the police will have something to go on."

"If he kills me, what will happen to Bronwyn?" Charlotte asked. "I can't let her suffer for something I did."

She would go back into rescue, of course, but that wasn't going to happen. Charlotte wasn't going to die. Bronwyn's new home would be forever.

"You didn't do anything except witness an accident," I said.

"I made the choice to drive down Huron Court to look at a field of flowers. A deadly field."

Well, yes, she had done that. But who could have known the consequence?

"Stay at Dark Gables," I repeated. "He won't know where to find you."

"I'm to be a prisoner then. Not that it isn't lovely here. Lucy is a perfect hostess. It seems like I've known her for years."

"I'll talk to Crane," I said, "and I'll see you soon."

That evening after dinner, Crane and I discussed the murder of Jeff Handlon. He had been shot in the back, apparently at some other location, and dumped in the woods.

"Mac has a clue," Crane said. "Whether it'll pan out, I can't say. But here's what I see. A man who's desperate. He's killed two people. Sooner or later, he'll make a mistake and Charlotte's ordeal will be over."

"And if he doesn't?"

"We'll still catch him."

Crane, like Julia, was an optimist.

"It may take time," he added.

Time for Charlotte to live in fear, to isolate herself at Dark Gables, to wonder if this would be the day when Long Beard would strike.

I wanted to help her, but at present, what else could I do?

~ * ~

On Saturday the string of sun-warmed autumn days ended with a depressing dark sky and the promise of thunderstorms. I already heard thunder rumbling in the west, and Sky had scrambled to her safe place under the dining room table, a sure sign of impending wild weather.

I stayed home, finished my household chores early, and found a Gothic novel I hadn't read yet, but instead of settling into the rocker to read, I turned on the haunted television. Just in case.

The movie was on!

I stepped with ease into the action on the Main Street of Jubilee. The newcomer in town strolled languidly toward the Pink Palace hotel. She was a vision in shades of blue trimmed with ecru lace. An expensive vision, I imagined, as her dress appeared to be made of the finest fabrics and trim. Flaxen curls spilled out from an elaborate bonnet to frame her face with its rare peaches-and-cream complexion.

All she needed to complete the picture was a parasol to protect her from the burning sun.

Luke was sitting in front of the hotel with his bewhiskered friend, whose Confederate uniform seemed to be tearing at the seams. They both greeted the new lady with admiring glances, but she didn't pay any attention to them.

Was she pretty enough to make Luke forget about Susanna?

She disappeared into the hotel, and the scene changed to a charming Victorian living room. Susanna sat sipping tea with her cousin. Alicia's eyes were alight with curiosity.

"Did you enjoy your visit to the L Bar E?" she asked.

"Very much."

"Luke Emerson is the wealthiest rancher in Jubilee," Alicia said. "You couldn't possibly find a better husband."

Susanna looked down into her teacup. "I'm not looking for a husband, Alicia."

"Oh? But what else would you do?"

Eagerly waiting for Susanna's answer, I hardly noticed when Misty padded up to me with her toy goat in her mouth. She dropped it at my feet and gave a plaintive little whimper. I ran my hand along her back, my eyes transfixed on the screen.

Susanna said, "I might teach school. The town doesn't have a teacher yet. I could do that."

"And end up a spinster? You wouldn't like that."

"I'm too young to be married."

"You're twenty-five years old, Susanna. If you want to have a family, you'd better find a husband soon."

Susanna sighed and took a sip of her tea, a long sip. "Everything is so new and exciting in the West. I just want to enjoy myself."

"That's well and good, but a man like Luke won't be available forever," Alicia said.

"I disagree." Susanna smiled and after a while added, "To tell the truth, I *do* like him."

Wait, I thought, *wait until you see your competition, who already caught Luke's eye. You'd better heed Alicia's advice.*

"There's a dance next week," Susanna said. "Luke invited me to accompany him."

"Well, then, I won't worry about you. What will you wear?"

"I only have one appropriate dress, my green silk."

"You'll look beautiful in it. I'll lend you my pearl necklace."

The cozy indoors scene faded to be replaced by a hitherto unseen area with hills and brush, similar to the backdrop of many a Western movie. Four horsemen rode heavily against a background of stormy sky.

I blinked, and the screen went dark. Once again I'd lost the movie at a particularly interesting point.

Frustrated, I turned the 'off' knob. A flash of lightning sliced across the sky, and the clock chimed six times.

The forecast rain had come. It sounded more like hail, striking the windows with icy needles. Foxglove Corners would turn into a mire. There would be no walks with the dogs tonight.

I got up and almost stepped on the toy goat. Misty still lay at my feet, her dark eyes ever hopeful. I was the world's worst collie mistress.

How could it be six already? I'd just turned the TV on. Crane would be home any minute, and I hadn't started dinner, hadn't even thought about a menu.

What could I do? Suggest we go out? In this downpour?

Think!

There must be something I could defrost? Stew? Stuffed cabbages? Either would do.

Crane wouldn't mind dinner being late. He was wondrously adaptable. Nonetheless, I was thankful that the storm and the clock had recalled me to the present. I was losing more time than seemed possible, gazing in a state of entrancement at the short scenes of the elusive movie.

But then, I hadn't really looked at the clock when I turned on the TV.

Misty followed me into the kitchen, holding her goat gently in her mouth. I threw it into the dining room for her. Finding the stuffed cabbages in the freezer, I slipped them in the microwave. Thank heavens for modern appliances. Now what else could I prepare—quickly?

As I practically threw my dinner together, I wondered. What was happening in Susanna's world? How pretty she would look in green. Would the new blonde be at the dance and would Luke notice her? And who were the riders heading toward Jubilee in the rain?

Twenty-five

The grounds of the Foxglove Corners Public Library had been raked, but more leaves continued to fall even as I walked up to the porch. They were mostly crimson, drifting down from the many maple trees on the property. I felt one land on my hair and brushed it off.

Miss Eidt's cat, Blackberry, lay in front of the burning bush, creating a striking study in contrast. I reached for my phone, intending to take her picture, but she dashed around the side of the house, out of sight.

The silly cat. She'd lost her chance to be immortalized in Jennet's Photo Album.

I had told myself I needed more reading material, specifically some of the classics from the Gothic Nook, but what I really wanted was to talk to Miss Eidt. It had been her idea to visit the estate sale, and she had been with me when I'd first noticed the antique television set. I thought it was time I took concrete steps to solve the eerie mystery.

In truth I had tired of the pattern. Turn on the TV at the right time—whenever that was—and the Western movie was on. Without warning it vanished to be replaced by the same modern day program I could watch on the flat screen television. Or the screen turned black.

I resented being left hanging. There had to be a logical explanation for the phenomenon, although I hadn't discovered it yet.

Didn't there?

In Foxglove Corners, capital of the Inexplicable, couldn't I simply have a haunted TV that had frozen when airing the story I found so enthralling?

That made sense. But why did the movie always begin again exactly where it had stopped, even when days passed between its playing?

Try as I might, I couldn't come up with an explanation for the anomaly. And why was the cabinet warm when the TV hadn't been turned on? It felt as if it had been running continuously.

Elementary, Jennet. It's haunted and 'haunted' doesn't bow to rationality.

I stepped inside the library. Miss Eidt sat at her desk with a stack of glossy new hard covers at her elbow. She was dressed a little differently today. Instead of her signature pastel suit, she wore a floral dress in shades of greens and blues with a pearl choker around her neck. No matter what her clothing choice, she always looked cool and serene.

"Good afternoon, Jennet," she said. "How nice to see you! It's been a while."

I agreed. "Too long. I'm here to explore your Gothic Nook, but first, do you have a few minutes to talk?"

"Of course. Debby?"

Miss Eidt's young assistant appeared from behind the paperback carousel, pushing back her single long braid.

"I know, Miss Eidt. I'll take over."

Debby liked nothing more than to sit at Miss Eidt's desk and rule over the dozen or so patrons who sat at tables reading or browsing in the stacks. One day she aspired to be the head of her own library.

Miss Eidt opened her office door. "Let's go inside and be comfortable. Is anything wrong?"

"Nothing new. That antique television is driving me over the edge."

She frowned. "How can it do that?"

"It plays the same movie, when it wants to, only that one. I'm hooked on the story and baffled by what makes the set tick. I have an idea I'd like to run by you."

She plugged in her electric teakettle. Good. Everything seemed better when accompanied by a cup of Earl Gray, Miss Eidt's current choice of brand.

"Let's hear it," she said.

"I don't think the TV suddenly exhibited its strange properties when I brought it home. Someone else must have been aware of its weird ways."

Miss Eidt nodded. "The person who owned it before you. The lady who passed away. It *was* an estate sale, remember."

"True and somebody put the estate sale together or authorized it. How did you hear about it?"

"In an article in the *Banner* about weekend activities. I don't remember any names mentioned, but we're in luck. I clipped the article for my vertical file."

Miss Eidt's vertical file was a holdover from another age. She refused to retire it, as she had refused to discard her favorite teacup when its handle broke. She clipped articles of note and filed them in pastel manila folders. An Internet search would be easier but lacked the charm of handling actual news clippings.

My anticipation rose as she brewed the tea and searched for the maple cookies she'd ordered from the Vermont Country Store Catalog.

"It'll just be a minute," she said. "It was the last story in."

She soon found the folder. "Here it is. I remember thinking this would be fun and you'd enjoy it, too."

She set the article on the table and we read it together:

Estate Sale Set for September 7

Sponsored by the Foxglove Corners Historical Society, an estate sale will be held at the home of the late Eustacia Stirling on 51 Grovelane on September 7. Sale items include rare first editions, original art and sculpture, and collections of all kinds, along with nineteenth century furniture for all rooms.

"And a collie," I murmured, remembering Bronwyn.

"A collie? Oh, yes, of course. Where is she now?"

"Bronwyn found a loving mistress," I said. "But back to the sale. I'll have to contact a member of the Foxglove Corners Historical Society. I didn't know we had one."

"Neither did I, until I saw the article. It must be new."

Miss Eidt busied herself arranging cookies on a paper plate. "What do you hope to find out?"

"The name of a person who knew the owner. Possibly the heir."

"Everything inside the house was for sale," she reminded me. "Do you think anyone would know the properties of one old television set?"

"Possibly, if the original owner confided in a friend unless, of course, she bought it and never once used it. I have an electric knife that would fit into that category."

"Here's another option," Miss Eidt said. "Take the set apart. Maybe you'll find the miniature CD player Brent thinks is inside or something else that causes this weird glitch."

"In other words, dissect it?"

"You could say that."

A disturbing image formed in my mind. A vaporous spirit lying still on Crane's workbench, its innards spread around it, all of them warm and pulsating with life.

"I couldn't do that," I said. "It would be like murder."

"Surely not, Jennet. You're overreacting. All you'd be doing is destroying an intangible object for a good cause."

I thought about what she said but still wanted to keep the television set intact. Maybe that was the only way I could see the rest of Susanna's story.

"It'd be easier to find another person who heard about the TV's unusual qualities or maybe experienced them," I said.

Would anything be easy about solving this mystery, though?

"Do you remember the name of the woman who took our money at the sale?" I asked. "Something Bell? Christa Bell?"

"No, she had a more common first name," Miss Eidt said.

"Somebody at the Historical Society would know."

Research was the key. Along with the name of the previous owner, it would be helpful to know where the set had been made and where it'd been sold. Incidentally, how many of them had been produced? Was mine the only haunted television set in the lot?

Finally, if the antique television set I owned was truly one of a kind, how had it gotten that way?

Too many questions. I couldn't wait to start searching for answers.

Twenty-six

Her name was Anna Bell, and she was the founder and president of the Foxglove Corners Historical Society which had recently celebrated its third birthday. Anna's office was located in a renovated farmhouse, circa 1890, on the outskirts of Foxglove Corners. It had been purchased with funds raised by Mrs. Bell. The first (and presumably most generous) donor was Miss Eustacia Stirling.

All this I learned on the society's website, along with their contact information. I sent an e-mail to Anna Bell, expressing my interest in an antique television set acquired at the recent estate sale, then resigned myself to wait.

This waiting period gave me time to create a credible story. I didn't want to tell anyone about the Western movie that came and went apparently on a whim. Not at first anyway. And I wouldn't describe the television as being haunted.

What could I say then?

Perhaps a little bit of the truth. It didn't pick up local channels. Sometimes it didn't work properly at all. I couldn't find the one program it aired in any TV guide.

Well, that was certainly strange.

If I hoped to be successful, I had to be clear about what I wanted. Which was… I had to think about that. What would satisfy me?

The name of another person who might be familiar with the TV while it was in Miss Stirling's possession—if such a person existed.

There was another name, one I'd never known. I recalled the woman in the pink sundress who had been so disappointed that I'd already purchased the TV. I'd been afraid she'd grab it out of my hands and run. I felt she would be impossible to trace and probably had no prior knowledge of the television. Her eagerness to possess it, though, was suspicious.

It was as if she knew something about it that I didn't—at the time.

I had to settle for the possible. If I were lucky, Mrs. Bell would provide me with a name. In the meantime, I set out to do my own research. First, what company manufactured the television set?

You'd think that would be easy to find, a fact my mind had already registered during one of the many times I'd turned the TV on or dusted it.

You would be wrong. There was no name on the cabinet, not on the front where I expected to see it, nor in any other place. How exasperating!

How impossible. Everything had a name. Panasonic, Sony, Kenmore, Spectra, Dixie…

It's there somewhere. You just haven't found it yet.

Or for some reason it had been removed, leaving no trace of its existence.

I was well on my way to obsessing about the lack of manufacturer's information when I stopped myself. Why be surprised when I was dealing with a television set that was the essence of ghostliness?

I checked my e-mail before shutting the computer down, even though I knew it was too soon for Mrs. Bell to respond.

~ * ~

That evening, Lucy called. I knew immediately that something was wrong even as she said, "Don't be alarmed, Jennet, but I think you should know about this."

I glanced at Crane, feeling a need for his support even before knowing why.

"It's Charlotte," Lucy said. "She went home for a while this afternoon, and she isn't back yet. She said she'd only be gone an hour."

How could I be anything but alarmed?

"Why did she do that?" I asked.

"She wanted her wool skirts and turtleneck sweaters, she said, and her boots. She only brought one pair of shoes."

"Did she take Bronwyn?"

"Yes. Bronwyn went, too. They go everywhere together. This time they've been gone for almost three hours. I've been debating about whether to drive over to her house and check on her."

"I'll do it," I said. "I'm closer. Did you call her?"

"She doesn't answer, and her mailbox is full."

"That doesn't sound good."

"Charlotte impressed me as being considerate of other people's feelings. She knew I'd be worried about her."

"Something happened."

"Yes, I'm afraid it did," Lucy said. "Let me know what you find out. I'll call you if she shows up."

As I ended the call, Crane folded his paper. He'd been listening. "I'll drive you, honey," he said.

~ * ~

She wasn't there. Neither was the blue car. There was no sign that anyone on two legs or four had disturbed the layer of leaves that carpeted the walkway. Her neighbor wasn't at home either.

A sense of *déjà vu* settled over me. Charlotte had gone away again, taking Bronwyn with her.

I looked up and down Sagramore Lake Road and didn't see her car. The lake was still and silent, shimmering in the late afternoon sunshine. I half hoped to see Molly and Jennifer with Ginger, but the beach was deserted. They'd probably been in school when Charlotte had left Dark Gables for her own house.

If they had anything to tell me, they would call.

"What do you think?" I asked Crane.

"She never reached her house."

"I wonder if she went back to her cottage up north," I said.

"That would be foolish. She was safe with Lucy."

We walked back to Crane's Jeep. "I don't believe Charlotte lied about wanting her warmer clothes. That was her intention. Someone derailed it."

"The hit-and-run driver," Crane said. "Who just happened to be where she was?"

"That's unlikely, but possible. I hope we're not too late to change the outcome."

An unwelcome image took shape in my mind: Charlotte lying dead in an autumn field or wood, buried under leaves. We might never know what happened unless a hiker or hunter stumbled on her body.

And Bronwyn?

She went where Charlotte went.

From the beginning, that adoption had been steeped in mystery.

But that was unfair. When Charlotte had taken Bronwyn home, she couldn't have known that a leisurely drive on a country road with her new dog would lead to danger for both of them. It was fall, for heaven's sake. People took color tours all the time. They viewed the changing leaves and marveled at nature's wonders, and nothing untoward happened.

"Do you have the address of Charlotte's cottage?" Crane asked.

"I didn't know she had one till she mentioned it," I said.

"Does Sue Appleton have it?"

"I doubt it, and I'd rather Sue didn't hear about this."

"You and Lucy can try to call Charlotte."

"We can."

Would her mailbox still be full, though? Would she have a signal, wherever she was?

"I can try," I added.

And if Charlotte never got in touch with us, well then she was lying in that deadly autumn field covered with leaves.

With Bronwyn at her side.

Twenty-seven

The days whirled by with the blowing wind. Leaves danced through the air on their downward flight, and pumpkins of all sizes grew on vines or decorated porches. While the mornings were cool, the days remained unseasonably warm. September stepped aside to make way for golden, glorious October.

The hours filled with everyday concerns: dinner, the needs of seven collies, lesson plans, classes, then dinner again.

Julia had accepted an offer to teach at Maplewood University and set out to find a suitable house to purchase. From Foxglove Corners she would have a long commute of an hour and a half in good weather.

"A half hour tops is what I'm looking for," she'd said.

After school one day I took Halley, Gemmy, and Sky on a walk to Sue Appleton's horse farm, needing to breathe fresh air and enjoy a taste of freedom, albeit a brief one. The fall day was picture perfect with cotton-fluff clouds in an azure sky and sunshine that set the maple leaves on Sue's trees on fire.

We sat on the porch surrounded by six collies. In other words, in collie heaven. In spite of being surrounded by brightness, our mood was somber.

Neither Lucy nor I had heard from Charlotte. She was officially a missing person. By now I'd told Sue about Charlotte's second disappearance.

"Charlotte must be dead," Sue said. "That man killed her to keep her from identifying him. Otherwise she'd be in touch with one of us. And what became of our Bronwyn? I can't bear not knowing."

"Let's not bury Charlotte yet," I said.

Sue didn't seem to hear me.

"All because she stopped to help a stranger at an accident scene. She should have just driven on."

A stranger who subsequently died of her injuries. Ignoring an unuttered cry for help simply wasn't human.

"You don't mean that," I said.

"If she had, she'd be alive. So would Bronwyn."

There was no point in trying to change Sue's mind. She was upset, but at heart she was a good person who had often gone out of her way to help others.

"I'm going to believe that Charlotte is alive until I see her body," I said.

"You realize we may never know what happened to her. Or to our poor rescue." She paused. "A retired couple inquired about available collies this morning. They want to adopt an older dog, perhaps one nobody else wants."

"Do we have a collie for them?" I asked.

"There's Dasher, who's nine. Emma Brock is fostering him. His picture isn't on our website yet."

"That's good. When will they meet him?"

"Tomorrow. It sounds perfect, but I'm leery."

"Why?" I asked.

"After what happened to Bronwyn. Something similar could happen again."

We'd had this kind of conversation before. It couldn't be allowed to affect our new program.

"If everything is perfect, as you say, there's no reason not to approve the adoption," I said.

"I suppose so."

"You know I'm right." I tugged gently on the leashes. "It's so lovely here I'd love to stay longer, but I'd better go home."

I had four collies waiting for me and dinner to make. Always dinner.

~ * ~

The next day after school I stopped at Dark Gables to visit Lucy. Leonora had called in sick which gave me ten free minutes. We sat in the sunroom drinking tea and talking about Charlotte while watching the wind blow golden leaves into the fountain.

"Sue thinks that Charlotte is dead," I said.

"I feel she's still alive but in danger."

"Based on what?" I asked.

"One of my feelings."

"And Bronwyn?"

"I don't know, but Bronwyn was always at Charlotte's side. You'd think they'd been together since Bronwyn was a puppy. What happens to one happens to the other. I miss them," she added. "So does Sky."

Sky nudged my hand and set her gaze on a plate of oatmeal cookies, the picture of a happy, expectant collie.

"Are you saying that Bronwyn is in danger, too?" I asked.

"I guess I am."

Silently I drained the excess tea into the saucer and watched the tea leaves form their patterns.

"Let's see what the teacup says," I said.

Lucy studied the arrangement of leaves in my cup. She was frowning. That was never good.

"I still see the Viper," she said.

Veronica. Crane's not-so-secret admirer. She'd been silent lately, but isn't that the way of vipers? Stay out of sight until it's time to strike?

"I wish she'd slither out into the open so I could smash her," I said.

"That may happen sooner than you think."

"How can you tell?" I asked.

"Each time I read your tea leaves that initial *V* is closer to your home." Lucy pointed her lavender-tinted fingernail to an innocuous light leaf. It *did* look like a capital *V*.

"When she makes her move, I hope I'll be ready for her," I said. "What else do you see?"

"Your wish. And here's a crossroad. Soon you'll have to make a major decision. One road leads to darkness."

"And of course I won't know which one to choose," I said.

"You'll have to follow your heart."

Well, that was vague. Lately my heart had been uncommunicative.

"Do you see any sign of Charlotte and Bronwyn?" I asked.

"Not today," she said. "Not in your cup."

~ * ~

Julia was home for dinner that evening. It was an occasion. She had been seeing an English professor who taught at Maplewood University. He was only a friend, she insisted, but he was extremely knowledgeable about Victorian literature. Presumably they had much in common.

She cut carrots and radishes for a salad while I prepared breaded pork chops, both of us supervised by Candy and Misty.

"I'd love for you to see the house I'm considering," she said. "Tomorrow's Saturday. Could you go with me then? We can stop for lunch on the way back."

"Sure," I said. "Tell me about it."

"Well, it's perfect for me. It's white with gables and purple trim. There are mature trees on the property and a small old-fashioned flower garden that looks sort of droopy at this time of the year. I can see myself planting larkspur and foxglove and cloves. I love the scent of cloves."

"What about the inside?" I asked.

"There's a library with built-in shelves on three sides and three bedrooms. One of them can be my office. It has a basement and a sunroom and a wonderful veranda. I can sit outside and read in the spring. The existing bushes are straggly, but I'll dig them out and plant whatever I like. I'm thinking of blue hydrangeas."

"It sounds ideal," I said.

"I'm pretty sure I'm going to make an offer, but I want you to see it first."

"It's a date," I said. "Saturday morning."

The sun was shining, and Julia had returned from her long sojourn in Italy. She had a new position, a compatible gentleman friend, and the prospect of becoming a homeowner. These were all good things, but thoughts of Charlotte and Bronwyn simmered beneath them. They wouldn't go away.

Twenty-eight

Doing something out of the ordinary on a breezy Saturday morning lent an air of adventure to our excursion. Not that I expected to take a detour and discover a ghost town. That had been a once-in-a-lifetime happening. Still, I had a feeling that something momentous was right around the corner.

I often had these feelings, but that momentous something had yet to appear.

"Maplewood is a picturesque little town," Julia said as we left the freeway and drove down Main Street with its stately Victorian mansions. "It'll probably grow now that the college is here. There's plenty of room for expansion."

We turned onto a quiet street of mature maple trees and charming vintage houses. The address we wanted was 51 Rosebriar.

Julia's description hadn't done justice to the 1930s' bungalow. It was set comfortably in a bed of crisp russet leaves. Its twin window boxes were empty, but a grapevine wreath decorated with yellow leaves, red berries, and glitter-speckled branches set off the lavender front door. Orange and crimson chrysanthemums arranged amidst pumpkins on the porch steps completed the autumnal look.

We had a glimpse of the fading flower garden for which Julia had high hopes. We parked in front of the house and stepped out of the car. I took a breath of fresh air, lightly scented with burning leaves, and looked around, slowly becoming aware of a certain nostalgic atmosphere in the surroundings. I could almost believe that I'd stepped into a Norman Rockwell painting or several decades back in time.

"The owners have already moved out of the state," Julia said. "I wish you could see the inside, but the realtor had another commitment today. All the walls are freshly painted and the floors are refinished. The windows look like they've just been washed. They're new. What do you think?"

They sparkled in the sunlight. A good omen.

"I think you should make an offer for the house before someone steals it from you."

"This is supposed to be a quiet neighborhood," Julia said, "but it won't be like living on Jonquil Lane."

"Did you want to live in the country?"

"Not really. This is perfect for me, and it has a big backyard. I could walk to Maplewood if I wanted to."

"Let's drive by the school," I said.

Julia was right. She could conceivably walk to Maplewood University, but she probably wouldn't want to, especially in the wintertime.

I drove through winding, tree-lined streets, mesmerized by the kaleidoscope display of color, and turned on University Lane. My first impression of the college was one of freshness, of bright new buildings and subdued landscaping. Even on a Saturday morning, the university pulsed with life, albeit on a smaller scale.

We sat on a stone bench and watched students stroll by alone or in small groups. It was almost noon. Lunchtime. Memories from my own college days at Oakland University unfolded in my mind. Eating a quick lunch, rushing to class, taking notes on splendid fall days with my future spread out before me like a magic carpet.

Julia pointed to the closest buildings. "That's the library, the Marella Latham Hall where I have my office—well, a small one. Over there is the Student Union and the newest co-ed dorms. I'll be teaching composition classes at first, but one day I'll have courses in nineteenth century literature. I can hardly wait."

Seeing Julia so enthusiastic and confident about her future restored my belief in happy days to come. It was as if I'd been able to tune out my problems for a little while, anyway. After all, were they so insurmountable? Not from this vantage point.

"Promise me you'll make an offer for the house," I said.

She didn't hesitate. "I intend to. As soon as we get home."

~ * ~

We stopped for sandwiches and cold drinks at a restaurant built on a small lake. We'd done this often in the past, combining shopping trips with lunch. Before Julia moved to the West Coast, then to England. Before the tornado. In those days we'd looked tirelessly for clothes and jewelry and make-up. Never a major purchase like a house.

It was as good as old times, and Julia, settled in her new life, would be close enough for us to visit often. If the sale went through.

It had to. Julia was counting on it. So was I.

Julia finished her Coca-Cola and swished a straw through the ice at the bottom of the glass. "I'll need everything. You'll have to help me, Jennet."

"You know I will. I'd love to."

"The thought of filling an entire house with furniture is overwhelming. The previous owners left the stove and refrigerator, but I'll need staples and dishes for the kitchen, sheets and towels. Oh, and cleaning supplies. Like I said, everything."

"You won't have to buy everything at once," I pointed out. "Take one room at a time. Start with the bedroom."

"I'd like to be faithful to the era of the house," Julia said. "That'll take a bit of research."

"That's something you're well-equipped to do. It'll be fun."

I thought again about the unmatched excitement of new beginnings, wishing in a way that I could start all over furnishing our green Victorian farmhouse with antiques for the living room, window treatments for the kitchen, different lamps, and more paintings.

Crane would be incredulous. He didn't like change, not even when I rearranged the existing furniture.

"We can start at the Green House of Antiques," I said. "That's always been my favorite place to shop."

"First I'll make a list and prioritize."

The sense of having a grand adventure continued. We skipped dessert and resumed our drive home, entering the freeway when we had a chance.

While we'd been in the restaurant, there had been a change in the weather. Low clouds pressed on the trees that grew close together on either side of the freeway. And was that thunder in the distance? What else?

The sun had disappeared. I remembered the day's weather forecast. 'Slight chance of a thunderstorm.' Well, the rain had held off for the important part of the day.

I turned on my lights and glanced at the speedometer. At seventy, I seemed to be speeding but was keeping up with the traffic which was heavier than I'd anticipated. For some reason I thought about the trip that Annica and I had taken up north when I'd impulsively exited the freeway and driven into a storm.

That wouldn't happen today. The route home was straightforward, and I had no intention of veering off course. But I *did* want to be home before the storm.

Oh, darn. Too late. I'd scarcely completed the thought when large drops splattered on the window, raindrops mixed with blowing leaves. I turned on the windshield wipers.

Beside me, Julia shifted nervously in her seat. Had I communicated my unease to her?

Rain, rain, go away," she sang. *Come again another day.*

"The farmers will be happy," I said. "They claim we didn't have enough rain this summer."

I glanced in the rear view mirror—and didn't like what I saw.

"That black car is following me too closely," I said. "What's wrong with him? If I had to stop suddenly, he'd crash into me."

"Don't stop." Julia turned to look at the offending car, and her tone changed. "Maybe you'd better change lanes, Jennet."

"If I can."

The cars behind me were in every lane, a veritable flotilla, travelling at what seemed like warp speed. The black car was even closer to mine, if that were possible.

"I can't," I said.

A deafening horn blast drowned out Julia's reply. Not content with one antagonistic bellow, the driver kept his hand pressed down on the horn until no other sound could be heard, or so it seemed. Obviously he wanted me to go faster. I couldn't do that either, not safely, and he couldn't pass me. I could hardly stop in the middle of the freeway. That would be suicide.

"He's crazy," Julia cried.

"Angry," I said.

Road rage.

I wasn't going fast enough to suit him. Well, I wasn't about to increase my speed and risk skidding on slick pavement.

"There should be an exit coming up." I could hardly hear Julia's voice. "About a half mile."

I didn't want to exit in some backwater. But it might be better if I did and left the freeway to the fool in the black car. I could always reenter it, by which time he would be far ahead.

The rain came in slanting sheets pounding on the windows, diminishing visibility. Lightning sliced the sky. The cars that had once hemmed me in were now far ahead.

When did that happen?

The black car was still on my tail, which didn't make sense. Why hadn't he passed me?

Julia sat forward to peer through the curtain of rain. "There's the exit coming up! Just ahead."

I turned on my blinkers and eased into the 'exit only' lane, following the curve onto a narrow country road leading to heaven knew where.

"Thank God," I said. "We're safe."

But I had spoken too soon. The driver of the black car had exited with me and increased his speed until he was tailing me again.

Twenty-nine

We're in trouble.

I wished myself back on the freeway where the next wave of cars would be catching up to the exit lane. Right about now.

One of the drivers would be certain to notice what was going on. Someone would stop. Someone always stopped when they saw another in peril.

Julia glanced at the glove compartment. "Did you bring your gun?"

"No."

It was at home, locked in the cabinet where Crane kept his firearms when he was off duty.

"Is there anything we can use—like a baseball bat?"

I didn't have to think about it. "Nothing."

I stepped on the accelerator, watched as my speed approached eighty… eighty-five. I felt as if I were airborne. Felt sick and cold.

The black car still tailed me.

I looked right and left, desperately hoping to see a turn-off. A makeshift country path. A farmhouse. Any house.

A sign swam by. *Deer X-ing*.

In an incredible burst of speed, the black car zoomed well past me and turned sideways on the narrow road. My way was blocked. The only exit was a cornfield on one side. On the other, meadowland rolled away into infinity. Neither offered an escape route.

What could I do? Except stop?

He'd anticipated that, had somehow known I wouldn't crash into his vehicle.

The door flew open, and the driver emerged.

He was a hulking giant of a man, burly, oozing belligerence, with a long black beard and a fierce expression that radiated violence.

Bearded?

It can't be. There has to be more than one man in Michigan with a long black beard.

Julia's voice was tremulous. "What are we going to do?"

A blank screen came down over my mind.

Was it to end like this? My happy, carefree day with my sister disintegrating in a blast of mindless road rage?

Crane, I thought. *Oh, Crane...*

Julia grabbed my arm. "Lock the door, Jennet."

They were locked, for all the good that would do.

Shouting obscenities, the man punched the window with a fist that looked like a hamhock. His eyes were burning. His face, above the beard, was blood-red.

"You cut me off back there, bitch. Nobody cuts me off."

I had done no such thing.

It didn't matter. In his eyes, I'd done the unthinkable. Crossed him.

He punched the window again. And again. It shattered. Shards of glass flew through the jagged opening, landing in my lap. Julia screamed.

I *did* have something. In my purse. A small can of *Halt!* I kept it there in case I encountered a menacing dog.

Did I have time to reach it?

My purse was on the floor, along with Julia's, at her feet.

"My purse," I whispered. "Get the spray."

She'd have to understand.

I'd aim for his eyes. Then? Let him rage. While he was blinded, turn the car and backtrack. Where there was an exit, there must be an entrance.

With luck, I'd buy us a few minutes.

He'd cut his hand on glass. He waved it angrily in my face. Drops of blood flew through the air. Landed on his pants. On his plaid shirt.

Good! Anything to slow him down.

Julia pressed the cylinder into my hands.

Now! Quick!

I took aim and pressed the lever as an enormous shape burst out of the cornfield and barreled into him. With a screech, he fell back on the road. The animal leaped into the meadow.

"It's a deer," Julia whispered.

"Dear God," I said, staring at the motionless body in the road.

"Is he dead?" she asked.

"Not likely. I don't care."

I turned the car, making a semi-circle in the field, and headed back the way I'd come. Seconds ticked by. I kept an eye on the rear view mirror, kept expecting to see the black car come to life and start tailing me again.

I didn't see anything. I could only hope that the shot of *Halt!* together with the deer's assault had rendered the madman harmless.

I had seen Black Beard fall but couldn't count on him being incapacitated for long.

Look for the freeway entrance.

"Look for an entrance, Julia," I said.

She fumbled in her purse, wiped her eyes with a tissue. "That was close."

"Too close. We almost… Well, we didn't."

"I thought deer only came out at dawn and dusk," she said. "This isn't dawn and it sure isn't dusk."

"True. I can't explain it. I'm just glad this one came along."

My heart had settled back into its normal rhythm, but I was still cold, every part of my body inside and out. To come so close to death…

Jennet Ferguson and Julia Greenway, sisters, died today, victims of apparent road rage…

Best not to dwell on it. I was alive. I was going to see Crane again and all my beloved collies. Julia was going to have her life in academia.

"It isn't raining anymore," I said. "When did it stop?"

"I have no idea. Where *is* that entrance? We can never eat venison again," she added.

"I don't eat it at all. The taste is too gamey for me. But I know what you're saying."

"That deer saved us," Julia said. "I hope it didn't get killed."

"Well, we were stopped. If I'd been driving eighty when he leaped across the road, that would have been a different story. I saw it running away. I think."

"I'm still shaking," Julia said.

"I wish…"

Had I used up my allotment of wishes?

"I'm going to report this," I said. "In case that man is dead. I wish I'd thought to jot down his license plate number. Did you notice the make of the car?"

"Just that it was black."

"That won't help… Oh, there it is!"

The freeway. With a hasty prayer of thanks, I turned off the country road and was able to merge into the right lane almost immediately.

After a moment, Julia said, "If he's dead, they won't think you killed him. Will they?"

"If he's dead," I repeated. "The deer killed him. What I did, with the spray, it was self- defense. All anyone has to do is look at my window. And the blood."

It had splattered on my white skirt and my green shell, ruined them. I'd never wear them again.

"There's something you should know," I said.

She waited. "Something bad?"

"Maybe. We'll have to wait and see. I think that man may be the one who's been threatening Charlotte Gray. The hit-and-run driver."

"Why do you say that?" she asked.

"A feeling," I said, "and the black beard. No, it's more than a feeling. I'm almost certain of it."

Thirty

It had rained in Foxglove Corners, and the green Victorian farmhouse fairly shimmered in the afternoon light. The sun struck the stained glass window between the twin gables, turning glass into myriads of shining jewels. My home had never looked more beautiful to me.

Everything was more precious when you believed it might be forever lost to you.

Candy's face appeared in the bay window. In another second, Misty joined her. Soon all the dogs were barking.

"Our welcoming committee," Julia said quietly.

Her expression was grave. I knew how she felt. Now that we had escaped the black bearded man, scenarios of what might have been tumbled through my mind.

Stop thinking about it. It's over.

I forced my thoughts back to my life. Crane wouldn't be home yet. Although I could hardly wait to see him, I wanted time to shower and change my clothes.

"I need a cup of tea," Julia said.

"One pot of tea coming up. That is, as soon as I get out of this bloody skirt and shell."

"I'll get it."

We went inside, and the dogs lost no time in congregating at the kitchen door to meet us. First Misty, then Candy, sniffed at my skirt.

Sky scurried under the dining room table, while Misty began to growl.

"Good heavens," Julia said. "It's like she knows what happened."

My psychic collie.

"Maybe she does."

Julia filled the teapot and set it on the stove while Misty followed me upstairs into the bathroom. I stepped out of the skirt and yanked the shell over my head. Ugh. They had his blood on them.

I'd loved that skirt. Loved. Past tense. I tossed it on the floor on top of the shell. I couldn't get it out of the house fast enough.

Wait! I froze, aghast at what I'd been about to do. Blood… DNA… It could lead us to a match. If Black Beard had a record, we could identify him.

I retrieved the discarded clothing and folded it neatly. That murderous jerk would rue the day he'd waved his bloody fist in my face.

~ * ~

Julia and I lost ourselves in dinner preparations. A pot roast with rice, we decided, and blueberry pie for dessert. Julia loved to cook but had pretty much eaten in restaurants during her long stay abroad. She appeared to have recovered from our trauma and was encouraged by the possibility of our assailant being apprehended.

As for myself I had a headache. Delayed reaction.

I sprinkled sugar on the crust and put the pie in the oven. All this time Misty had stayed at my side, moving whenever I did, even though I'd changed into a clean dress.

She knows, I thought.

Incredibly, Crane also knew that something had happened even before I told him.

"I had the strangest feeling that you were in danger," he said. "Then it passed."

My psychic husband?

"I thought I was the one who had forebodings," I said.

"I can't explain it." His voice acquired a steely edge, that deputy sheriff tone, and his gray eyes glittered with icy flecks. As I told him about the encounter, his eyes grew colder and colder. "That man isn't going to get away with this. He left his blood behind. That'll be his death sentence."

"I'll settle for jail time," I said. "Today was bad enough, but what if he's the hit-and-run killer?"

That reminded me of Charlotte. I'd forgotten about her disappearance in the harrowing events of the day.

"That's right," Julia said. "Charlotte can identify him."

"We have to redouble our efforts to find her."

Julia nodded. "We have a dangerous maniac on the road, and… Oh, I have to take the freeway to school on Monday."

"Chances are you won't meet up with him again," I said.

Julia looked worried. "Unless he trolls the freeway looking for victims. Female victims," she added.

Crane locked his gun in the cabinet. "Don't worry. Sooner or later, we're going to nail him."

~ * ~

If ever there was an evening when Brent's company was needed, this was it. He hadn't seen Julia since her return, which meant he hadn't come over for several days. I missed his bluster and bonhomie.

He had two enormous bouquets filled with orange roses and sunflowers. The dogs wagged their tails expectantly. Candy nudged his leg. "They're in my jacket pocket," he said, anticipating her concern.

"My goodness," Julia said as he hugged her. "They're gorgeous. Thank you, Brent."

She was holding both of the bouquets, and they were in danger of getting crushed. I took them and hunted for two vases.

"Something smells good," Brent said.

"It could be the pot roast or the blueberry pie."

Crane took his jacket. Brent quickly pulled three packages of treats from his pocket. “I have good stuff here. Liver, salmon, and turkey.”

“Sit down, Fowler,” Crane said. “We have a lowlife to catch.”

“Julia and I almost got killed today,” I added.

We all found a seat, and I told them what had happened. The story grew more chilling in the retelling.

“I never had to use that *Halt*! on a dangerous dog,” I said, “but I’m glad I had it today.”

“He’s not going to forget that,” Brent said.

“Mmm. I never considered that.” I didn’t need another enemy out there in the world plotting revenge. “Well, a little spraying of *Halt!* didn’t do any lasting damage.

Except to his ego.

“Besides, the deer did him in,” I added. “Will you give me in a hand in the kitchen, Julia?”

Misty sprang up and followed us. How long would she shadow me? And Candy was beside her, but Candy’s attention was on the pot roast.

“Crane will carve it,” I said, arranging carrots around the roast. “The rice is done. I hope the pie will be cool enough to eat.”

Candy whined as if to remind me of something I’d forgotten. The roast, of course. She rested her chin on the counter as close as she dared get to it.

Dogs and guests and the perfect moment to slice a pie—all mundane matters, and every one of them was easier to deal with than an elusive killer who nursed a grudge.

~ * ~

I couldn’t fall asleep that night. An hour passed, then two.

Don’t think about the time, I told myself. *Think about lovely things.*

I closed my eyes, and the scene on the country road played itself in my mind, a variation on the theme.

Julia couldn't find the spray. And the deer was miles away. The man with the black beard waved his fist in my face, splattering me with his blood. He pulled a gun out of his pocket and aimed it at Misty who growled at him from the back seat.

I woke up.

Well, I'd fallen asleep after all. How real that dream had been! How close to mimicking a possibility.

If I had forgotten the *Halt!* when I'd changed purses? If the deer had waited until dusk to leap?

I reached out to touch Crane. To assure myself that he slept beside me. At the moment I was safe in the house. But I had to leave it eventually.

Thirty-one

Monday found me in my classroom at Marston High School, warm and dry, while a heavy rain pummeled the woods outside the window.

The string of warm October days had broken. Ironically today's short story, *All Summer in a Day*, dealt with rain on the planet Venus, as imagined by Ray Bradbury.

On Bradbury's Venus it had rained steadily for five long years. The sun was due to appear briefly on this particular day, after which the rain would return. Naturally that day of sunshine was a much-anticipated occasion for the sun-starved colonists.

The story was really about cruelty, specifically children's cruelty to one another, which had given me an idea to assign a composition on the subject of bullying. As Bradbury customarily packed multiple ideas into his work, I could see additional composition ideas suggested by this one short story.

On the whole, my World Literature class was well-behaved with an occasional rebel who seized his chance to claim the limelight.

"But that's stupid," Will said when we finished the reading. "That's not how it is on Venus."

"How do you know?" demanded Tori. "Did you ever go there?"

"Yeah," he said. "Did you?"

"Yeah."

It was time to intervene, to introduce the concept of a willing suspense of disbelief in terms my tenth graders could understand.

"Nobody knows for sure what the surface of Venus is like," I said. "Therefore, science-fiction writers are free to describe planets any way they like. Please note the date on the board. That's when Ray Bradbury wrote the story. He's making a point. Who can tell me what it is?"

"He's talking about how mean people can be," Judy said.

Point taken.

"Good," I said. "Also how much pain people can cause others."

"And also ignorance," pointed out Annemarie. "The kids didn't realize what they were doing to Margot by locking her in the closet until they saw the sun for themselves."

I stole a glance at the dispirited scene on the other side of the window. Trees almost stripped of their leaves, broken branches lying on the soggy ground, and mud. This area, part of the school's property, was off-limits to the students, which naturally made it a favorite hang-out. I didn't imagine it would be popular today.

Like the earth people living on Venus, I longed for a glimpse of the sun.

After additional discussion about remembered incidents of cruelty in their past classrooms, my students began writing their compositions. No one seemed at a loss for words. I had chosen my subject well. After all, the world was full of bullies. Here in Oakpoint, Michigan, Marston High School had its fair share.

As the class fell silent and no one appeared to need help, my mind drifted to a place I definitely didn't want to revisit.

The man with the black beard was a bully. Selecting a victim who appeared vulnerable—a woman driving the speed limit on a freeway. Forcing her to stop on a lonely country road. Threatening her with physical harm. And damaging her vehicle. Don't forget that.

My car was at the dealership for repair, which meant that Leonora was driving this week, and I was more or less grounded until Crane or Julia came home.

But for the timely intervention of the deer, I might not be in this room, teaching my class. And how often would a deer leap out of the wild and take down a killer? That was, quite definitely, an act of God.

Lord, thank you for my life.

I didn't think the man was dead. A hard fall on a country road would probably not be fatal, although he might have broken a bone or two. He was still out there, still a bully, and for all their talk of revenge, what could Crane and Brent do? They didn't know his name or anything about him.

Julia had been able to give Mac Dalby, our friend on the police force, the approximate location of the freeway exit from which the man had followed me and forced me to stop. There was no black car on the country road, no telltale sign of blood—the rain would have taken care of that—and no dead deer. The incident might never have happened.

I was glad the deer had gotten away uninjured.

In my classroom, reasonably safe from danger, a feeling insinuated its way into my thoughts. A foreboding. I would meet him again, the man whose name I didn't know, and this time I couldn't count on the appearance of a roving deer.

The bell rang. The composition wasn't due until tomorrow, but a few papers landed haphazardly on my desk as the class hurried out of the door.

Next was my rowdy American Lit class. For the first time ever I was happy to see them. They would keep me so busy that I wouldn't have time for unpleasant thoughts.

~ * ~

At home I looked out at my empty driveway and wished my car were there, washed clean of dark memories, with its window and damaged door repaired. Not that I had any place to go. A storm was brewing. I just wanted to be able to leave the house if it became necessary. What if one of the dogs got sick?

You'd wait for Crane or Julia to get home.

I probably should have arranged for a rental car. I could still do it. In the meantime, I'd get a head start on dinner.

After stirring celery and carrots into the stew—the last step—I set it on the stove to cook and contemplated the haunted television. I hadn't given it a thought lately.

Sky whimpered as lightning knifed through the clouds. She scurried under the dining room table and waited, trembling, for the worst to happen.

"It's all right, baby," I said, grateful that I didn't have seven fearful collies.

Maybe I shouldn't turn the television on until the storm was over.

Oh, well… Why not take a chance? It would probably be okay.

I turned the 'on' knob, and a picture quivered into focus on the screen. It was the main street of Jubilee, quiet and dusty and, strangely, familiar. It might have been a street I'd once walked down in a town I knew well.

Horses tethered outside the Nugget, a saloon, waited patiently for their riders to return. The door of the barber shop opened, and a cowboy strutted out. Welcome lights shone from inside the Pink Palace Hotel. A dog leaped up on a wagon and started barking.

Happily, I settled down in the rocker to see what was happening in Susanna's world, hoping to catch a glimpse of Luke.

Pedestrians strolled along wooden plank sidewalks, most of them intent on their destinations, some of them dawdling. I saw Susanna in her green-striped dress talking to an older lady clad in black with silver curls spilling out of her bonnet.

The peaceful scene shattered with a thunder of hooves and a cloud of dust as four horsemen rode into town, their faces covered with dark bandanas. Townspeople melted into the background.

The riders dismounted, guns drawn, and burst into the Jubilee bank which looked like every bank I'd ever seen in a Western movie. A veritable giant with a gruff, take-no-prisoners voice, demanded money of the thin bespectacled man who'd been taken unaware.

"Hand it over," he barked.

"W-we don't have any money yet this morning, the bank clerk said. "If you come back later…"

The robber aimed his gun at the unfortunate man's face.

From outside the bank I heard gunfire, followed by a scream that went on and on.

And from outside the house, in my world, lightning electrified the sky. The picture vanished. The screen was dark.

Was that it? One short scene?

For heaven's sake! The movie always stopped at a pivotal point. Were the robbers going to get away with stealing the bank's money? Had the clerk's feeble attempt at wit antagonized the gunman? What was going on outside the bank? Who screamed? Had a runaway bullet struck Susanna or her elderly companion?

Obviously I wasn't fated to know today. I might as well turn the television off and check on the stew.

Sky gave a little 'remember me' whimper."

"Come on out," I said, but she refused to leave her haven under the table. Halley and Misty followed me into the kitchen, tails wagging.

The stew smelled… Like it was burning!

I grabbed the tall spoon and scraped chunks of beef from the bottom of the Dutch oven, then added water. Saved. Just in time.

But hadn't I just turned it on? Quickly I checked the temperature. Medium heat.

Next to the controls, the stove clock told me what had gone wrong. Forty-five minutes had passed while Sky hid from the storm and I lost myself in the movie.

But how was that possible? Not that much had happened in the story. A glimpse of Susanna and her silver-haired companion on Main Street, the scene in the bank…

I shouldn't be surprised. It had happened before. I had quite literally lost myself in the strange movie that came and went at will. In other words, under the spell of the old Western, I'd lost track of time.

It was as good an explanation as any.

Thirty-two

After the storm moved out of the Foxglove Corners, I turned on the haunted television set again—in the middle of breaking news about flood alerts. The movie was as lost as I was.

Suddenly I was impatient with the entire mystery. Absolutely fed up. I was minutes away from taking the set apart. That's what I told myself, but, in the end, I knew I wouldn't be able to do it. I'd find another way. Later. No, soon because I was tired of being taunted and held captive by demented electronics.

The stew was done. Crane and Julia would be home any minute, once again too late to see the movie. I was lucky they believed me. Most people would think I was delusional.

"Let's go outside, girls," I said.

Sky ventured out from under the table and trailed after the rest of the pack with Raven. Raven's walking was better, but she showed no interest in her doghouse, which was good. She was never going to live outside again.

While the dogs padded around in the wet grass, I admired the yellow Victorian across the lane. Camille and Gilbert had decorated the wraparound porch with pumpkins and tiny orange fairy lights that looked like glittering stars.

Halloween was two weeks away. We should do something similar, perhaps attach pumpkins as heads to our scarecrows. Yes, that would work, and while I was at it, I'd set myself a goal: solve the mystery of the rogue TV by the end of October.

Misty found a red ball buried in a fall of soggy leaves. She brought it to me, eyes bright and tail wagging.

"Let's play in the house," I said, taking the muddy ball reluctantly, and called the dogs to heel.

Back inside, I turned on the TV again, this time to a cooking show. Sheets of Halloween cookies waited to be frosted. A cook in a witch costume was turning cats and pumpkins from plain to fantastic with black and orange sprinkles.

Baking cookies was something else I could do.

Waiting led to thinking, not particularly about Halloween treats and seasonal decorations. I turned the TV off and wondered what determined its slip into the familiar pattern. Was there a common denominator other than the fact that I was always alone when the movie started playing? Which in itself was vaguely suspicious.

The answer came so quickly that it must have been on the edge of my awareness all along.

Rain.

It had been raining every time the movie aired.

Every time?

I leaned back in the rocker and thought about that.

Yes, every time. All the way back to the day when I'd first seen the antique television set at the estate sale. It had rained just before we'd arrived. I remembered clearly. Miss Eidt had been afraid the weather would spoil our day. We had both worn raincoats. She'd added a pretty paisley scarf. When I led Bronwyn out to the car, her fur was damp.

Not just rain, though. Stormy weather with lightning flashes and thunder crashes.

Every time.

I smiled, feeling proud of myself. Except, why hadn't I realized it sooner? The sky darkened, the rain came, lightning crackled in the sky. On the small screen the movie played, only to stop in mid-scene.

What could the connection be?

Because there had to be one. I felt as if I'd made a huge, unanticipated breakthrough.

Fine, but where would it lead me?

One problem remained. Thunder and lightning didn't explain the eerie way the movie restarted exactly where it had been cut off, even though days separated the two airings.

Perhaps I'd be able to solve this mystery, too.

~ * ~

I needed more. I needed help. The next day, as if she heard my plea, Anna Bell called from the Foxglove Corners Historical Society in response to the message I'd left on her voice mail.

"I'm not sure I understand what you're asking, Mrs. Ferguson," she said. "Is there a problem with one of the estate sale items? All sales are final, you know."

"Yes, it isn't that I'm dissatisfied with the television set. It has some unusual properties. If possible, I'd like to talk to someone familiar with it."

"That would have been Miss Stirling," she said.

"Is there anyone else?"

After a pause, Mrs. Bell said, "There's Stacia Emmalyn Stirling, the heir. Or you might contact Lida Ronan. Lida and Eustacia were best friends since their school days."

"Could you give me their phone numbers?" I asked.

"I'm not comfortable doing that, but they should be in the directory or online. Lida designed and maintains our website."

I thanked her and ended the call. Of the two women, I thought that Lida Ronan, the longtime friend, would be the person most likely to be familiar with Eustacia Stirling's possessions.

A commotion at the side door told me that Crane was home. The dogs didn't go into their welcome home frenzy for Julia yet.

It was time to put sleuthing on hold for homemaking.

~ * ~

The heir, Miss Stirling's grand-niece, was on vacation, but Lida Ronan agreed to meet me at Clovers for lunch on Saturday. She didn't understand my problem either. That was my fault. I didn't want to be more specific until we could talk face to face. However, when Saturday arrived, I still didn't know what I was going to say to make sure she didn't dismiss me as a crazy person.

I was still sorting through words as I walked through Clovers' doors to the tinkling of the green clover wind chimes. I didn't see Annica, but I recognized Lida Ronan from the society's website. She was waiting for me, already seated with a cup of coffee.

She looked too young to be a contemporary of Eustacia Stirling, but I noticed a cane hooked onto the table, and she seemed delicate. Her pink foxglove brooch gave a whimsical touch to her black turtleneck sweater.

She appeared to recognize me, too.

"I'm Jennet Ferguson," I said, going up to her table. "Thank you for meeting me."

She had a warm smile. "It's my pleasure. "I love to do something different on a fine fall day."

Well, this will be different, I thought.

Encouraged by her friendly tone, I told her how I'd been fascinated by the antique television set and how after I'd purchased it, another buyer expressed an interest in it. To put it mildly.

"I was afraid she'd grab it right out of my hand."

I didn't imagine the flash of comprehension in her eyes, nor the sudden pale cast her face acquired.

"I know the TV you're talking about," she said.

As if it were a person.

"Do you know how it's unique?" I asked.

Marcy chose this moment to interrupt us. Perhaps that was for the best. Annica wouldn't be able to contain her curiosity, and I hadn't told her about the haunted television set yet.

"Hi, Jennet," she said. "What can I get you to drink today?"

"I'll have iced tea with lemon," I said.

The situation called for a hot tea with Lucy Hazen sitting at the table ready to read tea leaves. But I'd settle for a cold drink.

When Marcy was out of earshot, Lida said, "That TV works—with a vengeance."

One of us had to be more specific.

"I know what you mean," I said. "Sometimes the programs follow the TV guide religiously. Other times, there's the same movie on all three channels and nothing else."

"Then the program goes off just like that…" Lida snapped her fingers, and her sapphire and diamond dinner ring flashed in the light. "And you're returned to regular programming. Eustacia was afraid of that TV."

"Did she see the Western movie, too?" I asked.

"No, for her it was *Peter, Paul, and Mary in Concert.* She loved that group, and at first she thought it *was* regularly programming. Until the same show kept coming on over and over again."

For the first time since I'd acquired the rogue TV, I felt vindicated. Somebody else had experienced its intricacies. I wasn't going crazy.

Well, I didn't really think I was.

"Did Miss Stirling ever try to find out why the television was like that?" I asked.

"Not to my knowledge. Who could she ask? What she did was have it stored in the attic. You know, out of sight, out of mind. Her niece took every single thing out of the house for the sale."

"Then it became somebody else's problem," I said. "I'm determined to find out what makes it tick."

"There's a tiny movie reel stuck inside," Lida suggested, but the gleam in her eyes was mischievous. I didn't take her seriously, although I imagined Brent would.

Marcy brought my tea, refilled Lida's cup, and gave us menus. I chaffed over the delay, but then we had come to Clovers for lunch.

After we'd ordered soup and sandwiches, I asked, "Do you know if this concert came on only when it rained?"

"If it did, Eustacia never mentioned it."

"It was raining on the day of the estate sale," I said.

"So it was."

"And every day after that, when I saw the movie, there was either lightning or thunder."

"That's truly bizarre," Lida said. "I know that Eustacia didn't keep using the TV. She was afraid that maybe her mind was slipping. I'll admit I thought so myself. After a while she asked me to take it up to the attic for her."

"I take it you never saw Peter, Paul, and Mary?"

"Never on that TV."

That matched my situation. I had one last question; then I had to start eating my lunch before the soup cooled off. "Do you know where Miss Stirling bought it?"

"I can help you with that," Lida said. "I was with her at the time. It was a little shop in Lakeville where I took my stereo for repairs. Roland Radio."

At last. A clue.

Thirty-three

The trees that lined Chestnut Street were making a brave attempt to hold onto their leaves in the high wind, even as I struggled to keep the hood of my raincoat from blowing back.

The sky was overcast with afternoon thunderstorms predicted. Before leaving the house, I'd turned on the television, hoping to see the aftermath of the bank robbery in the movie. Instead the noon newscast was just beginning.

The storm was still far off to the west. I'd try again later as soon as I heard the first thunder crash.

Lida Ronan didn't know the address of Roland Radio, but it was next door to a flower shop and across the street from a bookstore whose name eluded her.

Roland Radio… I walked to the intersection, crossed the street, and retraced my steps. There was no bookstore, no radio shop. Now that I thought about it, how could a radio shop support itself in today's economy?

With a sigh I watched my clue blow away in the wind. Ah, well, there would be another one.

But who would provide it?

Not wanting to go home empty handed, I walked over to the Green House of Antiques, which I hadn't visited in ages.

Julia's offer had been accepted, and she planned to move to her new house next month. This was a good opportunity to look for a housewarming gift for her and maybe something for myself. I hadn't bought a series book in months.

As always, the owner had decorated the window of the Green House with a creative and eye-catching touch. Witches and black cats prowled through a blanket of crinkled crimson leaves up to a cobweb-draped dollhouse. About a dozen spooky books formed a walkway to the porch, among them *Down a Dark Hall, Salem's Lot, Dracula, The Secret in the Old Attic, Hansel and Gretel,* and *Tale of the Witch Doll.*

I opened the door, and a rubbery spider on a black ribbon slid down from the ceiling with a bone chilling screech. It did an eerie dance in the wind that blew in with me. The salesgirl wore a costume with a glittering tiara on her long yellow hair. I didn't recognize her. I *had* been away a long time.

"I'm Glinda Good," she said. "Really. Don't mind the insect. It's fake."

"What makes it screech?" I asked. "I never touched it."

Her eyes sparkled with humor. "Acoustics or black magic or a little bit of both. What can I help you with?"

A black cat, a real one, leaped up to the counter and stared at me with cold green eyes.

What are you doing in my domain?

"I'd like to look at old books in a series," I said. "Like Judy Bolton and Beverly Gray. Also I need a housewarming gift."

"Our books are scattered around the shop." She pointed to a volume with a jagged-edged dust cover on top of a mahogany table. "Here's *The Ghost Parade* by Margaret Sutton. Are you a collector?"

"Well, an amateur one," I said. "I have that book."

"Let me know if you have any questions."

Browsing in an antique shop was one of my favorite pastimes, and I'd never once left the Green House without at least one purchase. I found two Beverly Grays I hadn't read yet and a lovely Gone-with-the-Wind lamp for Julia.

The spider screeched, and two young women in jeans and jackets entered the shop. Surprised, they added their own screams to the wind's howl.

"Ugh," one said. "Arachnid."

I brought the lamp and books up to the check-out counter and went back to see if I had overlooked something good.

And there it was, an antique television set, a duplicate of the one currently on my living room table. I'd know it anywhere.

Glinda stood behind me, so close that I almost stepped on her pink, pointed-toe shoe.

"Isn't it exquisite?" she said. "It's a true relic from another age."

"Before the remote was invented."

"Yes, indeed. Can't you just see a family gathering around it watching—uh—*Tom Corbett, Space Cadet*?"

I could, possibly because a print propped up next to the TV depicted the scene she described. A mother and father, a sandy-haired boy and a girl with long braids, all watching a vintage television with a small screen.

"Does it still work?" I asked.

"I'm sure it does, but let's check."

It was already plugged in. Glinda turned the 'on' knob, and a talk show filled the screen with a lot of chatter and cleavage. A contemporary program, judging by the women's dresses and hairstyles.

"It's a steal at a hundred and fifty dollars," Glinda said.

I had already decided to buy the TV without knowing why. Perhaps I suspected that once I brought it into my house, it would exhibit a preference for old Western movies.

I didn't really believe that, but I didn't have to justify my decision. I simply wanted it.

"Do you know where it came from?" I asked.

"Probably a private sale, but you'd have to ask the owner."

I could do that. I knew her, although we hadn't seen each other in a long time.

"I'll take it," I said as the door opened, and the spider screeched again.

At the counter I reached for my credit card. Maybe I'd give this set to Crane as a late birthday present to make up for the one I'd kept.

~ * ~

All the way home, while the wind set the trees along the road to swaying and tossed leaves at my windshield, I thought about my second antique television. What if it were another rogue with its unfathomable agenda? Would it start the western movie or a concert from the beginning or be further along?

Maybe I would take this one apart. And find a miniature CD player inside? The thought made me smile. As for Crane, well the idea to give him the set had been fleeting. I already had plans for this one.

I carried all of my purchases inside but left Julia's present in the trunk since she was home. The dogs cut their customary ear-splitting welcome short to sniff at the packages looking for their treats which, luckily, I'd remembered to buy. I set the new television on the kitchen table and passed out liver chip dog cookies to all. I was happy to see that Julia had the teakettle on and filled a plate with cinnamon-something muffins.

"Did you buy another haunted TV?" Julia asked.

"Maybe," I said. "We'll see when it starts to storm. I'll turn both of them on at once."

And most likely both of them would be airing contemporary programs because I wasn't alone. The phenomenon was reserved for me. So I could keep doubting my sanity?

Julia poured boiling water in the teapot and gave the leaves a rigorous stir. "I had a scare on the freeway, Jennet. I'm pretty sure I saw that man."

I didn't have to ask her who she meant.

"He still had the black beard. He was wearing a red checked hunter's cap."

"Did he see you?" I asked.

"I don't think so. He caused quite a commotion cutting across three lanes to exit. People were blasting their horns at him."

"What kind of car was he driving?"

"All I noticed was the garish yellow color. It would make me ill if I had to look at it in my driveway every day."

"He'll be easy to spot in a car that color," I said. "But that's odd. You'd think he'd want to keep a low profile. Perhaps change his appearance. At least shave his beard."

"Maybe he's not afraid of being recognized anymore," she said.

*Because he eliminated the witness, s*he might have added.

I didn't want to believe that Charlotte had been murdered, leaving Bronwyn on her own in a hostile world, but it had been so long since she'd left Dark Gables with her dog and dropped out of sight. What other explanation was there?

The man was nearby. He probably wouldn't recognize Julia, but he would remember me and the burn of *Halt!* spray in his eyes.

On that fearful thought, I poured our tea and took a satisfying, restorative sip. That might happen in the future, but it wasn't happening today.

Thirty-four

At Clovers, painted pumpkins and miniature scarecrows decorated the tables and booths. My centerpiece scarecrow bore an unmistakable resemblance to Raggedy Ann, complete with red yarn hair.

She looked coy, as if she had a secret she'd never divulge. Which was my imagination running wild. How could black button eyes communicate any emotion?

"Happy Halloween!" Annica approached my booth and set an orange and black menu in front of me. Her empire-style dress was bright red, and a pair of Raggedy Ann earrings swung amidst strands of red-gold hair. She tapped one earring lightly with a frosted crimson fingernail.

"It's our theme this year," she said.

"Raggedy Ann?"

"No. Story book characters. Marcy is Snow White, and Mary Jeanne is Cleopatra.

Everyone in Foxglove Corners was decorating or dressing up for Halloween, while I waited for a lightning flash to bring back an old Western movie.

"You'll have to try our pumpkin soup," Annica said.

"I'd rather have something more ordinary."

"A piece of pumpkin pie with a nice cup of tea? We have pumpkin spice."

"That sounds good, but I'd like the kind of tea you always have."

"We hardly ever see each other since school started." She lowered her voice. "I've been wanting to talk to you alone, Jennet, but I didn't want to call you at home. I have some news you'll be interested in."

Annica caught Marcy's attention and nodded imperceptibly. It was her signal to Marcy to cover for her. Later, she'd return the favor.

"I'll just say it before I take your order," Annica said. "Your nemesis has been in again, telling lies."

My heart sank—almost literally. Like a stone, it sat at the bottom of my stomach, and my heart began to race.

I tried to speak in a normal tone. "You're referring to Veronica."

"The snake-in-the-grass. Where was Crane this past Wednesday afternoon?"

The sudden change in subject threw me into a state of confusion. "Why, he was home. Same as always."

"Was he late?"

I had to think about that, but my memory refused to cooperate. All of the recent days were running together in my mind with nothing to differentiate one from another.

"I don't remember," I said. "He might have been a little late. I don't keep track of the time."

Not true. I had to be aware of time because of dinner. I almost always had something on the stove or in the oven an hour before I expected him.

"What did Veronica say now?" I asked. "The same?"

"Not exactly. She said she and Crane had dinner together, just the two of them."

Among all the questions I wanted to ask, the least important leaped to the forefront. "Did she say that out of the blue?"

"Not quite. She ordered the filet well done and said she hoped it would be as good as the one she had with Crane at the Adriatica on Wednesday."

"I don't believe it," I said.

"Neither do I, but I thought you'd want to know."

"I do. I suppose she knew you'd tell me."

"Of course, but I almost didn't," Annica said. "I don't want you to worry. She's only trying to stir up trouble. The witch."

"The viper."

"Witch, viper—they're both poisonous. Shall I get your pie?"

"No," I said. "I think I'll just have a cup of tea."

I had planned to tell Annica about the haunted television set, about Julia's new house, and Charlotte's disappearance. I didn't. I'd tell her another time.

Now I sat still, contemplating the Raggedy Ann doll and waiting for Annica to bring my tea. I remembered the dinner I'd cooked for Crane on Wednesday. Turkey breast, stuffing, and sweet potatoes. He'd eaten with his usual enthusiasm and took a second helping. He certainly didn't act as if he'd just had a filet at a restaurant.

~ * ~

I drove out to Crispian road in a whirlwind of leaves. It was blowing our many-colored autumn world apart. My thoughts were whirling, too.

Crane might have had a cup of coffee with Veronica at a diner when both stopped for a break. She had changed the details to make it sound like a dinner date.

Just ask him, I told myself.

Then at Clovers, by ordering a filet, she had created a situation in which she could casually mention having a steak dinner with Crane.

Don't ask him. Tell him that for some reason Veronica has been lying to Annica, knowing she would pass the message on to me.

That was a better approach. Said that way, it wouldn't seem as if I believed it.

And I didn't. I knew how Veronica operated. A chocolate cake for Crane's birthday… Baking a cake for a beloved husband was a wife's privilege.

What else? Hints of a relationship that didn't exist.

The wind was shrieking. My Ford Focus felt like the Volkswagen I'd driven to and from college. It had been so light that a good wind could send it flying down the wooded slope to the icy lake below.

There's no good wind. It's all dangerous.

I gripped the steering wheel so tightly my fingers hurt.

All right. Calm down. Concentrate on the road, on slippery patches and leaping deer. And snakes. It was almost the end of October. Shouldn't snakes be hibernating or slithering off to wherever they spent the winter months?

Snakes, yes, but not a determined female deputy sheriff with a warped sense of honor.

The wind was so loud it was making my head ache, but I should be nearing Jonquil Lane soon. Home had never seemed more of a haven.

~ * ~

That evening, before we sat down to eat, I said, "I heard something disturbing from Annica today. Veronica told her that the two of you had dinner together at the Adriatic on Wednesday."

"She told her *what*?"

He looked surprised. Genuinely surprised.

"I know you don't agree that Veronica is up to no good," I said, "but why would she say that?"

"I have no idea."

"Unless she's delusional."

"She always seemed normal to me," he said. "Do you think Annica is making it up?"

"Absolutely not."

"Or maybe Annica misunderstood her?"

"I have faith in Annica," I said. "This isn't the first time Veronica has said something about her and you. Then there was that cake for your birthday…"

Candy nudged me. She knew the dogs' dinners were ready, on the counter, and had no patience for human conversation.

"It isn't true, Jennet," Crane said.

"I never thought it was."

"I don't know what she hopes to accomplish."

"That's easy. She wants to undermine my faith in you. That'll never happen," I added quickly.

"Why?"

"Who knows? I'm concerned that Veronica might be dangerous. Her obsession with you is troubling. If she thinks this dinner at the Adriatic really happened, where will it end?"

He was quiet for a moment, frowning, his gray eyes reflective. "I'm going to talk to her tomorrow," he said. "In the meantime, don't worry about it."

Thirty-five

Annica didn't want me to worry. Crane told me not to worry. But I couldn't help worrying, not because I was afraid Veronica would steal my husband. I was certain she was delusional. If she believed the dinner with Crane at the Adriatica had really happened, what was next?

I was glad Crane intended to talk to her. Still, I wondered if I should have confronted her myself.

"Accuse a lunatic of lying?" Julia was flabbergasted. "That's a horrible idea. Who knows how she'd retaliate?"

We were having tea and gingersnaps in the kitchen, a relaxing ritual we'd begun shortly after Julia came home. I was going to miss her when she moved to her own house.

"I like to handle my problems myself," I said.

"Not this one. The lady is armed—and dangerous."

"I wonder. Don't you have to pass a psychological evaluation to be a deputy sheriff?"

"You'd think so. Or if you were deranged, one of your fellow officers would notice something off."

"Crane has always been a good judge of character," I pointed out.

But at one time Veronica had him fooled. He'd thought she was just lonely, being new in town. He'd insisted she only wanted to make friends. Until the cake episode.

"Maybe she's just off her rocker when it comes to Crane," Julia said. "She wants him. She's hoping you'll think he's been seeing her behind your back and break up with him."

The unmitigated arrogance of the woman.

I bit down hard on a gingersnap. "I'd like to squash her," I said.

"Remember she has a gun."

"So do I."

"Jennet!"

I didn't mean to imply that I'd use it, but it felt good to say it. I wouldn't even be able to squash a snake—or chop its head off.

"I consider myself a match for her," I said. "It won't come to violence."

"Once she's aware that Crane knows about her lie, she may give up," Julia said.

"I'm not counting on it."

The topic was destroying my enjoyment in our quiet alone time. I refilled our teacups. I'd have to visit Dark Gables soon and ask Lucy to read my tea leaves.

"Well, enough about Veronica the Viper," I said. "Tell me about your classes."

She did, and her enthusiasm warmed the chill that had settled in the air. Afterward I turned the antique television sets on. Both were airing the same contemporary programs, but then once again I wasn't alone, and it wasn't storming. I'd wait for the proper conditions to see whether I'd brought another rogue into the house.

~ * ~

When Crane came home, he looked happy. He roughhoused with the dogs and glanced at the stove where the beef stew was bubbling merrily in the Dutch oven.

"Looks good," he said.

I couldn't wait. "Did you talk to Veronica?"

He locked his gun in the cabinet. "She claims that Annica must have misunderstood her. She *did* make the remark about having a steak at the Adriatic but didn't say a word about me being there."

I waited.

"I don't believe her," he said. "I told her to be careful of what she says from now on. I'm a happily married man, and I don't want even a hint of scandal attached to my name."

"Then that's the end of it?"

"I hope so. I don't know why she's fixated on me."

"I do."

He hugged me. "We have a new deputy sheriff in the department. Henry. He's interested in Veronica. He's working up the nerve to ask her for a date."

But Crane was the man Veronica had set her sights on. I *did* understand. He was a genuine treasure. My treasure.

I kissed him and went back to my dinner, piercing a chunk of beef to see if the meat was done. Not quite yet.

"I'm glad," I said. "Thanks for setting the record straight."

I wasn't entirely out of the woods, though. If I knew Veronica, she would retreat and return with a new attack. I didn't intend to let my guard down.

But I kept that last thought to myself.

~ * ~

I turned off the stew and stepped back from the stove as Candy jumped up and led the race to the door. All of the dogs were barking, and someone was knocking on the door. Something outside the door was barking, too. A coyote? Another dog?

I glanced through the bay window. Brent's vintage white Plymouth Belvedere with the green fins was parked behind my car, and a dark sable collie trotted along at his heel. A thin layer of white covered the ground and glistened in the trees. Snow lay lightly on Brent's dark red hair and the new dog's coat.

I told the dogs to Stay and opened the door. My pack converged on Brent. He held out a restraining hand to Misty who looked ready to leap into his arms. The new collie hung back, her ears flat against her head. She looked familiar.

I looked at her closely. "Is that…?"

"A stray," Brent said. "I found her lying in the road with the snow falling on her. I thought she was dead. Turns out she was just sleeping, so I brought her to you."

The stray shook the snow from her coat and gave a little whine. Candy bared her teeth in a half-hearted warning to the newcomer. One of my gentle collies growled.

"Candy, no!" I said.

She grumbled but sat down.

"I knew you'd have an extra collar and leash lying around," Brent said. "I do, too, but once I got her in the car, I didn't want to backtrack."

Crane took his coat and closed the door on the cold air that was trying to force its way inside along with a few snowflakes. "Look around, Fowler. How many collies do you see?"

"A lot."

"It's Bronwyn," I cried.

Hearing her name, Bronwyn wagged her tail. I laid my hand on her head. Yes, there was no doubt. It was Bronwyn.

"I've been calling her Snowy," Brent said. "You know her?"

"This is the dog Charlotte Gray adopted. Charlotte had Bronwyn with her when she disappeared."

"Isn't Charlotte the lady you think the hit-and-run killer did away with?" Brent asked.

"Charlotte adopted Bronwyn, yes. I don't think she's dead. This proves it."

"I don't see how."

It was ninety percent a strong feeling. I searched for words to explain it. "Charlotte and Bronwyn were always together. If her collie is alive, then so is she."

I looked into Bronwyn's soulful eyes. "Where is Charlotte, Bronwyn? If only you could talk."

She looked at me and wagged her tail.

"Where did you find her, Brent?" I asked.

"On Wolf Lake Road, about a half mile from my house."

"That may be a starting place to look for Charlotte."

"Not necessarily," Crane said. "She could have come from anywhere."

"Wherever she was, I think it was fairly close to Foxglove Corners. It isn't likely that she traveled a long distance."

Back to Foxglove Corners.

I took another look at her. The snow had melted from her coat, and I saw that burrs had worked their way into her fur. She had a cluster of them behind each ear. Her paws were crusted with old mud and something that might be dried blood.

It was a wonder she hadn't been killed as she took on the Michigan countryside. What had she eaten? Where had she found water?

Bronwyn whined and nudged my hand.

It was time to bring a halt to speculation and take care of my unexpected guest. She would need food and water.

"Is that beef stew I smell?" Brent asked.

"It is, and there's plenty for all of us. I have to take Bronwyn to Sue. She's been fretting over her ever since I told her that Charlotte disappeared.

"Before you do that, let's eat," Brent said. "Is there pie, by chance?"

"Julia baked two apple pies."

As if on cue, Julia came down the stairs in beige slacks and a green turtleneck sweater, her golden hair freshly washed and shining.

"Hi, Brent," she said. "Jennet, do I see eight collies?"

"This is Charlotte's adopted collie, Bronwyn," I said.

"Right. Now where's Charlotte?"

Thirty-six

The moon was bright as I drove up Jonquil Lane with Bronwyn. Its light illuminated the snow that lay motionless on the frozen countryside. Stray moonbeams danced among from the shadows of the abandoned development, making it seem somehow less forbidding.

Still I was glad I was in a car and not on foot.

It was too cold for the snow to melt tonight, and too early for snow. It wasn't even Halloween yet.

Try telling that to Mother Nature.

An unwelcome thought slipped into my mind. If we had passed the season of thunderstorms, I might not see my Western movie again until spring.

Michigan weather could be capricious, though. Next week we might have a warm-up. A single flash of lightning could bring the movie back from wherever it had gone.

So many months… Would I have forgotten the plot by then? I didn't think so. Susanna and Luke, the handsome rancher who looked like Crane, and the newcomer to Jubilee in her fancy attire? In the last scene, an outlaw was robbing the bank, and someone had screamed outside in the street. At this point, the movie had vanished.

I turned on Squill Lane, and Bronwyn whimpered in the back seat. I wondered how often she had been in a car traveling to an unknown destination since I'd taken her from the estate sale.

"We're going back to the horse farm," I told her. "To Sue. To wait for Charlotte."

She yelped, and I could swear she understood what I'd said.

The lights were on in Sue's ranch house, and dogs were barking. Would they remember Bronwyn? I hoped they'd make her feel welcome—Icy, Bluebell, and Echo. They should be used to other dogs in their house as Sue often brought a rescue home.

She opened the door and cried out in delight at the sight of the collie at my side. She recognized her immediately. I was glad I hadn't called to alert her to Bronwyn's arrival. There's nothing like a happy surprise.

"It's our Bronwyn," she said.

"Brent found her near his place. She was sleeping in the road."

"In the road? In the snow?"

"It doesn't seem to have harmed her."

"That's a miracle. She doesn't look malnourished. What about Charlotte?" she added.

"She's still missing."

Still missing, I thought. *Presumed dead by everybody but me.*

I hoped Bronwyn didn't sense what I was thinking.

"Bronwyn, girl," Sue said. "Let me look at you."

Ears flattened, Bronwyn came to Sue, dancing around her, nudging her and whimpering like a little puppy. It was as if Bronwyn had been Sue's dog for years.

Sue stroked her head and promptly encountered the burrs behind her ears.

"I didn't brush her," I said, wishing I had. "Brent was over, and I was making dinner… You know. Overload."

"I can groom her. I'm just so glad to have her back. She's staying with me for a while."

"Of course," I said. "You can't let anybody else adopt her. Bronwyn is Charlotte's collie."

"I know that. Can you stay for a while, Jennet? I was just about to make some hot chocolate."

"A very short while. I left Brent alone with Crane. Who knows what those two will cook up while I'm gone?"

I settled in a chair in the family room, surrounded by dogs and warmed by the flames in Sue's wood burning stove.

Sue was still fussing over Bronwyn. When she looked up, I saw the glint of tears in her eyes. "I'm so glad to see Bronwyn, but I hope this doesn't mean Charlotte is dead," she said.

"I think of her as being lost. So was Bronwyn, but she found her way home."

Well, almost home. What would have happened if Brent hadn't discovered her lying in the middle of Wolf Lake Road? Another car might have run over her. That didn't bear thinking about.

Charlotte would find her way home, too.

Bronwyn was safe with Sue. I could only hope she'd soon be reunited with her true owner.

~ * ~

On the one hand, there was my life with its problems and mysteries. A missing woman, an unknown killer, and a deputy sheriff with her own warped moral compass.

On the other, there was school. Along with the two hours spent commuting to and from Oakpoint, my teaching job occupied most of my weekdays.

Holidays sent ripples of unease throughout the student body, even quasi holidays like Halloween. Student Council members were selling candi-cards to convey Halloween wishes to friends—and sometimes to teachers. The cards contained personal messages. A chocolate marshmallow ghost, witch, pumpkin, or cat accompanied each card.

The activity was fun and worthwhile. Funds raised would be added to those from the Thanksgiving collection to feed needy families in the community next month. It was also a distraction. Candi-cards were sold in the cafeteria, the halls, and during class. Hence the distraction. They would be delivered during the second period on Halloween.

"That's a nice early trick-or-treat," I said to Leonora at lunch.

She gave a pretend shudder. "Don't say trick in school."

"It's a nice way to get someone's attention," I said. "Somebody loves you. Guess who? It's ideal for a shy kid."

I remembered a certain Halloween when I was a high school freshman. We'd had a similar custom of sending spooky cards without the candy. I'd received a love message from M. B. I'd never figured out who he was.

"Think of the downside," Leonora pointed out. "Off-the-wall energy, wrappers on the floor."

"Scrooge," I said.

"Wrong holiday. How about the kid who doesn't receive one?"

She had a point. "But that's life," I said. "Like the girl who isn't asked to the Homecoming Dance."

I unwrapped my sandwich. Turkey with lettuce on whole wheat bread with a healthful treat, an apple. What had I been thinking when I'd packed my lunch? Last night, Julia had baked a batch of pumpkin-chocolate chip cookies.

"Are you going to Miss Eidt's Halloween party at the library?" Leonora asked.

"I'd like to. I forgot about it."

"She's hoping people will come in costume."

"I don't know that I'll go that far."

But it would be fun to dress up as a glamorous witch again.

"I haven't had time to go to the library lately," I said.

How could I have let that happen? I had missed Miss Eidt and the cozy white Victorian library filled with books and decorated for the current season, and missed coffee and doughnuts in Miss Eidt's private office. The Gothic Nook… I'd only been there once. This Saturday I would make it a point to go. I couldn't celebrate Halloween properly without a new Gothic novel.

I glanced at the clock. When I was at school, I was always glancing at the clock—to see if I had time to run to the faculty lounge between classes or how much more of a period was left, and, at present, to see how many minutes remained of our so-called lunch hour.

Ten minutes, enough to finish my sandwich and eat the apple.

"How is the class from hell?" Leonora asked. "I haven't heard you complain about them lately."

"Surprisingly they're good. It makes me uneasy. I suspect treachery in the making."

"Now who's a Scrooge?"

"How does that apply?"

In answer she offered me a chocolate frosted brownie, her husband Jake's favorite dessert. She always had brownies in her lunch these days.

I took it, happily dropping the apple back in my lunch bag.

"I have one exceptionally good group," I added. "My afternoon World Literature class. We're having a week of spooky stories for Halloween. Today it's *The Invisible Hand.* A good class and a good story add up to fun for everyone."

"We could read *The Lottery* in American Literature classes even though it's out of chronological order," Leonora said. "It's a good harvest story, and October is a harvest month. Draw the paper with the black *X* and get stoned to death. This year's harvest will be good."

I considered. Shirley Jackson's chilling little story was certainly appropriate. However…

"We don't need to give them ideas," I said.

Thirty-seven

Every holiday Miss Eidt unpacked her white Victorian dollhouse, built in imitation of the library when it was her family home, and added miniature seasonal decorations. For Halloween she had tiny ghosts and witches, along with cats, bats, and rats. I stood in front of it, trying to see the title of the red book that lay on a table in the living room.

The microscopic letters were real: *Dracula.*

"What do you think?" Miss Eidt stood behind me holding two mini jack-o'-lanterns.

"It's fantastic," I said. "I always wanted a dollhouse."

She set one jack-o'-lantern on either side of the entrance. "Are you coming to my Halloween party?" she asked.

"I hope to, if nothing happens to prevent it."

"Don't let anything happen," she said. "Maybe you can bring your haunted television set."

"It won't perform on command. I figured out that it needs a thunderstorm to malfunction. Lightning appears to turn it on and off."

"How odd. I thought you'd have solved that mystery by now."

"I'm still working on it."

"You'll wear a costume for the party, I hope," she added. "You're always so imaginative."

I was saved from answering by Debby, who held a vampire figure in her hand.

"I found him. Where does he go?"

"How about in one of the bedrooms?" She placed the black-cloaked vampire so that it hovered over a bed. "Like this."

For a gentle lady, Miss Eidt had a ghoulish streak that emerged at this time of the year.

"I'm going to look for some good Halloween reading," I said, and headed to the Gothic Nook.

Anyone would think it was strange for me to celebrate a night devoted to spirits and frights when at times my life was a ghostly carnival. But who doesn't like to experience fear while sitting by a roaring fire, knowing all along that you're safe in your house?

I had the Gothic Nook to myself. Miss Eidt had added to her collection. The best Gothic novels, in my opinion, were the old paperbacks that had their heyday in the sixties and seventies. An occasional torn cover, carefully mended by Debby or Miss Eidt, only meant that the book had been well read. I chose *To See a Stranger, Who Rides a Tiger, The Legend of Witchwynd, Ravenscroft,* and *Legacy*, which I'd read twice before.

Miss Eidt was putting the finishing touches on the dollhouse, supervised by Blackberry. I said goodbye to them and went outside. While I'd been in the library, the sky had darkened, and a smell of rain permeated the chill air.

I'd better hurry home. Conditions were perfect for the rogue television to broadcast the Western movie. Julia had gone to a downstate mall to shop for clothes, and Crane, of course, was patrolling the roads of Foxglove Corners.

Except for the seven collies, I would be alone in the house, which is what the haunted TV wanted.

~ * ~

The storm began with a bolt of lightning that electrified the sky. Shielding the books under my raincoat, I ran from the car to the side door, straight into a jumping, yipping pack of collies. One of them nipped at my ankle.

In their minds, I had been gone all day, and they wanted treats and fresh water. Only Candy and Misty needed to go out, and they didn't stay long. The other collies backed up into the kitchen.

I filled water bowls and passed out Camille's homemade dog biscuits, then hung up my dripping raincoat. Now to see if the lightning had summoned the movie.

I remembered then. I had two television sets, the original and the one I'd bought at the Green House and stored on the credenza.

Turning the second set on, I found it was airing a soap opera scheduled for this time. A man and a woman were exchanging snappy dialogue peppered with clichés and flirtatious remarks. In other words, it was performing normally.

Crane was in luck. He'd get his belated birthday present after all.

It appeared that I was in luck, too. On the other TV, the main street of Jubilee shivered into colorful life. It had changed from tranquil to chaotic. Every inhabitant of Jubilee seemed to be gathered around the young woman lying in the street.

"Susanna!" Luke ran to her side. A splotch of blood high on her right arm had soaked through the green stripes of her dress.

"Is she dead?" Susanna's elderly companion held her hand over her heart, a theatrical gesture. She looked frantically around at the crowd as if hoping for a favorable answer. "That boy shot her!"

"She's alive, Mrs. Mills," Luke said. "What boy?"

"He rode off with the gang."

Luke lifted Susanna carefully and cast a quick, dark look toward the east, but the outlaws were lost in billowing clouds of dust.

"He was aiming at the sheriff, but he missed," Mrs. Mills said. "Susanna was in his way. Land sakes, can't a body walk down the street of her own town anymore and not fear for her life?"

"Sometimes, no."

Luke carried Susanna to a small white house. Mrs. Mills followed close behind him.

"I hope Doc Limmerton is in," Luke said. "You're going to be okay, Miss Susanna."

She didn't answer. Her eyes were closed; her long dark hair streamed down her back.

The doctor emerged from a back room, rubbing his eyes. He had a bushy mustache and spectacles. "What have we here?"

Silently he examined Susanna's wound.

"Gunshot wound. Stay with her, Mrs. Mills." Luke rushed out the door and into the street. He mounted his horse and galloped east after the outlaws.

In the doctor's office, Susanna lay on a narrow bed while the doctor examined her.

"Could be worse."

"You just rest, dear," Mrs. Mills said. "The doctor will tend to that—that little injury."

Darkness gave way to light. Sunshine streamed through the window. It looked as if Mrs. Mills had kept her lonely vigil throughout the night.

Susanna stirred, struggled to move, to speak. "Luke? Where's Luke?"

"He went after them," Mrs. Mills said.

"Alone?"

"The sheriff and his deputy probably went with him."

Susanna's voice was weak. "One against... How many of them were there?

"Four, I think."

"Was anyone else hurt?"

"Only you."

"My dress is ruined," Susanna said.

"Better the dress than you, dear. It's only cloth. You need to rest that arm."

The scene changed to a barren expanse of countryside lit by a fiery morning sky, to Luke, the sheriff, and five riders, probably townsmen. The camera lingered lovingly on the weathered planes of Luke's face as if it had finally found its perfect subject.

"I say we keep going," he said. "Are y'all with me?"

Lightning flashed, and the screen suddenly filled with blue sky and an airplane flying above the clouds. The movie was gone, as I knew it would be. The lightning brought it, and the lightning took it away. I turned off the TV and glanced at the clock.

Almost an hour had passed, which was what I expected. Misty lay at my feet, but the other dogs had retreated quietly to their favorite places to wait for the rain to pass. It was on the way out, a light pattering on the windows.

My library books lay scattered on the coffee table where I'd dropped them.

I heard Julie's key turn in the lock.

Back to the real world. To treading on slippery leaves and wiping muddy paws, to making dinner, correcting essays, and waiting for Crane. Back to my life.

I met Julia in the kitchen and helped her unload her packages on the kitchen table.

"I found a great blue dress on sale," she said. "I bought lots of lingerie, enough to carry me through the winter… What's wrong?"

I'd been listening to her, but a part of my mind was with Luke and the posse. Would they find the bank robbers and bring them back to Jubilee to hang? What a gruesome way to die. But that was justice in the Old West. Live by the sword, perish by the sword. Even the boy who had shot Susanna.

"Nothing," I said. "I was watching the movie."

"Darn it. I missed it again."

"It only plays for me," I said.

"Suppose it only plays when someone—not necessarily you—is alone?"

"I don't think that's likely."

"Let's experiment. The next time it storms, you leave the house, and I'll turn on the TV."

"But it's my phenomenon," I said.

Yes, I was owning it.

"Well, it was just a thought," Julia said. "What happened to sisters sharing?"

"Let's think about dinner," I said. "What should we make?"

Thirty-eight

The pumpkins in Clovers appeared to have multiplied. Most of them had grotesque or sly faces, courtesy of Mary Jeanne and her carving knife. Annica continued the theme with crystal pumpkin earrings that glittered through strands of her red-gold hair.

"I'm getting tired of wearing orange," she said. Her turtleneck sweater was pale peach, not quite a fall color. "What can I get for you today?"

"I'd like hot tea and an apple muffin—and information. Have you seen my arch-enemy lately?"

"Veronica the Viper?"

"None other."

"She came in for breakfast yesterday. I wanted to wring her neck, making me out to be a liar like she did."

I'd told Annica what Veronica had said about misunderstanding her, and Annica hadn't taken it well. Maybe I shouldn't have mentioned it.

"I was one step away from spilling maple syrup on her uniform," Annica said.

"I'm glad you didn't."

"Yeah, I need this job."

"Did she say anything about Crane?" I asked.

"Not a word. She placed her order, didn't thank me, and left me two dimes and a nickel for a tip. She had six pancakes and bacon, too."

"Could her little campaign to win Crane be over?"

I half hoped Annica would think Veronica had given up. Instead, she mirrored my own thoughts.

"She's the kind who'll come up with a Plan B. But she'd better leave me out of it."

I was grateful that, except for one occasion, Veronica and I hadn't been in Clovers at the same time. She wouldn't allow me to ignore her, and I might say something I'd regret.

"Are you and Crane going to the Halloween party at the library?" Annica asked.

"I am. Crane will probably keep the home fires burning."

"What are you going to wear?"

"I'll put together a witch costume. I still have that peaked hat somewhere."

"That's what you wore the last time."

"And I got a few compliments for my efforts. What are you going to be?"

"A medieval lady. I'm looking forward to being someone else for the night," she said. "I've been memorizing Chaucerian phrases. How's this? *Whan that April with his showres soote/ The droughte of March hath perced to the roote...*"

"Nobody will understand you. Or people will wonder why you're talking about April in October."

"I'll try to find a better quote."

Whatever she said, Annica would be magnificent. She was made for brilliant colors and glamour.

"You'll win first prize," I said.

Unless *I* did. I'd better start looking for witch quotations.

"I'm going with Brent," she added. "He'll be himself. The Huntsman. I'd better get your tea. Marcy called in sick, and I'm working alone."

~ * ~

On the way home, I stopped at Sue Appleton's horse farm. I'd been thinking about Bronwyn, hoping she was adjusting to being back with Sue.

"I'm worried about Bronwyn," Sue said. "She's changed."

I saw what she meant. Bluebell, Icy, and Echo were chasing one another around the property, sending leaves shooting into the air in high waves. Bronwyn lay on the porch, her gaze on the driveway that led out to the road.

Of course she was older than the other dogs. Still, my Star held her own in collie games with the rest of the pack who were younger.

"When you first brought her to me, she took an interest in her surroundings and played nicely with my three," Sue said.

"That was before Charlotte came into her life."

"Now she's restless. Even in the house, she sits on the sofa where she can see the road. I have a feeling that Bronwyn would like to go back to wherever she came from, so I keep an eye on her."

"If she truly wanted to leave, wouldn't she have done so by now?" I asked.

"Maybe. Who knows?" Sue rose and called to the dogs. "Let's go in. It's getting too cold to sit on the porch."

The wind was growing stronger by the minute, contributing to the chill in the air. We trooped inside and settled down in the family room.

"Has Bronwyn ever tried to leave the farm?" I asked.

"No, but sometimes I think she'd like me to follow her—to some place."

"Why don't you let her? She might lead you to Charlotte."

At the mention of her owner's name, Bronwyn tilted her head and gave a small whimper. There was no doubt in my mind that she knew what we were talking about.

"For many reasons. This is a busy time of the year for me with my riding students, and I'm not a detective. Even if I were, I'd need a better clue than a dog's intuition."

"I wonder if Bronwyn would take *me* to Charlotte," I said.

"It's not like you can ask her."

I wasn't so sure about that. Bronwyn wasn't a search and rescue dog. She had always been a pet. But she had formed a deep attachment to Charlotte. I thought it likely that she knew where Charlotte was. If she could come as far as Wolf Lake Road on her own, she could retrace her steps.

But how we would begin? Go back to Wolf Lake Road, choose a direction, and start walking?

"This wasn't the way our geriatric collie program was supposed to work," Sue said. "We placed Bronwyn with a good owner, and now she's adrift."

"You *are* going to keep her, though, aren't you?" I asked. "Until Charlotte comes home."

"Of course, but I want her to be happy."

Bronwyn hadn't joined us in the family room. I'd seen her leap into the sofa with a clear view of the road and the autumn leaves dancing in the wind.

The scene was heart-wrenching. If only I could reunite Bronwyn with her owner. If only it were still possible. I felt like crying at the sight of the faithful collie waiting for her owner to return. Once again I renewed my resolve to make that happen. Whatever it took.

~ * ~

The fields were murky, their spent wildflowers reduced to bare stalks and brown powder. The only color was a cluster of purple violets.

I must have been traveling on that accursed Huron Court.

Someone was chasing me, a man whose face was familiar, who meant to harm me. He might be hiding behind the taller stalks, waiting to grab me.

Choose a direction, and start walking.

I'd said that before in another place.

A gust of wind blew me out of the fields and into my car. The wind's wail turned into a siren.

Veronica said, "You shouldn't be driving on this road, Jennet. It's forbidden. That'll cost you a hundred dollars."

As she reached for my license and registration, I grabbed a pitcher and poured maple syrup over her crisp, clean uniform sleeve.

I couldn't have awakened at a better time.

Thirty-nine

A witch cut-out with a leering green face greeted me as I walked up to the porch at Dark Gables. She had a platter in her hands, as if waiting to fill it with an oven-roasted Gretel.

Lucy opened the door before I could knock and saw me looking askance at the witch. "A bit of Halloween whimsy," she said. "I couldn't resist."

"She doesn't exactly say *Welcome*."

"What witch says that? Unless she's trying to lure you into her cottage? Sky is afraid of her," she added.

Lucy's pretty blue merle collie was hiding behind Lucy's black midi-dress. Only her face was visible.

"I had a feeling I'd see you today," Lucy said. "Come in."

In the sunroom, Lucy filled the electric teakettle with water and plugged it in. I sat in the wicker loveseat and looked out through the French doors. Like the flowers in my garden, Lucy's plants were dying or dead, and leaves shivered in the wind as if in agitation, knowing their death was near.

"What's new?" Lucy asked.

"I'm not having any luck finding Charlotte," I said. "Bronwyn is grieving. I haven't figured out what makes the haunted television set malfunction yet. But—and this is good—Crane knows that Veronica lied about having a dinner date with him."

I told her about Veronica's latest ploy and how it had fallen flat when Crane confronted her.

"She had to backtrack. She said Annica misunderstood her, which didn't go over well with Annica."

"This is cause for rejoicing," Lucy said. "We'll see if she's still in your teacup. I take it that Bronwyn came home," she added.

"Brent found her near his house. She's back with Sue, waiting for Charlotte to join her."

"Strange," Lucy said. "I think about Charlotte often. Sometimes I can call up images of a missing person's surroundings, but for Charlotte, there's only a black screen. Sort of like your TV when it cuts the Western movie off."

"I hope that doesn't mean she's dead."

"I don't believe she is, but something is keeping her away from us. It's like she's frozen in place. Figuratively speaking, of course."

An image of Charlotte trapped in a giant ice cube took shape in my mind. Quickly I sent it away.

"What's new with you?" I asked.

"They've finally started shooting *Devilwish*," Lucy said. "I visited the set yesterday."

Devilwish was Lucy's best-selling horror novel for young adults. Soon it would enjoy renewed popularity as a movie. Lucy was interested in following the progress of her work's transformation, while I was content to wait for the completed film and see the bizarre plot unfold all at once.

"Seeing my book come to life is an extraordinary experience," Lucy said. "The actors are perfect in their roles. Just a little older than I imagined them."

The teakettle whistled. While Lucy poured the tea and assembled a plate of cookies, I contemplated the view of her garden and the woods beyond. Branches swayed in the wind and leaves fell into the fountain's basin. The trees were almost bare, gaunt skeletons against an icy blue sky.

"Our beautiful autumn will soon be gone," Lucy said. "Well, nothing lasts forever."

Foxglove Corners was heading into winter, an inhospitable season for those who needed to be outside. Or were trapped there.

"Thank heavens Bronwyn at least is safe, I said.

~ * ~

We drank our tea, and a wondrous feeling of warmth settled around me. Hoping to hear a good fortune, I handed Lucy the cup, with the tea leaf patterns set.

"I still see her." Lucy pointed to a long light tea leaf that, according to her, represented Veronica the Viper. "She hasn't gone from your life. My advice to you is to beware." She turned the cup around and added, "I don't see your wish. Your cup is rather a mishmash today."

"Like my life. My wish was to be rid of Veronica once and for all."

"It'll take more than a wish to get that hussy out of your life," Lucy said.

"Crane knows she's chasing him now," I said. "Inventing assignations. Making sure I hear about them."

"She thought you'd just brood in silence. She was hoping to cause a rift between you two."

"I won't let her do that."

But it frightened me when I remembered how close I'd once come to keeping Veronica's not-so-subtle harassment of me a secret from Crane.

"You'll have a better cup the next time," Lucy said. "And always remember, you don't have to believe what I tell you."

She moved the plate of sugar cookies on the coffee table closer to me. They were pumpkin-shaped and covered with orange frosting.

"Have one," she said. "Get into the spirit of the season."

Sky yelped and sat up, an endearing trick that none of my girls had mastered. Trust a collie to make everything better.

"Pumpkin is good for collies," Lucy said, rewarding Sky with a cookie of her own.

I bit into mine. It was too sweet, but that was all right. I had another one and surprisingly felt a little better.

~ * ~

The wind sounded like the wail of a coyote caught in a trap.

Struggling to stay upright in an especially strong gust, I hurried to my car. The cold tore away the sense of comfort created by having tea and cookies with my friend.

Hurry home, I told myself. *As fast as the law allows.*

I wouldn't want to be stopped for speeding by Veronica in her role as deputy sheriff.

There was little traffic on Spruce Road; there rarely is. I drove the speed limit, thankful for the spruce trees that grew on ground that was level with the road. My greatest driving nightmare was to be blown from the road down to a deep wooded slope. Down…Down…I could almost feel this happening, even though the Focus was hardly a tin can.

I had seven collies waiting for me at home. I couldn't afford to lose control of my car.

But the wind was a mighty adversary, ever increasing, and this section of Spruce Road was notorious for curves with many 'no passing' lines. And Deer X-ing signs.

Even without the curves, nobody in his right mind would try to pass another vehicle with such limited visibility, and the weather was worsening. Leaves filled the air. They looked like large snowflakes, landing on the windshield, sticking to it.

Perhaps they were. Enough precipitation had already fallen on the road to make its surface slick.

I turned on the windshield wipers and the low lights, felt the car begin to go into a skid, and slowed to a safer speed. And I kept my hands on the wheel. This was no day to be driving, and it was later than I'd thought.

Remember the collies. Remember home.

Crane was out patrolling the roads of Foxglove Corners, but he was a master driver. He could handle any car in any weather. As for me, driving had never been my favorite activity. I drove because it was necessary for the life I'd chosen.

I should have stayed home today, but when I'd left for Dark Gables earlier this afternoon, there'd been manageable wind. It was almost always windy in Foxglove Corners. Today the weather had changed abruptly, the temperature dropping as the wind gained strength.

The car came out of nowhere. It was behind me, racing toward me, a splash of garish yellow. Its lights were off and it was traveling too fast for the curves and the condition of the road. The horn blasted. It was too close to me. Too close…

That fool driver was going to try to pass me!

Well, let him. It would be his funeral.

He did, all the time leaning on the horn and leaving only an inch, if that, between his car and mine.

In that instant I saw his face clearly in the fading light. He had a long black mustache, and his eyes blazed with recognition.

Oh, no. Not him. Not now.

A feeling of *déjà vu* hit me with the suddenness of a lightning bolt.

Something like this had happened before.

To Charlotte and to me.

Forty

He sped past the Focus and disappeared around the next curve. I listened for a telltale crash but heard only the howling wind. Was I safe now?

Possibly, but I didn't relax. It wasn't like the man to drive away from a perceived grievance.

Remember the freeway.

I was currently traveling through an isolated section of Spruce Road, but if I remembered correctly, I should be near a tiny town with the odd name of Dingle. It consisted of a few blocks of houses, a general store, and a small church, Saint Irmagard.

There would be people in Dingle. If I were lucky, a few of the population would be out and about. In every one of the scenarios that played through my mind, someone came forward to help me.

I drove on, watching for Dingle Road, and thinking. I'd obviously annoyed Black Beard by driving slowly on a little-traveled road. As I'd angered him on the freeway when he claimed I'd cut him off. As I must have enraged him when I aimed a burst of *Halt!* directly into his eyes.

That I was still alive was a miracle, given the man's track record.

He might have seen my license plate number, in which case he might be able to find me.

Or he could be waiting on some lonely by-road to intercept me. Or parked beyond the next curve.

None of that happened.

I drove past Dingle. A blue truck lurched toward me from the opposite direction, then another Ford, an older dull blue model passed. Nowhere in the dim landscape did I see a garish yellow car. Again, I'd dodged a bullet.

But my heartbeat never slowed until I turned on Jonquil Lane. Unmolested. Safe. Home.

~ * ~

Trust a collie to make everything better. In my home, make that seven collies.

I stood in the vestibule shaking, battling an unreasonable urge to burst into tears. I couldn't summon the energy to take off my raincoat.

Misty whined and nudged me, her bright eyes full of questions. Halley pushed past her, asserting her place as leader of the pack—the first collie in the house—and thrust her long nose in my hand.

"Good girl," I said. "It's all right. I'm all right."

Even if I wasn't.

I had to keep telling myself that I was safe with seven sharp-toothed collies to protect me. I'd have another cup of tea and let the fright drain out of my memory.

Ha! That wouldn't happen anytime soon. And I couldn't stay barricaded in the house.

It's over, I thought. *Go on with the day. Turn on the haunted TV? Not today. I wanted my real-life husband, not a cowboy lookalike.*

~ * ~

Having a caring audience went a long way to dispelling my lingering fright.

Crane was incredulous. "All the cops in Foxglove Corners are on the lookout for this guy, and you keep running into him."

"So do I," Julia reminded him.

"Every time I've met up with him, he's driving a different car," I said.

"With different license plates." Crane locked his gun in its cabinet, which reminded me of my own gun. It would be more effective than *Halt!* which I still carried in my purse.

"He definitely lives in the area," Julia said. "You'd think somebody would see him stopping for gas, buying groceries, or eating in a restaurant. Somewhere."

"Or driving on the freeway," I added.

"We're the only ones looking for him," Crane pointed out.

"I've seen several men with beards," Julia said. "It's not unusual for this time of year."

"Around Halloween, you mean?"

"No, hunting season. They think they look manly, all rugged and macho."

Crane ignored that. "Beyond a certain point, Spruce Road has dangerous curves and woods and lakes."

"That describes most of Foxglove Corners," I said. "Spruce Road is the best route to Lucy's house. Who'd think a pleasant afternoon would end in terror?"

"Bad things can happen anywhere, at any time," Crane reminded me.

He was right, and the same held true for him. For any law enforcer, a run-of-the-mill encounter or often a traffic stop could result in a senseless shooting. It had happened to Crane once. I tried not to think that it could happen again.

Well, I thought. *It won't happen here in our home. We're safe.*

~ * ~

The strident ringing of the landline disrupted the peace of our evening.

I let my book fall to the floor and rushed to the kitchen. Almost everyone used their cell phones these days. I'd almost forgotten what the landline sounded like, or the weight of the receiver in my hand.

"Hello," said an unknown voice. "I'd like to speak to Jennet Ferguson."

"This is Jennet."

"Finally. I've been trying to reach you. My name is Stacia EmmalynWinters." As she paused, I reviewed my acquaintances with these names. Could my caller be one of my students named Stacia?

"We've never met, but Eustacia Stirling was my great-aunt," she said. "I was talking to Mrs. Bell about the recent estate sale."

Of course. Eustacia—Stacia. The heir who'd been on vacation.

"I'm calling because I understand you bought my aunt's old television set at the estate sale," she said.

I reached for a pen and a pad of paper in case I was about to hear important information. I wondered if I should mention the TV's unique properties. No, it would be better to let Ms. Winters speak.

"I'm curious," she said. "Is the set working?"

"Yes. All three channels." I almost added 'with a vengeance.'

"Well, it *is* an antique." Another pause. "Did you find anything unusual about it?"

"Only its propensity for airing a movie in parts instead of regular programming."

"Ah," she said. "A movie. Not a concert. The TV used to have a fondness for *Peter, Paul, and Mary in Concert.*"

"Sometimes, the programs are contemporary," I added. "But I'm hooked on that movie. I want to know how it ends."

"You have a most unusual TV," Stacia said. "Aunt Eustacia was fascinated by it—at first. Then it frightened her. She thought it was cursed."

"I've been thinking it's haunted."

"Something's wrong with it," she said. "I tried to find out everything I could about it to set my aunt's mind at ease."

"What did you learn?"

"A few commonplace facts and a few bizarre ones. Actually, the television wasn't supposed to be included in the sale. I planned to take it, but what's done is done. Even so, I can't let go of this mystery. Could we get together sometime to share experiences?"

If Stacia hadn't suggested a meeting, I would have.

"I'd like that," I said, "but I'm a teacher. My school is an hour away from Foxglove Corners."

"That's all right. How about late Tuesday afternoon? Do you know where the Foxglove Corners Historical Society is located?"

"Vaguely."

"I'll give you directions and the address. We're closed to the public for repainting, but we can meet in my office. It'll be more private."

And privacy was desirable for two people who were going to discuss a ghostly phenomenon.

I jotted down the directions and said I'd see her on Tuesday.

I stepped over Halley, who showed no inclination to move out of my way. Crane and Julia were sitting quietly in the living room where I'd left them. Crane was still reading the *Banner*, and Julia was studying her Composition textbook for her class, pen in hand.

Crane looked up. "Bad news, honey?"

"Just the opposite. My caller was Stacia Winters, Eustacia Stirling's great-niece."

Julia closed her book. "Who's that?"

"Eustacia Stirling was the last owner of my television set."

As soon as I'd told them what she'd said, Julia jumped up. "Let's turn it on now."

"There's no storm," I said. "No lightning, and I'm not alone."

"It can't hurt." Crane rose. "I'll do it."

He turned the 'on' button, and a pair of glamorous skeletons in flashy transparent evening attire danced across a stage that would have made Dracula feel at home.

Julia stated the obvious. "The movie isn't on, but this looks good."

"It looks like you'll have to share your mystery with this lady," Crane said.

"That's okay. Maybe she'll have some answers. Besides, if this strangeness continues, I'll begin to fear for my sanity."

I didn't tell him that I'd already done that.

Forty-one

Stacia Winter and I arrived at the Historical Society headquarters at the same time. I couldn't have asked for a more private meeting place. Situated on the outskirts of Foxglove Corners, the old white house sat in an acre of farmland, lonely and silent, with the nearest neighbor at least a mile away.

Stacia was younger than I'd anticipated, knowing she was the niece of Eustacia Stirling. *Grand*-niece, I corrected myself. She wore a vintage denim jacket over a blue polka dot dress, and her dark chestnut hair fell in soft waves just below her shoulders. She carried a leather briefcase over her arm and two tall Starbuck containers in her hands.

"I hope you like coffee," she said. "There's cream and sugar inside."

I took one. "Thanks so much. Black is perfect. It's just what I wanted after a long day at Marston High School."

"I've taken over my aunt's office on the first story," she said, "but I'm still in the process of sorting her papers."

She unlocked the front door, and I followed her through cozy rooms furnished in the style of the house's era. In her spacious office, every bit of wall space was filled with small paintings of local scenery. A smell of fresh paint hung in the air, and a ladder leaned against a door at the end of the hall.

"I taught middle school history," Stacia said. "After two years, I rethought my career, but you have no idea how much I admire teachers."

"Teaching has its moments," I said.

She opened her briefcase and took out a notebook and a sheaf of loose papers. "When Mrs. Bell mentioned that the TV had been sold at the estate sale and the new owner was asking questions, I knew I had to contact you."

"I'm so glad you did," I said.

"Let's start with a weird little detail. A previous owner had the television blessed by a priest, the Reverend George Drake. He's now retired and living in South Carolina."

"That *is* serious." I settled myself in a hardwood chair, while Stacia took her place at the desk.

"It sounds like the owner believed the television was possessed," I added.

Stacia nodded. "My thought exactly. And he or she convinced a priest that it needed blessing. That's why my aunt decided the set was cursed."

Or haunted, I thought.

"Aunt Eustacia told me her new television was unusual, but that I had to see for myself. That first time, it appeared to be just an ordinary TV. I couldn't see what all the fuss was about. She insisted that on three occasions, all she could get was a Peter, Paul, and Mary concert. She used to say that the television was evil and she wanted it gone. In the end, her friend, Lida Ronan, carried it up to the attic."

"I'm convinced the weather determines what it plays," I said. "For me, a lightning bolt brings the movie on. Maybe, way back, it was struck by lightning, and that set the anomaly in motion. It turned the set into a Stephen King monster.

"That's an interesting theory, but if it were true, my aunt never made the connection."

I took a sip of my coffee which was the right temperature for me and delicious, better than the coffee I brewed at home.

"How did you know about the TV being blessed?" I asked.

Stacia rifled through the papers and withdrew a blue sheet torn from the kind of pad that comes in four pastel colors. She handed it to me. "Because of this note."

The few sentences appeared to be hastily written, possibly scrawled under duress.

At my request, Father Drake blessed this television set in an attempt to alter its unnatural behavior. It didn't work.

The note was unsigned.

"It was taped to the side of a cabinet," Stacia said. "Now I have my own information here."

She glanced at her notes. "Aunt Eustacia saw the television at Roland Radio Repair. She wanted a small TV to keep in her bedroom for nights when she couldn't sleep.

"I was lucky enough to meet Mr. Roland. He had retired by then and sold the store. He claimed he didn't notice anything unusual about the set. The first he knew of a problem was when my aunt complained that she couldn't get even one of the three channels. When she turned it on to demonstrate, it showed a modern program."

"Naturally. It's the most perverse bit of electronics in the universe."

"Mr. Roland told me he'd purchased the TV from a man who said he found it in somebody's trash. He didn't usually operate this way, but there was something appealing about the set. He knew he could sell it."

I sipped more coffee and remembered a detail that might be relevant.

"I bought a TV exactly like it in the Green House of Antiques, but so far there's nothing strange about the duplicate."

"I think my aunt's television—now yours—must be the only one like it in existence."

"But why is it like that? A Western movie for me, a concert for your aunt, who knows what else for the owners who came before us? Because of lightning?"

"That's what we have to find out," she said. "I assume that's what you want, too."

"I do—definitely."

Although I also wanted to see the movie in its entirety. If I didn't manage to exorcise the demon that controlled the rogue TV, how would I ever know what happened to Susanna and Luke?

"The trail ends with the unknown person who took the TV out with the trash," Stacia said. "We can guess why he wanted to get rid of it. There's no way to know who he was, and no way to look farther back into its history."

I refused to accept that. When one reaches a dead end, what is there to do but take a few steps backward?

Stacia rose. "Will you let me know if you find out anything else?"

"I will, and you do the same."

All I could do then was go home and wait for the next electrical storm.

~ * ~

On Friday the spirit of Halloween pervaded every corner of Marston High School. The bulletin board in my classroom was covered with information about the Salem witch trials, although we'd passed that point of history in our chronology. In addition, the familiar motif of a witch riding her broomstick across the moon called attention to the theme.

It was going to be a disruptive day. During second period, the Student Council had sold doughnuts, which students were allowed to eat in the classroom on this day only. Now, during fourth hour, National Honor Society members were delivering personal messages and candy to certain lucky students, an event which had already elicited chattering and giggling and the rattling of wrappings.

The spell cast by sugar and secrets would last throughout the day. Enterprising students might also come to class masked although, we could hope, not in costume.

Happy Halloween, I thought as I opened a message addressed to me and accompanied by a chocolate marshmallow ghost.

You're a nice teacher, Mrs. Ferguson. Guess Who. ???

I glanced at my American Lit class and continued taking attendance. Did anyone who sat before me think I was nice?

Not likely. I dropped my message and the ghost into my shoulder bag.

Today's story, *The Outcasts of Poker Flat*, was one of my favorites, although it was sad, and I cringed at outmoded nonsense like 'her sister who had sinned.' For added color, outside the window snowflakes drifted along in the frigid air. As they were light, no one was in danger of being snowed in. In the unlikely event the snow increased, we had plenty of chocolate in the room for sustenance.

I turned my back on the class—always a risky move—to write a few background notes on the chalkboard. A shrill cry erupted at the back of the room. Jocelyn Masters stormed out of the room, her long blonde hair flapping in the air like wings. She took her purse but left her books on the desk.

"Jocelyn…"

But she slammed the door.

I opened it and looked for her in the hall. In seconds she had disappeared, and I couldn't leave the class unattended to follow her.

"What happened?" I demanded.

The two boys, Will and Rob, sitting closest to Jocelyn, looked like innocence personified, and the girl, Meghan, was turning pages in her textbook. I'd noticed that the four young people appeared to be the best of friends, often talking and laughing together during class when they should have been reading.

"Did somebody say something to Jocelyn?" I asked.

"She just got up and left," Will said.

"I saw that. Why?"

Will shrugged. "Girls."

"She wasn't feeling well, Mrs. Ferguson," Meghan said.

In that case, there was something I could do.

"Start reading the story," I said, and wrote a brief notice to the office, stating the time Jocelyn had left the classroom and the lack of an apparent reason. That would cover me in case Jocelyn left the building without permission.

"Now," I said. "When Mr. John Oakhurst steps out on the street of Poker Flat, what did he notice?"

Three hands waved in the air.

"Guys playing poker in the snow."

"Nothing."

"A lynch mob."

"Let's go back to paragraph one," I said.

I glanced at the clock. Forty-five more minutes of class. Forty-five minutes until lunch. Forty-five minutes with my favorite author and an uninterested class.

I thought of snow and being trapped and the chocolate marshmallow ghost in my purse—and started reading.

Forty-two

We plowed our way through *The Outcasts of Poker Flat* to the bitter end, as, one by one, the outcasts faced their destiny.

Joyce, one of the more emotional members of the class, peered into her compact mirror and wiped her eyes.

"Why did it end like that?" she demanded. "Why couldn't they be saved?"

"Get real, Joyce," Rob said. "Who would save them?"

Outside the school, in twenty-first century Michigan, it was snowing, still lightly, providing a perfect background for our story.

"People can get snowed in and starve to death even today," I said. "Sometimes they can't be saved."

"Not in Oakpoint, though." That was Rob, always wanting the last word. "You can always walk to a grocery store."

"I agree. It could happen in an isolated cabin up north or out west, in the mountains, though."

Five minutes before the bell rang, a shadow fell across the doorway. The new assistant principal, tall, intimidating Mr. Boski, said, "Excuse me, Mrs. Ferguson. Mr. Holloway, come with me."

"Who, me?" Will looked around, as if one of his classmates had the answer. "What'd I do?"

Mr. Boski glared at him. "Yes, you. Take your books with you."

With a sullen face, Will obeyed.

A hush fell over the class. When the bell rang, the usually rowdy group left the room in a near-decorous manner. The appearance of an administrator had that effect.

Later, as Leonora and I ate our sandwiches in her room, I described Jocelyn's dramatic exit.

"I can't imagine what that was about," I said.

"A lovers' quarrel?"

"Could be."

"Maybe she got a mean Halloween message from somebody," Leonora said.

That could happen, although sellers were cautioned to read the messages carefully to weed out any hint of insult or worse. But kids could be crafty and subtle, and not every exemplary student was above reproach.

Jocelyn's friend, Meghan, had taken Jocelyn's belongings, including the message and a chocolate pumpkin, with her. I had planned to question Meghan privately, but she made a dramatic exit of her own, practically the first one out of the door.

"I'm sure I'll find out eventually," I said.

Later that day, in my conference period, I looked up from grading papers to see Mr. Boski at my door again. This couldn't be good.

"The Holloway boy has been bullying Jocelyn," he said without preamble. "She asked to be transferred out of your class."

Nothing could have surprised me more.

"But they seemed like such good friends," I said, recalling all the times I'd seen them engaged in flirtatious banter and walking down the hall, hand in hand.

"I don't know about that, but he's been sexually harassing her. If she can't get a transfer, she wants you to change her seat."

And that would stop the harassment? Well, it would help if they weren't sitting close to each other.

"I had a talk with him," Mr. Boski said. "He's not to have any contact with Jocelyn in this school. If there's another incident, he's getting suspended. That won't sit well with Coach Barrett."

Will was on the varsity football team, one of their star players, I understood. He might have more to worry about than his grade point average.

"I'll move Jocelyn to the front of the room and keep an eye on Will," I said.

"Do that."

In the interest of being proactive, I added, "What about the other girl, Meghan?"

"I talked to her, too. Will hasn't been bothering her. Just Jocelyn."

Of all the problems I'd encountered in this second class from hell, harassment was one I had never anticipated. If Will and Jocelyn had been boyfriend and girlfriend at one time, their romance had obviously degenerated into something quite different.

"Thanks for letting me know," I said.

As if he'd do anything else.

When I was alone, I reflected on what had happened and might have happened on past occasions.

Sexual harassment was rampant, constantly in the news, and alive and well in my class where every student had a right to feel safe. How sad that Will had tarnished the happy spirit of Halloween Message Day with his behavior.

What could I do now? Give them a lecture on harassment and bullying? That would be helpful, but another idea came to me almost immediately. I would introduce *All Summer in a Day* into our course work, even though that it was a modern story and we were in the nineteenth century in our survey.

Like my World Lit students, they couldn't possibly miss its lesson, and we could follow up Bradbury's theme with discussion and writing.

~ * ~

I couldn't find my peaked witch's hat, but the rest of my costume was in the bedroom, in one drawer or another.

I didn't need a hat. I had my black midi-dress, a crystal cat pin, an onyx dinner ring, and black fingernail polish. I also had a shade of lipstick so dark a shade of red, it was almost black. But the hat would have been a nice touch.

Crane wouldn't see me in my witch's costume unless he stopped at the library after his shift.

"That's okay," he'd said this morning after breakfast. "Leave it on till I come home. We'll have our own Halloween party."

Julia was going with me. Among her possessions was a diamond tiara. When I asked her how she'd gotten it, she only said that it was a present. She intended to leave her long golden hair down and wear a pink dress with a sequined bodice.

"If anyone asks, I'm a princess," she said.

"You'll look like one." We'd be quite a contrast, two sisters, one a princess and one a witch. "This is going to be more fun than renting a costume."

Only when I was dressed, I looked like I did every day, although I rarely wore black and didn't care for dramatic makeup.

Misty had been lying in the doorway observing me while I dressed. When I sprayed Joy perfume on my wrists, she began to growl softly.

"What?"

I stared at her, remembering another time she'd objected to a scent I wore. It was the bottle of Ann Haviland's Wood Violet toilet water from the dime store in the ghost town known to us at the time as Forever.

There was nothing unique or threatening about Joy, nothing to cause a dog to growl. Of course Misty wasn't just any dog. She was my psychic collie.

I crossed the room to pet her, and she nudged my arm with a whimper.

Don't go. Stay with us.

What an inauspicious beginning to a Halloween party! I tried not to read anything sinister into her behavior. Maybe Misty just didn't like seeing me in black.

Forty-three

We drove to the library on a magical white road that glistened in the October moonlight. Snow clung to the branches, held there by the cold temperature. It was easy to think that one could stop the car and scoop up a handful of diamonds embedded in the ground cover.

"What a beautiful night!" Julia said. "But it looks more like Christmas Eve than Halloween."

A sudden wave of euphoria washed over me, bringing along with it an uncharacteristic bit of giddiness.

"At a time like this, I feel like I could ride my broomstick across the moon," I said.

"You didn't bring a broom," Julia pointed out.

"No, I didn't. Maybe Miss Eidt has one in her office."

Julia laughed. "She might at that. Jennet, If you could fly anywhere in the world, where would you go?"

"Wherever I could make the most mischief," I said.

"How unlike you, Jennet."

"Well, I'm a witch for the night."

The drive to the Corners was short but marginally hazardous as even a dusting of snow could turn a road into a skating rink. But, to Julia's chagrin, we made it without incident. She thought I was driving too fast.

Fairy lights hung from the lower branches of the library's trees, and it seemed as if Miss Eidt had turned on every lamp inside the old white Victorian and lit every candle. She had banned overhead lights for the party, which was ideal for atmosphere but possibly not so conducive to safety.

Blackberry, wearing a large orange ribbon around her neck, sat on the single wicker chair left on the porch for the winter, giving us her cold, jewel-eyed stare. From within, an eerie sound of agonized wind drifted out into the night. Miss Eidt had found her *Ghostly Sounds of Halloween* CD.

She was waiting in the entrance to welcome her guests, dressed as the Queen of Hearts and wearing a prodigious amount of Valentine jewelry. At her side, Debby was a demure Alice in Wonderland in blue and white with a long straight blonde wig.

"Jennet and Julia," Miss Eidt said, "welcome to Fantasyland. That's the name of the library tonight. Go and mingle. Sample our buffet. Lucy Hazen is in the Gothic Nook reading passages from her scariest books. Have a ball."

"At ten-thirty she'll be reading tea leaves. It'll be first come, first served," Debby added. "You won't want to miss that."

The mighty wind blew in a wolf howl that might have originated in the heart of the frozen north. I shivered, feeling as if, with one touch, my body had just been encased in ice.

"Good grief," Miss Eidt said. "What's that? Jennet, did you bring one of your pretty collies to the party?"

"I'm sure they're all at home," I said.

But were they?

I remembered Misty growling at the scent of Joy and following me anxiously as I went downstairs. But surely she was home. I'd said goodbye to each of my dogs in the kitchen before I left. That included Misty.

Don't be silly, I told myself. *It's the CD, not a dog.*

I followed Julia to a buffet table spread with desserts, picked up a Halloween-decorated paper plate, and eyed the selections.

"Look!" Julia said. "It's a Yule Log."

Behind us somebody said, "It's a *Halloween* Log. I made it."

The voice was familiar; so was the face. I'd met Edwina Endicott several times at the library, always browsing in the Supernatural section. Edwina was a self-proclaimed ghost hunter, the one other person who had seen the spirit of Violet Randall traveling on Huron Court with her collie. Or so she claimed. Edwina was also a little unhinged.

On the other hand, why doubt her? I knew Violet haunted that insidious road. Perhaps she had shown herself to Edwina.

"I'm a ghost," Edwina announced.

Her costume was a long white dress with wide, flapping sleeves. It looked like an exquisitely embroidered nightgown.

"You look—er—ghostly," I said.

Julia appeared to be captivated by Edwina's culinary creation. "It looks like a Yule Log to me."

"It's a Halloween Log," Edwina insisted. "Observe the orange icing and the chocolate bats on top."

She turned to me. "The ghosts of Foxglove Corners have been quiet lately, but maybe they'll come out tonight. This is their night, you know. That's why I decided to come as a ghost. To make them feel welcome."

I didn't agree with Edwina about the lessening of psychic energy in Foxglove Corners. I could tell her about the ghost dog who cried inconsolably in the untenanted house where she'd died. But that was a ghost I didn't want to share with her. In any event, it was futile to argue with Edwina about supernatural matters.

"Oh, I see someone I know," she announced and without another word dashed off into the milling crowd.

"Just look at all these gorgeous costumes!" Julia stepped aside to make way for a clown who was descending on the buffet. "This all reminds me of *The Masque of the Red Death*."

"Poe's story had a gruesome end, if you'll recall," I said.

"The only one wearing red tonight is Miss Eidt with all those Valentines pinned to her dress, and she certainly isn't the Red Death."

I chose a large gingerbread cookie shaped like a cat and bit into it. "Mm. Delicious."

"Let's mingle," Julia said. "Meet you back at the buffet in a half hour and we'll compare notes."

A scream pierced through the hum of party conversation, bringing the happy noise to a halt. Several people looked nervously at the dark between the stacks.

"What now?" Julia asked. "Is murder being committed in the library?"

Debby, adding cookies to the dessert carousel, overheard us. "It's Miss Eidt's CD. I told her that scream was going to scare people. She thinks it's perfect."

"It may be perfect for the party, but not for your guests' nerves," I said.

It seemed I could still hear the scream's echo.

~ * ~

Brent Fowler, the perennial huntsman, and his medieval lady, Annica, swept through the front door in a flurry of snowflakes. Near the entrance, heads turned. People gave the attractive red-haired couple admiring glances.

"You're a fantastic Huntsman, Brent," I said. "And Annica, you look beautiful. Green really is your color."

Brent gave me an outrageous wink and put his arm around Annica. "Look what I caught in my trap."

Annica tossed her head. "You wish."

I squelched a desire to laugh. Annica sounded flippant, but she was dead serious.

Dead?

Wrong word choice.

"Who screamed a minute ago?" Brent asked. "If there's trouble…"

"It's just one of the sounds on Miss Eidt's CD."

"Oh ho! Canned terror."

"It sounds like someone's being tortured," Annica said. "Are we going to find a mutilated corpse in a corner?"

"I doubt it."

The CD was giving us music now, a haunting tune that conjured images of isolated graveyards and ghostly shrieks.

Brent peered through the milling revelers. "What do they have at the buffet?"

"Lots of good stuff and a Halloween log."

"What? They're serving wood?"

"It's a cake shaped like a log," Annica said. "You'll love it."

"Have you sampled it, Jennet?" he asked, noticing the crumpled napkin in my hand.

"It's too rich for me."

Brent took Annica's hand. "Let's check it out. See you later, Jennet."

I glanced at my watch. Only ten minutes had gone by. I had time to visit Lucy in the Gothic Nook. I was eager to see whether she was wearing her signature black with gold chains or a costume.

Forty-four

As I crossed the library to the candlelit area where the stacks began, I saw another woman wearing my dress. Of course there were thousands of black mini-dresses in existence, but it seemed that the unknown wearer had deliberately imitated me, even copying my hair color and style with the long bangs. From a distance I could tell her fingernails were painted black.

Did she fancy herself a sister witch?

Well, I hadn't taken pains to put together an original Halloween costume. Obviously neither had she. At least she didn't have a crystal cat pin.

I stole a last quick glance at her and the man who stood behind a file cabinet draped in cobwebs. He was watching her intently. The man was a tall and burly pirate, complete with sword. He was masked and his beard was obviously fake. It looked like black yarn that had been left out in the rain.

The woman didn't appear to have noticed me or the man. I sailed past them to the Gothic Nook where Lucy presided over a small twig table set with plain white teacups, an electric teapot, and an orange pillar candle.

Lucy had forsaken her customary black attire in favor of a purple, red, green, and gold skirt with a scarlet blouse. Chains, hoop earrings, and bracelets, all gold, completed her look.

She pushed back a strand of long black hair. "Am I a credible gypsy?" she asked.

"I'm not sure what a real gypsy looks like," I said. "I've never seen one, but your setup here looks authentic enough."

"I had a large crowd for my readings from *Devilwish*," she said. "As soon as I finished, it all evaporated."

"They'll be back for your next act."

"I'm sure they will. The night is young. In the meantime, you can be the first."

She poured my tea quickly, and I drank it as fast as I could as it was still quite hot. When I was through, I let the excess liquid drain into the saucer and turned the cup slowly toward myself three times, letting the patterns form.

"I'll have to tell people how to do that over and over tonight," she said as I handed her my cup.

I wasn't prepared for her frown. She set the cup down and picked it up again, perusing the formations thoughtfully. Then she looked at me.

"What's wrong?" I asked.

"I'm not sure, but something is brewing."

"Something? What? You're scaring me."

"I wish I could be more specific. I can't." She reached across the table and laid her hand on mine. Her touch was warm. I imagined her transferring a modicum of energy to me.

"I only mean to warn you," she said. "It's coming. It'll be here soon."

It?

I took a deep breath. "I hope you don't say something like this to your other customers. You'll have people running out of the library."

"This message is for you only, Jennet. Beware. What's that saying you like so well? Forewarned is…"

"Forearmed," I said.

I heard a tapping of heels behind me on the hardwood floor. Lucy had another customer, and I didn't want to hear any more gloom and doom.

I would never let Lucy know that her reading had upset me. I'd been expecting a familiar fortune: a snake near my home, an initial *V*, three little dots indicating that my wish would be granted. What I'd received instead was this ambiguous warning.

You don't have to believe everything Lucy tells you.

I ordered my heart to stop pounding and my voice not to tremble. "Thank you for the reading, Lucy," I said. "I'll stop by a little later."

With a smile at the next in line, a plump lady dressed as an ear of corn, and the person waiting behind her, I left the Gothic Nook to Lucy and her dark visions.

~ * ~

Brent held a sugar cookie witch with orange sprinkles in his hand. "Hey, Jennet, that log *was* good. Do you know how to make one?"

"It's hard," I said. "I could try—if Annica will help me."

Annica cast a flirtatious look at Brent. "Sure thing."

"I went back for another slice, and it was all gone," Brent said.

"Annica and I will get together in the next day or so and bake one for you," I promised.

And, as an afterthought, we'd better bake another one for Crane because Brent would probably demolish the entire log.

Good grief, was my beloved husband now an afterthought?

"Annica wants Lucy to read our tea leaves," Brent said. "It's okay for her, but not me. I think it's all poppycock."

"You'd better hurry then. There's a line."

They headed to the Gothic Nook, and I started walking toward the buffet. Miss Eidt had borrowed one of her decoration ideas for the main desk—a large faux clock, its hand frozen at twelve o'clock.

I consulted my watch. It was about time to meet Julia. Not quite, though, and I wasn't hungry enough to visit the buffet again.

I looked through the window that gave the best view of the library's fountain. Like the trees, it wore a garland of fairy lights that turned the snow to a sparkling blanket. The statue cradled a faux bat in her arms. At least I hoped the bat wasn't alive.

How inviting the yard looked, and how lovely the brightly clad revelers were, their images reflected in the glass.

A pair of steely hands gripped my arms and turned me around into a rough embrace. The next instant a hard mouth smashed down on my lips. A rough cloth pressed on my face and throat.

Cloth? No, yarn. A fake beard made of yarn. The pirate who had been watching the other woman in black.

How dare he!

I tried to break loose, to cry out, but he held me in a death grip, keeping his mouth pressed against mine, his face mashed to mine. I couldn't breathe.

The handle of the sword cut into my ribs. I tried again to free myself. It was futile, and the CD was throwing wind gusts and cawings and screams around the library.

Was no one looking our way? Would a casual observer assume we were a pair of lovers overcome with passion?

Dear God, this couldn't be happening to me with over a hundred guests in the library.

I had to break away from this madman who had trapped me and rendered me incapable of speech.

My chance came when he removed one hand to open the library's side door. I wrenched away from him and freed my mouth.

"Help," I shouted. "Somebody, help me…"

The CD screamer drowned out my cry for help. A rush of cold air flew past me, and the next moment we were outside. I slipped on the snow-covered ground, and my abductor yanked me upright.

He spoke. "Go ahead and scream. No one will hear you."

I knew that voice. Knew the man. The hit-and-run driver had found me in the unlikeliest of places—a crowded Halloween party in the library.

"Let me go!" I demanded. "You don't know who you're dealing with. My husband is a deputy sheriff. You won't get away with this."

"Shut up." He dragged me through the garden, past the fountain out of the gate that was purely ornamental and never locked, into a Jeep, and shoved me inside. The next moment he was behind the wheel, starting the vehicle.

This is your chance! Get out now!

I couldn't. He'd locked the door, somehow made it impossible to open.

A tall policeman accompanied by another woman in black—a witch?—crossed behind us, so close the Jeep might have backed into him. I pounded on the window as hard as I could, but they never looked our way.

It was too late. We skidded in the library lot, slid into Park Street, and were off into the night.

Forty-five

He wouldn't talk to me. He wouldn't tell me why he had spirited me out of the library or where he was taking me.

I told him again about my deputy sheriff husband who would be on his trail and about Lieutenant Mac Dalby of the Foxglove Corners Police Department, a personal friend of mine. What I didn't mention was the girl whose death he had caused, and I thought it was prudent not to remind him of the *Halt!* incident.

He drove on and didn't speak. Before long I could no longer estimate the time that had elapsed since we left the library. I couldn't figure out how far we had traveled or what direction he had taken. North, I assumed.

The only sound in the car was the swish of the windshield wipers, clearing away snow that looked and sounded like freezing rain.

He was a careless driver, traveling too fast for roads that were rapidly acquiring a thin veneer of ice. Every time the Jeep slid, I felt certain we were going to crash into a tree, but the Jeep managed to hold the road.

The trees seemed endless. We were driving through dark woods, away from civilization and the people I knew—and Crane.

My arms burned where he'd held me, and I thought my lips must be cut. I reached for my compact…

My purse was gone!

All evening I had carried it over my shoulder on a long gold chain. I had it when I'd stood at the window gazing at the fountain, had up it to the moment the madman had grabbed me and held me in a vise like grip.

And after that?

After that I didn't remember having it. I must have dropped it.

I felt a brief surge of hope. Someone would find the purse on the library floor and know I'd been forcibly separated from it. I would never leave behind my keys, a twenty dollar bill…

My cell phone!

My link to the outside world, the only way to let Crane know what had happened to me. It was in my purse, wherever that was.

What if it had fallen off my shoulder into the snow-blanketed garden? Who would find it then?

I could have made a quick call while the man was distracted. Wouldn't he have to stop for a bathroom break or a sandwich or even a cup of coffee?

It depended on how far he intended to drive.

I halted this runaway train of thought. I couldn't do this without my cell phone.

My head began to ache. It started as it usually did, with a pinprick of pain above my right eye. Again I lamented the loss of my purse with two pain pills in plastic wrap inside.

I needed my purse!

I tried to make the pirate talk. "Aren't you ever going to stop?"

That inspired the longest sentence he'd uttered. "Not till we get to where we're going."

"Where's that?" I asked.

He didn't answer.

I closed my eyes and touched my temple. The pain seemed to be increasing.

Kidnapped by a pirate, I thought. *What a cliché. What an incredible, outrageous turn of events.*

~ * ~

I must have fallen asleep because it seemed that I was sailing on turbulent waters toward a fearsome destination. The ship flew a black flag emblazoned with a leering white skull and crossbones.

My dress was strange, made of a heavy material like brocade and emerald green in color. I was a lady kidnapped by the notorious Elizabethan pirate, Captain Blackbeard.

The wind shrieked. Men shouted. The ship tilted. It was going to sink in the roiling sea. The skull fell off the flag and landed at my feet. Surely this was a dire omen.

Then motion ceased. I was in a vehicle, not a ship. My dress was long and silky, and I wasn't wearing my coat. My head was pounding.

The pirate had brought the Jeep to a stop. He turned off the lights. It had stopped snowing, but icy traces remained on the windshield. By moonlight I saw our destination, a cabin as small as one of those tiny houses that are so popular today. It had two windows, one on either side of the door, and the view beyond them was dark.

The cabin was built in the middle of a rolling field. If there were trees, I couldn't see them.

It reminded me of a sepulcher.

If the man intended to leave me here, I had reached the end of the line.

~ * ~

He opened the passenger's side door. "Get out!"

I didn't move.

He grabbed my wrist and pulled me out of the Jeep, which had suddenly become my safe haven. I stood unsteadily on the ground, my shoes sinking down into at least three inches of snow. Immediately a cold wetness engulfed the hem of my dress.

The man released my arm and stood at the cabin door, struggling with the lock. He didn't have to worry about my trying to escape. There was nowhere to run.

As he pushed the door open, a tremulous voice called out, "Who's there? Whoever you are, help me. Please."

"Get inside," the pirate said to me. He felt along the wall. I heard a faint click, and pale light flooded the interior.

The woman on the cot shrank back to the wall. It was Charlotte—found at last.

~ * ~

He left the light on and went back outside, slamming the door.

"He's gone," Charlotte whispered. "We're safe for a while."

I walked over to her. "Thank God you're alive," I said. "Have you been here all this time?"

"Yes, all these weeks. Did Bronwyn find you?"

"In a way."

"I told her to find Jennet. I kept repeating it, but I didn't think she understood me. I didn't think she could do it."

"What happened?" I asked.

"He followed me when I left my house. I was afraid he'd hurt Bronwyn when she growled at him, but he just shoved her into the car with me."

I could see the picture clearly in my mind. Bronwyn growling, grabbed by the scruff of her neck and hurled into a strange vehicle by a rough hand. But they were together, Charlotte and her collie.

"How did she get free?" I asked.

"She's so fast. One day when he opened the door, she slipped out and ran across the field. He went after her with a gun. I didn't know till I saw you that she got away from him and found you."

It hadn't happened like that, but I didn't tell her.

"Bronwyn is safe with Sue Appleton," I said. "Now, how are *we* going to escape?"

Her hand dropped to her left thigh. "I can't go anywhere. I hurt my leg. I thought it was broken, but I can walk, a little. I don't know where we are," she added. "It's all one big endless field outside."

If only my headache would go away so I could think, so I could force my thoughts into order and make a plan. I sat on the edge of the cot and surveyed our prison. We must be in a hunter's cabin, roughhewn and filled with only utilitarian furniture.

Five other cots with drab old blankets were shoved close together against one wall. A retro kitchen table and four chairs occupied the other. On the table were a loaf of bread and a twelve pack of bottled water. I could see part of another room at the back, separated from the rest by a crude wood partition.

Seeing the direction of my gaze, Charlotte said, "He brings food. That is, a loaf of bread. There's a bathroom in back, a bar of soap, and a roll of toilet paper."

I absorbed this discouraging information. "I can guess why he wants us out of the way, but why didn't he just kill us?"

Not that I wanted that to happen. Even as I stared at the stark interior of the cabin, I was calculating our chances for escape. They were grim to non-existent, hampered by the fact that Charlotte couldn't walk well.

Things like this shouldn't happen in the real world. They were the stuff of the most melodramatic kind of soap opera. The villain catches his victim in a trap and…

…kills them.

No! I refused to let him win this demented game.

Bronwyn had escaped. So would we.

But how?

I pushed every extraneous thought out of my mind and tried to figure out how to do it.

Forty-six

I awoke from a disturbing dream of a sea storm and wild wind determined to fling me into the hungry water.

Why was it so cold in the room? I reached down for the blanket and grabbed a handful of coarse, gritty cloth—and knew immediately where I was. Lying on a hard cot in the pirate's cabin.

My head still hurt. So did the rest of my body. The past hours rushed back to me. The Halloween party, the pirate, the long ride in the dark, the cabin—Charlotte. Still, the timid voice across the room startled me.

"Are you awake, Jennet?"

"Sort of." I rubbed my eyes. "I will be."

I looked at her. Her face was thinner and drawn, and her eyes were haunted. Although she had apparently slept in her one outfit for several days, her pants didn't look wrinkled. The gray turtleneck sweater must keep her warm. Which reminded me. There was no heat in the cabin. Only a newer model wood burning stove with no wood in it.

It must be freezing outside. Was that lunatic killer hoping we would die here?

I was thankful that my dress had long sleeves and brushed my ankles. If only the material were heavier.

"Are you all right?" Charlotte asked. "I mean, did he hurt you?"

I ran my hands along my arms. “He roughed me up, but I’ll live.” I touched my mouth lightly. “My lips hurt.”

I didn’t mention the kiss. The memory infuriated me.

In truth, I felt miserable. It seemed as if I had actually been a passenger—or captive—on that imperiled ship of my nightmare, fighting the wind for my life. My mouth was dry. Oh, for the luxuries of home: a tooth brush, toothpaste, and clean water. A cup of tea.

“Didn’t he leave any food for us?” I asked.

“Just white bread and water,” she said. “Prisoners’ fare. We’ll share it. Open a bottle of water, Jennet. You’ll feel better if you drink something.”

That was a good idea. I took the bottle back to the cot and drank, trying not to think of whistling teakettles and tea leaves settling at the bottom of one of my cups at home.

Suddenly I knew I would pay any price for a cup of hot tea. I couldn’t stop thinking about it.

“I’m going to use the bathroom,” Charlotte said.

I drained the bottle, and although I didn’t feel any stronger, my mouth was a trifle fresher.

Faint daylight lured me to the closest window. A window to the world outside and freedom. I couldn’t budge it. But through the dirt of countless seasons I could see where I’d landed. Snow-covered acres stretched out to meet the horizon with only a few distant trees to break the monotony. No woods. No lake. A figure on a tall pole that might be a scarecrow overlooked the desolate vista.

Charlotte limped back to the cot and collapsed onto it. She had finger-combed her dark hair, but she still looked ghastly, a pale imitation of the glowing woman I’d known.

And I? I must be a frightful vision. A genuine witch leftover from a Halloween gala.

It’s the first of November, I thought. *A new month, an inauspicious beginning.*

What was Crane doing now? He would have known about my disappearance last night. I attempted to reconstruct the scene at the library. Julia must have panicked when she realized I wasn't anywhere in the library. Brent and Annica, Miss Eidt, and Lucy would have rallied around her. One of them had contacted Crane.

Would he think to call the school? For a moment I couldn't remember what day it was. Saturday? He'd have to call them on Monday.

If I were still missing on Monday.

And my dogs. What would they think? Did my psychic collie, Misty, know what had happened to me?

My purse, assuming somebody had found it, wouldn't tell the police where I'd gone, only that I'd gone.

Almost everybody was in costume or masked, which would complicate attempts to find me. As for the other woman in black who slightly resembled me, had one of my friends seen her from a distance and assumed he was looking at me? The whole night was a mishmash of confusion.

I realized that Charlotte was talking to me.

"I thought about breaking a window and just walking away. Then I knew I wasn't able to walk well. I couldn't even climb out of the window. Besides, where would I go? I don't know where we are or if there's a town nearby. But now that you're here, we have a real chance to get away."

Her faith in me was touching, if sadly misplaced. I could look for something to break the old glass; I could walk away from the cabin. Then what? Eventually I'd come to a house or a town. But now that I knew Charlotte was here, I wouldn't leave her.

"We're somewhere up north," I said. "This must be a hunter's cabin. It certainly isn't somebody's home."

Charlotte nodded. "There has to be a road nearby. There'll be cars and people. Someone would stop… If you can walk to it."

Possible scenarios ran through my mind. "I think our best bet is to wait for him to come back and maybe overpower him. Or outwit him. After all, there are two of us, and he can't be very bright. Does he come every day?"

"He was here last night. We might be alone for a whole day. And another night."

"That gives us plenty of time to plan. And to search. Maybe there's something in the cabin we can use."

"We need more to eat than a loaf of bread now that there's two of us," Charlotte said. "Or maybe he won't care."

I thought of bread, a loaf shared between two people, then about warm toast. Well, it was better than nothing.

"My guess is that he doesn't care," I said.

~ * ~

I searched the cabin. It didn't have a kitchen where I might find a knife. There was nothing in the bathroom we could use as a weapon. Clearly we had to rely on our wits. Rather I did. Charlotte had fallen silent. Her brief spark of hope had flickered out.

Well, I had been in seemingly hopeless situations before, and I had struggled my way out of them. It could happen again.

It has to.

"We keep calling him 'he'," I said. "Do you know his name?"

For a moment Charlotte didn't answer. I wondered if she'd heard me. Finally she said, "I don't. I was trying to remember if he told me at the accident. I don't think he did. Why would he if he was planning to drive away?"

"I have a dozen names for him," I said. "I'll go with the pirate."

"Last night I didn't recognize him at first."

"We were at a Halloween party at the library. He wore a mask, and that beard was fake. He must have shaved off the real one."

She sighed. "What will we do, Jennet?"

She was in desperate need of cheer.

"I had a run-in with him on the freeway," I said. "He followed me when I exited and forced me to stop my car. I had a can of *Halt!* in my purse, and I aimed it right for his eyes."

"Good! I wish I could have seen that."

"I wish I had that can with me now."

I looked at my watch. Eight-thirty. It was going to be a long day. Maybe the longest day of my life.

~ * ~

Charlotte was asleep, which was as good a way as any to escape the grim reality that had become our lives. Unless, of course, nightmares invaded your sleep.

I had time to think about the villains I'd confronted in the past. The first one came along during my first year in Foxglove Corners. I'd surprised her by throwing a bowl of salad in her face. Then the vile dognapper, Al Grimes, cornered me in my own home. I had smashed his head like a pumpkin with my rolling pin when the phantom Christmas tree distracted him.

Well, I didn't have a bowl of salad or a rolling pin now.

Other times supernatural manifestations had come to my aid. Unfortunately no ghosts would come to my aid today. I'd managed to live for a time in Foxglove Corners without encountering any ghostly phenomena.

Not true, my mind insisted. *What about the haunted television set?*

Yes, there was that, but it certainly couldn't help me now.

Forty-seven

At noon Charlotte was still sleeping. I imagined this was how she had coped with her long imprisonment. As for myself, I was wide awake, my mind spinning with ideas, none of which were feasible when examined in the light of day.

I could use a little ghostly intervention and a little food. Unfortunately the ghosts failed to materialize, and the food was unappealing. I hadn't eaten since last night when I never dreamed that a gingerbread cookie would have to sustain me indefinitely.

Also, exercise was essential lest I become as weak as Charlotte. But how was that possible? I'd already walked around the cabin several times. The thought of doing so again made me ill.

I ate a slice of bread, breaking it into small pieces to make it last as long as possible, and drank half a bottle of tepid water. As Charlotte had said, prisoners' fare.

When I finished my pathetic breakfast, I tried the door—and almost fainted when it opened. Why hadn't our captor locked us in? Was he that sure of our inability to escape from the cabin? Or that stupid?

No matter. Now I could go outside and explore. Perhaps I'd see something other than endless fields. Maybe a road.

I stepped outside into a blast of icy air. My mind was in such a muddle I didn't realize I didn't have a coat. My high heeled shoes, meant for evening wear, sank down in snow that called for tall boots.

Instantly my face and fingers began to burn. I ignored them and surveyed the vista I'd already seen from inside. Nothing had changed. I was looking at a field that seemed to go on into infinity.

Either it had snowed during the night or the wind had blown the snow into new locations. I could barely detect the impression made by the heavy Jeep or the tire tracks leading out to the road that must exist beyond my range of vision.

One minute, I thought. *I'll just stay outside for one minute, walk around the cabin, and go right back inside.*

Maybe the view from the back would be more promising. It was the same, but… Behind the cabin I saw a stack of logs most likely cut for the wood burning stove. Next to the wood pile, a red tool handle rose from a mound of snow that had formed around it.

If only…

It was! An axe. Heavy, wet, and lethal.

I had no need to look further. I had found my weapon.

~ * ~

"The fool left the door unlocked and an axe in the back."

Charlotte rose slowly to a sitting position. She was groggy, slow to join the waking world. "I'm so cold," she wailed. Then, "What did you say? What's that you have?"

"An axe. I was able to go outside. I found a wood pile and this axe."

"Then we can build a fire. Oh, thank God."

"Not without matches. But now I know what we'll do."

"To get out of here?"

"I hope so. He's going to come back, isn't he?"

"He usually does."

"Then listen. I suspected he wasn't very bright. Now I know it. There are two of us. We can take him down."

"But he has a gun."

"That's okay. We won't give him a chance to use it."

My plan had taken form as soon as I'd seen the axe. I knew what we'd do before I reentered the cabin.

"You provide the distraction," I said. "I'll hide the axe where I can get it quickly. Lie on the cot and tell him you're sick. You think you're dying. Anything to get his attention. When his back is turned, I'll hit him hard enough to knock him out."

"But he's so big. He's strong. Can you do it?"

"I have to. I'll do it quickly."

Like I'd hit the dognapper Grimes with a rolling pin. I couldn't afford to miss.

Now we had to wait for him to come. Charlotte, her eyes bright with hope, leaned back against the wall. I sat demurely on the cot with the axe hidden underneath but close at hand and waited.

Crane would be proud of me. I might go down, but I would go down fighting.

~ * ~

He came at the end of the day, carrying a white box that looked like it contained leftovers from his dinner. Charlotte was sitting on her cot, hunched over and holding her stomach.

"Please," she cried. "Help me. I have so much pain. I think it's my appendix."

He flung the box at the table. It landed on the floor. "Saves me the trouble of shooting you."

Her agonized cry almost convinced me the pain was real.

"Might as well dump you out in the snow," he said.

"No… Help me. For the love of God, get me to a hospital."

He bent over her and without a word yanked her to a sitting position. "This is better. The snow is nice and soft."

"Oh, God, I'm dying…"

Now! Be quick!

I grabbed the axe and struck a mighty blow to the back of his head. He fell heavily across Charlotte. Blood spilled out on the cot. He lay still. I imagined I could feel his blood, spraying out to bathe my face.

Dear God, I had killed him. One blow. I'd only meant to knock him out.

God forgive me.

I felt sick. Cold and shaky. Like I was coming apart, like I would end up in little pieces on the dirty floor… I was going to throw up. I swallowed.

Charlotte moaned softly. "Help me get out from under him."

I did. Slowly. Carefully. It wasn't easy. He was as heavy as a boulder and had all but buried Charlotte's lower body. But I managed. Soon she was standing, unsteady and tremulous but free.

But I… I'd killed a human being, an evil one who deserved to die. Still…

I'd killed him.

I don't care I don't care I don't care.

~ * ~

"What are we going to do now?" Charlotte asked, turning away from the fallen man.

"That's a good question."

What should we do? I'd like to tie him up, just in case he wasn't dead, but that was impossible. No one had left a length of rope in the cabin.

"Let me think. We have to leave."

"But he may come to. He'll follow us."

"He's dead," I said. "Can you walk at all, Charlotte?"

"I can do what I have to."

"Then we'll walk until we find a road. Oh, where's my brain? He didn't walk here. He came in his Jeep."

I rushed to the window, and there it was, the vehicle that had brought him to the cabin. Everything had happened so fast, it was probably still warm inside. Warmer than the cabin at any rate.

This was almost too easy. He leaves us untied, leaves the door unlocked, leaves an axe just waiting for someone to use it. Well, he wasn't very bright. That was an understatement. He was stupid.

"Ugh," Charlotte said. She'd picked up the white box and opened it. "Chicken bones, a couple of fried wings, hash browns, all mixed together. His garbage."

"Leave it. Let's look for the keys."

Then we could get out of the cabin. Borrow a cell phone. Let Crane know I was all right.

We could drive away from this unknown place straight to Foxglove Corners. Straight home.

Forty-eight

I found the keys in the pirate's pants pocket, and minutes later we were in the Jeep driving down the makeshift road through the fields. Snow flurries went twirling through the air, and the ground was slippery; but there was nothing in sight to hit.

We passed the scarecrow. Its tattered clothes flapped in the wind as it tried to free itself from the pole.

We must look tattered ourselves, two women wearing worn dresses without winter coats or boots.

"We have to find a police station," I said.

The tale we had to tell seemed fantastic. A kidnapping, imprisonment, a dead body. In our fevered rush to leave the cabin, I didn't think about the dead man. The moment I'd started the Jeep's engine and began driving, the enormity of what I had done crashed into me again.

But I'd done what I had to. Surely the police would see it that way.

Maybe they wouldn't.

Charlotte's thoughts ran along similar lines. We were nearing a town, Greenmill Falls, Population Five Hundred, when she broke her silence. "I don't think we should stop at a police station in one of these one horse towns, Jennet. How do we know they won't lock us up and go back to find the body?"

We didn't, of course, although I thought we looked like credible victims.

"You may be right," I said. "Let's push on to Foxglove Corners and deal with our own police department. We can stop at a gas station for a map and find out where we are. Greenmill Falls? I never heard of it."

Charlotte sighed. "I can't wait to pick up Bronwyn and have my life back again. The long nightmare is finally over."

"That'll all happen," I said, envisioning my first sight of Crane, feeling his arms around me and anticipating collie kisses from my dogs.

However I didn't share Charlotte's vision. For me the nightmare wouldn't be over yet. I'd bludgeoned a man to death.

~ * ~

We entered Greenmill Falls, bought a map with a five dollar bill Charlotte had found in her pocket, and drove on. Incredibly, no one at the gas station had a cell phone we could borrow. As we moved further south, we discovered that the snow had melted, which made our journey easier.

I had a general idea of where we were. We'd be in Foxglove Corners in another couple of hours.

Charlotte peered through the glass, shielding her eyes from the sun with her hand.

"There's something in the road, Jennet. I think it's a deer. You'd better slow down."

I did, but the animal didn't look like a deer to me. It wasn't tall enough, not long enough. Perhaps it was a fawn. We'd just passed a Deer X-ing sign.

"Jennet, it's a dog!" she cried. "A collie. He's going to get run over."

I slowed the Jeep.

"Not by us," I said, prepared to steer around the creature, whatever it was.

"Jennet, it's a collie. It looks just like Bronwyn. Could it be…?"

She broke off, moving her face closer to the glass.

A sable and white collie padded down the middle of the road toward us. By now I was close enough to see what Charlotte saw.

But how could this be? Bronwyn was safe in Foxglove Corners with Sue. She couldn't be in two places at once. The dog in the road had to be another collie who resembled her strongly.

Charlotte knew better.

I stopped the Jeep, and she eased herself down to the road, crying out as she wrenched her leg.

"Bronwyn!"

The collie ran joyfully to her, and Charlotte threw her arms around her. I'd never seen a happier, more excited dog, never saw a tail wag so fast. I wiped the tears from eyes with my hand.

"I know my dog," Charlotte said. "I would know her anywhere."

So would I, even though her coat was muddy with burrs and leaves and heaven know what caught in it. Like the time Brent had found her on Wolf Lake Road.

"This is her collar," Charlotte said. "My poor baby. She's so dirty."

I smiled. "We're not exactly clean ourselves. Look at us."

"This is what happened," she said. "Bronwyn couldn't get one of you to follow her, but she figured she had let our friends know we were still alive. Then she came back for me."

"That could have been," I said. "Who can tell what goes on in a dog's head?"

"But how could she come all this way? She made two trips. It's uncanny."

"Remember *Lassie Come-Home*," I said.

I chose to believe Charlotte's explanation. Bronwyn's sudden appearance was a bright light in the whole dark affair, and now we were on our way home to Foxglove Corners. All together.

~ * ~

We had to find a restaurant. We needed water for Bronwyn—and a hamburger, Charlotte insisted.

"And coffee to go for us," I added. I wasn't hungry, but my throat was dry; and we still had a distance to drive.

In the back of the Jeep Charlotte cradled Bronwyn in her lap, and the exhausted collie soon fell asleep. Charlotte leaned back in the seat and closed her eyes. Her hands never left the fur on Bronwyn's side and neck.

I drove on, counting the miles and wishing I were home with Crane and our collies. It had been a long night and most of a day since our separation, but it seemed more like a month. We'd been taken further north than I'd thought.

The day was fading. I hoped we'd be home before dark.

We made one stop at a roadside diner for water for Bronwyn and coffee for us.

Back on the road, I kept my mind free so that thoughts of home could claim center stage. Misty growling as I sprayed Joy on my wrists. Julia setting her diamond tiara on her golden hair. Crane's promising me a private Halloween party, Brent ordering his Halloween log, never doubting that he'd have it. Lucy telling me to beware of It.

Even then the man in the pirate costume was circulating through the crowd, biding his time.

The man I'd killed.

The hours and the miles passed. Bronwyn stirred in Charlotte's arms and whimpered.

Charlotte opened her eyes. She hadn't been asleep. "That's canine for 'Are we there yet'?"

I reached over to pet Bronwyn.

"Not yet, pretty girl. Soon."

"There's no snow," Charlotte said.

"We're lucky. That Halloween snow was a fluke."

"It won't be long now," Charlotte said.

"Sure."

"I'll have to let Sue know you have Bronwyn," I said. "She must have been frantic when Bronwyn took off."

I wouldn't do it right away, though. First came a stop at the police station; then my reunion with Crane and Julia. That done, I could be with my dogs, have a sandwich with a cup of the hot tea I'd been craving, take a shower, change clothes, call Lucy and Annica and Camille.

So much to do, but I was blessed with the gift of time. I couldn't complain.

Forty-nine

The daylight was almost gone when I turned off Jonquil Lane into my own driveway. At once the barking began, a full-throated clamor that carried beyond the walls of the house and reached all the way out to the Jeep.

My precious collies.

Their faces appeared in the front window, all squished together in a small space. Their bodies were in constant motion as they vied for the best viewing position. One of them broke into a howl.

The house was somber and dimly lit. Its stained glass window caught the last of the sun's rays, a sight that never failed to move me.

My home.

I parked behind Julia's new car and my Ford Focus. I didn't see Crane's Jeep. He'd be home soon, I hoped. And all the while the collies maintained their frantic welcome. They must sense that the driver of the strange vehicle in the driveway was their missing owner. To hear them carry on, you'd think I'd been gone for days.

As I walked to the side door, a strange feeling of unreality came over me. I felt as though I were floating up the walkway, seeing my beloved home through the eyes of a spirit returning home after a long time away. Like a lonely soul suspended between one life and the other, wondering what had changed, what had stayed the same.

But for the grace of God, I would have been a spirit.

I shook off the feeling. I had to knock on the door. Camille had my spare key, but the yellow Victorian was dark.

Knock then, I told myself. *What are you waiting for?*

The simple act increased the barking tenfold.

After what seemed like an eternity, Julia opened the door. She cried out, her hand over her heart. Her face was pale, her beautiful golden blonde hair was limp, and her eyes were bloodshot.

She burst into tears. "Jennet. Oh, Jennet. I was so afraid…"

The dogs swarmed around me with leaping paws, wagging tails, and wet tongues. Misty and Sky were in the lead; they had most likely been lying under the kitchen table. Halley and Candy pushed their way to my side. Gemmy, Raven, and Star were frantic at finding themselves at the outer rim of the circle with Julia.

It was pandemonium. I couldn't move. Neither could Julia.

"What happened to you?" she demanded. "Where were you?"

Over the dogs' incessant yelping, I said, "Kidnapped. It's a long story. I'll tell you everything later. Where's Crane?"

"He and Mac have been looking all over for you ever since Annica found your purse in the snow."

I saw my evening bag lying on the kitchen table. It was closed. My cell phone should be all right.

"Is it okay with you all if I sit down?" I asked the dogs.

They moved, reluctantly, but in the end they were still one pack as solid as a mountain.

I had no choice. I pushed my way through to the table and opened my purse. The cell phone was dry.

I dialed Crane's number, and, after all this time, all these hours, I had to leave him a voice message:

I'm all right, Crane. I'm home. Come home and I'll tell you what happened. Let Mac know. I have to see him. Love you.

There was so much more I wanted to say, but it could wait until we were together.

~ * ~

His kiss was everything I'd dreamed of, all I wanted. He seemed older to me, or perhaps worry had etched new lies at the corners of his eyes. In his arms I felt safe and loved. I never wanted the embrace to end, but we weren't alone.

We sat around the kitchen table drinking coffee, Crane and I, Julia and Mac Dalby. Misty and Halley lay closest to me. Misty kept nudging me with her nose as if to say, *I told you not to go.*

Julia had a box of tissues at her elbow. Periodically she wept new tears.

Mac was as down-to-earth as always. "How could you get yourself mixed up in a murder again, Jennet? You're going to send your husband to an early grave."

"I just went to a Halloween party at the library. That's hardly courting trouble."

"They told me they couldn't find you," Crane said. "You just disappeared without a trace except for your purse." He slammed his cup down on the table. "From now on, I want you to stay home all the time. I won't risk losing you again."

I was touched and chagrined at the same time. Had this latest foray into danger turned Crane into his dictatorial former self?

Julia didn't care for this sentiment. "Really, Crane. You sound like an old-fashioned tyrannical husband. This is the twenty-first century."

"I just went to a Halloween party at the library," I repeated.

As Crane reached for my hand, I realized I hadn't removed the black fingernail polish. "You're always in danger, honey. I've said it before, and I'll say it again. One of these days your luck will run out."

And I would lose everything I loved. Husband, sister, dogs, friends. Home.

"I plan to live a long life with you," I said. "I don't intend to make you a widower any time soon."

If that's what Veronica the Viper is counting on, I added to myself.

Mac cleared his throat. "Let's get back to this hit-and-run driver that snatched you out of the library."

"The man I killed," I said.

"We don't know that."

"The man whose Jeep I stole. We know *that*. It's parked outside."

"Where did he take you?" Mac demanded.

"I have no idea. A cabin somewhere up north."

I'd told him that Charlotte Gray had been his prisoner for weeks, but she was home now with her collie.

"Describe the cabin," Mac said.

I could still see it in my mind. I thought I always would.

"It was a small hunter's cabin built in an immense field. Maybe ten acres. I thought it was only a couple of hours from Foxglove Corners, but it was farther. There was a scarecrow on a pole and a wood pile in the back—and a body inside."

"Can you give me the name of a road?"

I hated to admit that I couldn't. "I was in such a state I didn't notice. All I wanted was to get away. It was near a little town called Greenmill Falls."

"I'll find it," he said, "and when we find him, we'll have our killer."

"I hope he's still there," I said.

Because if he wasn't, if by chance he wasn't dead, I'd have my enemy out there again. I'd done him more harm this time than I had with the *Halt!*

Mac had finished his second cup of coffee. Time was running out. I had to ask the question that had been tormenting me.

"Mac… Will I have to go to trial for killing him?"

"Let's not get ahead of ourselves," he said, rising abruptly. "Time to call it a night. Joanna has a special dinner waiting."

Crane walked him to the door.

I looked at Julia. "He didn't say no."

I felt a desperate need to touch a collie. I reached down to stroke the fur around Misty's neck and tried to feel better. I didn't.

"Julia, I'm going to be charged with murder."

"No you won't," she said. "It was clearly self-defense."

~ * ~

Julia yawned. "Well, goodnight, you two. I'm off to bed."

"It's eight o'clock," I pointed out.

"Well, it's been a long, tiring day. I'm worn out."

She went upstairs, followed by Gemmy and Star, leaving Crane and me alone. We sat on the sofa watching the fire, not speaking. Crane's arm rested heavily on my shoulder. Sometimes there is no need for words.

The dogs had chosen their favorite places and lay on their sides, drowsing, or just observing the goings-on. The fire crackled and flames danced, sending out warmth to banish the deadly chill that had settled around my heart.

Crane said, "It's going to be all right, honey. Whether the man lives or dies, you didn't do anything wrong. You saved two lives today. I don't doubt he'd have killed you and Charlotte eventually."

I believed him, and not just because I wanted to.

Fifty

Early Sunday morning, Camille and Gilbert crossed the lane to visit me. Their hands were full. Camille brought a baked ham, and Gilbert carried cornbread and a pound cake. All of Crane's and my favorites.

I was still in my nightgown, alone with the dogs. Julia was asleep, and Crane was on his shift.

When I opened the door, I didn't see the Jeep. Good. Another reminder of that terrible time gone.

"I don't want you to worry about cooking," Camille said. "Just rest and get your strength back."

"And as soon as you do, we want to hear everything," Gilbert added with a smile that reminded me so much of Crane it was painful. Gilbert resembled his nephew, Crane, in his features and in his voice with its light southern accent.

Camille took another box from Gilbert. "Don't forget you have school tomorrow, Jennet. I baked you a batch of pineapple-nut cookies."

Camille believed that good food, muffins, and cookies were the solution to all of life's problems. Even the one I currently faced. Their love and care surrounded me. I was going to be all right.

Camille took charge of the coffeemaker while Gilbert sat in the rocker with half of our pack at his feet while the other half stayed in the kitchen where the food was.

"Now," Gilbert said, "how did that kidnapper get you out of the library with no one noticing?"

"Mac told me his name," I said. "It's Ryland Anders. He calls himself Ry."

I didn't have to call him the hit and run killer or the pirate anymore.

"Miss Eidt told us there were over two hundred people at the party, although not at the same time," Gilbert said. "I don't see how he pulled it off."

"We were all in costume," I said. "Well, most of us. If anyone noticed us, they'd think we were acting in a scene: a pirate kidnapping a lady."

I imagined I would tell my story over and over again in the coming days. Eventually I hoped I'd be able to talk about it without being overcome by emotion.

I said, "I was looking out the window at the statue in the fountain. It had a fake bat in its arms. He came up behind me and…"

Every time I thought of Anders, in his pirate costume, forcing his vile kisses on me, I felt like hitting him again.

When I finished, Camille was crying. "That blow might only have stunned him for a second. Then what would you have done?"

"The story would have had a different ending," Gilbert said.

Camille pulled a handkerchief out of her sweater sleeve. "God was with you, Jennet. And to think, while all that was going on, Bronwyn was making her way back to Charlotte. It's incredible."

I'd have to call Charlotte as soon as Camille and Gilbert left, and Annica to thank her for finding my evening bag, and Leonora who had decided to skip the party. I had time to do all of this. Thank God for time.

~ * ~

Around noon Brent arrived with Annica, Lucy, and Miss Eidt. Miss Eidt brought food, too, a dozen doughnuts from the Hometown Bakery, and Brent presented me with a bouquet of yellow roses from all of them.

"Am I still going to get my Halloween log?" he asked.

"Brent!" Annica said. "Have a little discretion."

"It's okay," I said. "Annica and I will bake them as soon as things settle down."

"I wish I'd known what that jerk was up to," Brent said. "I could have stopped him in his tracks."

"None of us could know what Anders intended."

"They ought to ban masks at Halloween parties," Annica said.

Miss Eidt said, "Bringing so many people together in one place is risky. I should never have had that party."

"Don't think that way," I said. "There are risks all over. You can't just stop living. I'm looking forward to next Halloween. I didn't get to enjoy myself this year."

"When you vanished, it brought the party to a stop," Annica said. "We looked in every corner for you, even in the secret room. Then we called Crane and the police. I remembered how much you liked the fountain. That's when I found your purse. Not that it helped."

Julia said, "I waited at the buffet and waited. I thought you'd found a friend and were talking to her. I even saw you once."

"You saw a woman in a black dress who had dark hair and wore it the same way I do," I said.

"So I wasted precious time before it dawned on me that something bad had happened to you."

"It wouldn't have made any difference," I assured her. "By then I was in a Jeep heading north."

I'd never been able to figure out where the cabin was located. It didn't matter. Mac said he was able to trace Anders' address through the Jeep's registration, and Anders' neighbor told him about the cabin.

"All's well that ends well," I said.

I liked that line.

~ * ~

Mac came home with Crane.

"We got Anders," Mac said.

The great joy surging through me took me by surprise. "I didn't kill him?"

"Let's just say you didn't do him any good," Crane said. "He lost a lot of blood and had no way to get to a hospital."

"Because I took his Jeep."

"He took *you*," Crane pointed out.

Mac sat at the oak table and glanced at the coffeemaker. "What are the chances of getting a cup of coffee?"

"I'll get it," Julia said and brought one of our tallest mugs down from the cabinet.

"Is he going to live?" I asked.

"It's touch and go. I'm betting on go. But don't worry. He won't be around to bother you. We're not the only ones who want him. Five years ago, he killed his own kid and tried to blame the mother before leaving town. He's been arrested several times for domestic abuse. He likes to hurt women. Then when he hit that young woman who died, he left the scene. I hope to prove he killed that young medical student who witnessed the crash. I'd say the world is better off without Ryland Anders in it."

"Then I won't go to trial?"

He winked at me. "Not this time, Jennet, but try to stay out of trouble, for all our sakes."

There was Mac's signature condescension. In a way, I'd missed it.

Welcome back, I thought.

~ * ~

After a dinner of Camille's stew and cornbread, after coffee and pound cake in front of the fireplace with Crane and Julia, I called Charlotte.

"How are you settling in?" I asked.

"It's heaven to be home," she said. "I'm just so happy. My poor Bronwyn was starving. She can't get enough to eat. I have a Porterhouse for us tonight. I had too many days on bread and water," she added.

I told her about Anders' capture and his appalling background.

"Then you didn't kill him?"

"Apparently not."

"That's good, isn't it? Let someone else do it. I just want to forget the whole episode. I will, in time."

I agreed with her. Time was, after all, the greatest healer.

"Come over soon and bring Bronwyn," I said. "She can play with my dogs."

A few minutes later, Sue called.

"I was delaying this as long as I could, but you have to know," she said. "Bronwyn got away from me. I opened the door, and she just slipped through. I've tried to find her, but…"

"She's with Charlotte," I said. "I'm sorry I didn't let you know sooner. It's been hectic."

And I told my story again.

~ * ~

Leonora and Jake were my last visitors. By then, I didn't think I would ever drink a cup of coffee again. While Crane and Jake took the dogs outside to play, I told Leonora what had happened.

"I always miss out on all the action," she said.

"You're lucky. For a while I thought Charlotte and I would be prisoners forever, and no one would ever know where we were."

Crane and Jake came in, windblown and red-cheeked with the entire collie pack prancing around them. Jake asked me to tell him about my experience.

I obliged, but for the last time, I hoped. At least for tonight.

"You'll have a good story for your classes tomorrow," Jake said.

I was horrified. "I'll never do that."

"We try to keep our personal lives private," Leonora told her husband. "Nothing could be more personal than Jennet's experience."

Jake was unconvinced. "Just imagine all the attention you'd get."

I could imagine only too well. My American Lit students would find my survival story laughable, and parts of it I could never reveal.

No, there was a time for everything. As far as my Marston classes were concerned, this was a time for silence.

Fifty-one

I didn't know whether it was too much company in one day, too much coffee, or a combination of both, but when I woke on Monday morning, I knew it wasn't going to be a good day. I'd had a frightful dream of floating in mid-air over my house, unable to land. I had tried to breathe and couldn't fill my lungs with air.

It's only a dream, I told myself. *Get up. Be thankful that you can.*

I always gave myself the best advice.

Crane was downstairs frying bacon, judging from the delicious smell traveling up the staircase. Our bedroom guardians, Halley and Misty, had deserted me. The scent of bacon can do that.

I wanted to be up and alert before Crane left for his shift, but if I closed my eyes, I knew I would fall asleep. That would never do. Swinging out of bed, I took a breath, relieved to discover that it was possible, and walked to the window.

Only a dream. Breathe.

The view from the bedroom was dismal. Branches, stripped bare of leaves, blew back and forth against the sky. Yesterday Brent had said something about a warm-up with possible thunderstorms on Monday, a departure from Halloween's early snowfall.

Crazy weather.

I took a red corduroy shirtwaist dress out of the closet and a double strand of pearls from my jewelry box. The color would cheer me on a dull day, and I was in dire need of cheer.

The rush of depression took me unaware. Delayed reactions are the worst. I didn't know where this one had come from or how long it planned to stay, but I couldn't afford to let it overpower me. I had to teach today, and Mondays are particularly challenging.

As I reached the landing, Candy dashed past me with a pancake hanging from her mouth. Crane's shout followed her from the kitchen: "Candy, bring that back, you devil!"

He should know it was too late.

"Morning, honey," he said as I kissed him. He was already in his uniform, complete with badge and gun, and ready for the day. "Do you think you can eat some pancakes?"

"Mm, yes."

The food of home was so much better than dry bread and bottled water. Oddly, though, I hadn't been able to eat much last night even though I thought I was hungry.

Crane's looked at me for a moment and didn't say anything. Then he asked, "Are you sure you feel up to going to school today?"

I thought about it, thought about trying to catch my breath while my class waited for instruction. What if I couldn't do it?

"Maybe I should take a sick day," I said.

"You're been through an ordeal. You need to sit and do nothing. Or play with the dogs. Whatever you feel like doing."

"I could look for a recipe for Brent's yule log," I said.

How exciting.

Candy slipped back into the kitchen, unabashed, licking her chops. She padded up to Crane and fixed her eye on the stove, clearly looking for more.

Crane frowned. "Lie down, Candy."

"I'll call the school and Leonora," I said.

"Morning all." Like Crane, Julia was already dressed. She wore her new winter-white suit with her hair in a French twist.

"I'm staying home today," I said.

"Have fun. I'll be home late. We have an English department meeting, then we're going out to dinner."

I took a breath, thought about it, and was afraid for a moment that I couldn't take another one. But I did. Was this a symptom of a panic attack? After breakfast, I'd have to search for the disorder on the Internet.

"The dogs were out, and I fed them," Crane said. "They have fresh water. Sit down, girls. Pancakes and bacon are coming up."

Crane was unusually cheerful this morning. I wondered why. It couldn't be the weather, which looked even less promising from the kitchen window.

We ate breakfast quickly; then Crane and Julia went their separate ways. I was alone with the dogs and a whole day to myself and no idea of what I wanted to do.

Would my breathing return to normal if I rested all day?

I didn't want to have to see a doctor. With luck, this new obsession would pass. Breathing was something you just do. You don't think about it.

You'll be all right. You don't need a doctor's opinion. Believe it.

The worst was over, after all.

~ * ~

The dogs enjoyed their extra walk and playtime, all finished before the gray sky turned dark and threatening. Thunder rumbled over the Corners. The storm would break earlier than expected.

I rummaged through the stack of Gothic paperbacks and CDs I'd brought from the library. Here was a video I'd borrowed weeks ago and never watched, the one with rainbow colored horses on the cover.

Horses reminded me of my Western movie. In the trauma of the Halloween episode, I'd almost forgotten my haunted television set. With a storm on the way, the conditions were ripe for the movie's reappearance. That is, as soon as lightning flashed in the sky.

Today might well be the day.

In the kitchen I filled a bowl with popcorn. Halley and Candy followed me to the sofa and lay down, Misty beside me and Candy on the floor. The thunder grew louder, and Misty, who had never been afraid during storms before, moved closer to me. Sky was already in her safe place, under the dining room table.

I ate popcorn mindlessly and waited for the lightning. Rain began to fall, splattering on the windowpanes. Lulled by the sound, I felt my eyes grow heavy. And close.

I woke to an inferno of wild sound.

Lightning streaked lines of fire across the sky. For a fraction of a moment, the living room burst into unnatural brightness. In the woods across the lane, a tree crashed to the ground.

Coming out of my doze, I hurried to the TV and turned it on. Shrill feminine laughter erupted from the screen. Instead of a dusty main street in the Old West, three women sat at a round table giggling and talking about a racy new best seller. These weren't the faces I looked for.

I turned the volume down, took another handful of popcorn from the bowl, and closed my eyes again.

The storm worked its fiery magic all around the house, flinging lightning at the earth. Thunder rolled across the sky over the roof and back again. The splattering sound turned into smashing as rain beat against the windows, trying its best to break them.

In spite of the noise, I felt drowsy. I closed my eyes to the chattering women and relaxed. I was breathing normally now. Thank God. And I needed more sleep.

A jaunty tune woke me. The chatty women were gone. Animated lemons with fancy hats danced around a picture of a cake on a box of sponge cake mix.

Either I'd missed the movie or it hadn't played at all. I'd never know, but a quick glance at the clock told me I'd only been asleep for fifteen minutes. Usually, whole chunks of time passed while I lost myself in Susanna's adventure.

In those fifteen minutes, Candy and Misty had eaten all the popcorn and licked the bowl clean.

"Naughty dogs," I said half-heartedly. "Don't be sick tonight."

I sighed, setting my disappointment aside. There would be another storm and another chance to visit Susanna's world. I'd find out if she recovered from the gunshot wound and if Luke caught the bank robbers and who the new lady in town was.

In the meantime it was early, and the rest of the day lay before me, taunting me with waiting chores and unfinished projects.

I wished I'd put the red dress and pearls on and gone to school.

~ * ~

In the afternoon, the sky cleared. Everyone I knew was away. Crane on the road, Julia lecturing her class, Annica serving late lunches at Clovers. Miss Eidt would be behind her desk in the library, twisting her rope of pearls as she waited for one of the library's patrons to need her.

I could go to the library.

It didn't occur to me to avoid the library after my horrible experience at the party. I could take back my overdue books, an errand I'd been putting off. It had been a never-to-be-repeated happening.

Sensing my wandering attention, Candy reminded me with a vigorous nudge that the dogs would enjoy a walk now that I was home.

"Later," I told her. "We'll go for two walks. All right?"

At my desk I began collecting books to take back to the library. Here was *The Place of Sapphires*. Miss Eidt would enjoy that one. Here were the Western videos. We'd long since viewed them, but I hadn't seen the one with the horses on the cover. I might as well return it.

Before adding it to the stack, I took one last look at the cover. Rainbow colored horses galloping across the plains. It contained four Western shows that had played on television, obscure series I'd never heard of.

I couldn't believe what I was seeing. The fourth movie was titled *Susanna of the West.*

Fifty-two

Susanna of the West was an obscure series, a women's Western that had a brief run in the mid-seventies. It had been cancelled after a mere fifteen episodes. The movie on the rainbow horses CD was a compilation of two of the programs. All those days I searched for the movie! It had never been a product of Hollywood.

I saw the names of the cast, some of them now deceased. There was the handsome actor who played the part of Luke, the man who reminded me of Crane. And Susanna. I recognized the actress' name. Older now, she still appeared on television from time to time.

Maybe I could find more episodes. Someone, somewhere, must have loved Susanna's story and copied them on VHS tapes. I didn't have to wait for a lightning bolt to bring the movie to my haunted television set. I could search the Internet.

I shut down the computer, for the first time optimistic about finding what I wanted. Another day.

Wait! Wait a minute!

This was a welcome development, but it didn't solve the mystery of the TV. Why did the movie appear when lightning struck? Why was I the only one who had ever seen it? The mysteries seemed to multiply. Why did I see consecutive scenes even when the viewings were spaced over days? And why did Eustacia Stirling see Peter, Paul, and Mary in concert? Did we see our ideal show, the kind of program we enjoyed the most?

Would I ever know? Did it matter now that I'd be able—I hoped—to find the whole series?

Candy and Misty stood in front of me, wagging their tails, reminding me of my promise of a walk. The rain had stopped. Also, where was their fresh water?

I pulled myself out of the fog of speculation that had wrapped itself around me. I had responsibilities in the here-and-now. Activities I loved. For instance, walking with my collies in the rain-fresh lanes of Foxglove Corners.

As I spread gravy bones on a newspaper for my hungry crew, my thoughts took another direction. I remembered saying that perhaps a lightning strike had turned the television into a freak. I liked that idea better than Brent's suggestion of a tiny CD imbedded in the TV's inner workings.

All, right. Accept it and go on from there.

After all, not every mystery has a neatly tied up solution. Take the violets that grew in Brent's wildflower field on Huron Court. What governed their bizarre behavior? Would I ever know? And did the phantom Christmas tree still exist on some unknown plane? Would I turn on the haunted TV one day and see Susanna and Luke in each other's arms?

Perhaps. Who knew? I'd have to wait and see.

I took the leashes from their hooks and contemplated which three dogs I would take for the first walk of the day.

~ * ~

Crane came home with a large box that attracted the immediate attention of every one of the seven collies.

"I hope you didn't start dinner," he said. "I have a pizza."

I'd thought about everything except cooking. "We could finish the stew and cornbread."

"Save it for another day. We're going to have pizza tonight. I bought a large one so there'll be some for Julia. I'm glad she'll be home late. Not that I don't love her, but…"

"I know."

I plowed through the ravenous collies and went straight into his arms. "I want it to be just us tonight."

"And forever," he said.

Meet Dorothy Bodoin

Dorothy Bodoin lives in Royal Oak, Michigan, a city which is an hour's drive from the town that serves as a setting for her Foxglove Corners cozy mystery series. Dorothy graduated from Oakland University in Rochester, Michigan, with Bachelor's and Master's degrees in English, and taught secondary English for several years until she left education to write full time. She has written one Gothic romance and six novels of romantic suspense, along with the Foxglove Corners series.

Having lost her best friend, rough collie Wolf Manor Kinder Brightstar, in December, she is at present living without a collie. Kinder was a rough collie. For those unfamiliar with the term, think of Lassie. The smooth collie is exactly like Lassie except with short hair. Dorothy hopes by the time her next Foxglove Corners book is released, she'll have a collie in her home again.

Other Works From The Pen Of

Dorothy Bodoin

Treasure at Trail's End (Gothic romance) - The House at Trail's End seemed to beckon to Mara Marsden, promising the happy future she longed for. But could she discover its secret without forfeiting her life?

Ghost across the Water (romantic suspense) - Water falling from an invisible force and a ghostly man who appears across Spearmint Lake draw Joanna Larne into a haunting twenty-year-old mystery.

Darkness at Foxglove Corners - Foxglove Corners offers tornado survivor Jennet Greenway country peace and romance, but the secret of the yellow Victorian house across the lane holds a threat to her new life. (#1)

Winter's Tale - On her first winter in Foxglove Corners Jennet Greenway battles dognappers, investigates the murder of the town's beloved veterinarian, and tries to outwit a dangerous enemy. (#3)

A Shortcut through the Shadows - Jennet Greenway's search for the missing owner of her rescue collie, Winter, sets her on a collision course with an unknown killer. (#4)

Cry for the Fox - In Foxglove Corners, the fox runs from the hunters, the animal activists target the Hunt Club, and a killer stalks human prey on the fox trail. (#2)

The Witches of Foxglove Corners - With a haunting in the library, a demented prankster who invades her home, and a murder in Foxglove Corners, Halloween turns deadly for Jennet Greenway. (#5)

The Snow Dogs of Lost Lake - A ghostly white collie and a lost locket lead Jennet Greenway to a body in the woods and a dangerous new mystery. (#6)

The Collie Connection - As Jennet Greenway's wedding to Crane Ferguson approaches, her happiness is shattered when a Good Samaritan deed leaves her without her beloved black collie, Halley, and ultimately in grave danger. (#7)

A Time of Storms - When a stranger threatens her collie and she hears a cry for help in a vacant house, Jennet Ferguson suspects that her first summer as a wife may be tumultuous. (#8)

The Dog from the Sky - Jennet's life takes a dangerous turn when she rescues an abused collie. Soon afterward, a girl vanishes without a trace. Ironically she had also rescued an abused collie. Is there a connection between the two incidents? (#9)

Spirit of the Season - Mystery mixes with holiday cheer as a phantom ice skater returns to the lake where she died, and a collie is accused of plotting her owner's fatal accident. (#10)

Another Part of the Forest - Danger rides the air when a kidnapper whisks his victims away in a hot air balloon, and a false friend puts a curses on a collie breeder's first litter. (#11)

Where Have All the Dogs Gone? - An animal activist frees the shelter dogs in and around Foxglove Corners to save them from being destroyed. Running wild in the countryside, they face an equally distressing fate and post a risk to those who come in contact with them. (#12)

The Secret Room of Eidt House - A rabid dog that should have died months ago from the dread disease runs free in the woods of

Foxglove Corners, and the library's long-kept secret unleashes a series of other strange events. (#13)

Follow a Shadow - A shadowy intruder haunts Jennet's woods by night, and a woman who can't accept the death of her collie asks Jennet to help her find Rainbow Bridge where she believes her dog waits for her. (#14)

The Snow Queen's Collie - A white collie puppy appears on the porch of the Ferguson farmhouse during a Christmas Eve snowstorm. In another part of Foxglove Corners a collie breeder's show prospect disappears. Meanwhile, the painting Jennet's sister gave her for Christmas begins to exhibit strange qualities. (#15)

The Door in the Fog - A wounded dog disappears in the fog. A blue door on the side of a barn vanishes. Strange wildflowers and a sound of weeping haunt a meadow. The woods keep their secret, and a curse refuses to die. (#16)

Dreams and Bones - At Brent Fowler's newly purchased Spirit Lamp Inn, a renovation turns up human bones buried in the inn's backyard, rekindling interest in the case of a young woman who disappeared from the inn several decades ago. As Jennet tries to solve this mystery, she doesn't realize it may be her last. (#17)

A Ghost of Gunfire - Months after gunfire erupted in her classroom at Marston High School, leaving one student dead and one seriously wounded, Jennet begins to hear a sound of gunshots inaudible to anyone else. Meanwhile, she resolves to find the demented person who is tying dogs to trees and leaving them to die. (#18)

The Silver Sleigh - Rosalyn Everett was missing and presumed dead. Her collies had been rescued, and her house was abandoned. But a blue merle collie haunts her woods and a figure in bridal white traverses the property. (#19)

The Stone Collie - Jennet's discovery of a collie puppy chained in the yard of a vacant house sets her on a search for a man whose activities may threaten Foxglove Corners' security. Meanwhile, horror story novelist Lucy Hazen is mystified when scenes from her work-in-progress are duplicated in real life. (#20)

The Mists of Huron Court - The house was beautiful, a vintage pink Victorian in a picturesque but lonely country setting, and the girl playing ball with her dog in the yard was friendly, suggesting that she and Jennet walk their dogs together some time. Jennet thinks she has made a new friend until she returns to the house and finds a tumbling down ruin where the Victorian once stood and no sign that the girl and dog have ever been there. ((#21)

Down a Dark Path - What hold does the pink Victorian on Huron Court have on Brent Fowler who is determined to re-create the home of long-dead Violet Randall? When he disappears, could he have been cast adrift in time? (#22)

Shadow of the Ghost Dog - An invisible dog grieves inside the house chosen as a setting for a movie based on Lucy Hazen's book, *Devilwish,* and a landscaper unearths a human skeleton in the backyard while planting shrubs. (#23)

The Dark Beyond the Bridge - An antique television set that airs an obscure Western at random times, and a woman who disappears with her newly adopted rescue collie draw Jennet into a puzzling mystery. (#24)

Made in the USA
Columbia, SC
16 May 2018